Demon Rising

Dark Rising Trilogy Book 1

DEANNA BROWNE

DEMON RISING
Copyright © 2017
Celtic Moon Press
Cover Design by Kimberly Killion
All cover art copyright © 2018
All Rights Reserved
ISBN: 978-1-948884-07-5

First Publication: AUGUST 12, 2017

DEDICATION

To Spencer, for believing I could.

CHAPTER 1

T he tattoo on Becca's neck prickled as she walked the crowded path to work. Searching for the possible source of magic, she continued forward, with coffee in one hand and the other resting by the knife at her waist.

She moved amid a throng of people, shuffling along the worn walkways. Heavy clouds were scattered across the sky, while dilapidated buildings surrounded them, a haunting reminder of what once was. A young man pushed past Becca, dressed in blue coveralls. *He must be heading to the line.*

The warehouse traveled up twenty stories high, the tallest building in town with a large fountain in front. It must have once been a beauty. Now the fountain, covered in graffiti, ran dry and the boarded-up windows could barely keep the wind out.

A familiar, lanky guard stood watch on the side of the road. Could he have been the source of the magic warming her tattoo? He scanned the crowd with a demon dog at his side, a German shepherd with unnaturally large black eyes.

Turning forward, she let her dark hair fall into her face, not wanting to draw his attention. She stepped past the guard undisturbed. She could handle herself with the guards, but her boss, Nikko, constantly nagged her about keeping a low profile.

The crowds pressed together, and a large man knocked into Becca's side, tripping her. She stumbled, spilling the remains of her coffee all over her black jeans. Someone swore as the crowd surged forward, and she stepped to the side.

At five-foot-five, she was on the small side, but strong enough to cause pain and scrappy enough to avoid it when she could. The crowds weren't her problem, though. That would be the presence behind her, causing her tattoo to burn.

She whipped around and grabbed the small hand, reaching for her hunting knife. A young boy, maybe ten or twelve years old, struggled in her grasp. Blond hair curled around his ears. His face was lined with dirt. Once she glimpsed his eyes, she tightened her grip and shoved him back against a brick storefront.

A hellish black, his eyes revealed the demon residing inside of his body. Becca clamped down on any sympathy she might have had for this child, for he was no longer a child but a Soultorn. Fury rose, fast and fierce. Some wizard had corrupted this boy past repair by summoning a demon and using the boy's body as a host.

She pinned him against the wall with her forearm, her knife pointed at his throat. "Where's your master?"

"It could be you if you want," he lied.

His lips twisted into a wretched smile, revealing broken and stained teeth. The sour smell of his fetid breath turned her stomach. There could be only one master a Soultorn would ever answer to, and that magician must be an idiot to let a Soultorn roam free. Maybe they wanted someone else to dispose of it.

She should just kill this body. It would be a kind mercy for this poor boy whose body had been stolen. His blond curls and freckles tugged at her gut, reminding her of a past she didn't want to remember.

"Come on, lady. A kid's gotta eat," the demon whined, trying to force his expression into something pathetic.

A black leather jacket and steel toed boots didn't scream "lady." Ladies didn't work as a runner for the local drug lord either, but at twenty-four, it was the best job she could get. "You're a demon. All you eat is other's pain." Becca edged the knife deeper against his neck.

Demons could eat food. The human bodies they stole preferred it, but death and destruction were a demon's main course. The Soultorn in her grip struggled to swallow against the blade's lethal edge.

Her lips pressed into a tight dark smile. "What? Realizing that a lesser spawn of hell like yourself may not have a shot at the afterlife?" Not that she knew much about demon realms, but she'd heard that demons never enjoyed returning.

What idiot summoned this lesser demon? Weak magicians recklessly played with demons in a hopeless attempt to grasp power. Demon pets and Soultorns were not allowed in the Mundane market streets without a leash. The law, weak as it was, helped to keep the Mundanes somewhat safe from being enslaved by every two-bit magician. It wouldn't do any good for the wizards to kill off the work force.

The Soultorn spoke in a foreign tongue. Her tattoo tingled and dark spots filled her vision. She focused on maintaining her grip. As the Soultorn's dirty fingers dug into her jacket, pain shot up the arm that clutched the knife. Her tattoo protected her against minor magic, but not direct attacks.

Out of time, Becca grabbed its hair and rammed its head into the wall, hoping to weaken it and break the spell. It took several hits before those pitch black eyes rolled back, and it collapsed on the ground.

Her breath left in a rush. Her fingers tingled with the return of feeling. She shook them out and stepped back, knocking into her now empty coffee cup. Dang demons, she'd lost her coffee and had to deal with a minor demon before nine a.m. Yeah, it was a Monday.

The Soultorn fell at an awkward angle, knocked out but still breathing. She didn't have the stomach to kill a child host this morning. Now the magician who created it? That was a different story.

"Are you going to finish it?" Ted, the local coven guard from across the street, appeared behind her, placing a hand on her arm. His vicious grin and long brown hair almost mirrored the look of the possessed German shepherd at his side. The dog's tail wagged high in the air, his teeth sharp and white. Not only could demons reside in humans, but magicians could put them into animals as well—changing the whole meaning of family pet.

Becca shuddered in disgust and backed away from his touch. "Isn't that your job?" It was the one useful thing maggots like Ted did to help the Mundane.

"Yes, but I like a girl with a little blood on her hands." As if in agreement, the demon dog at his side barked.

The only blood she wanted to spill was his. Wizards like him caused deaths like this without a second thought. "Just do your job," she said, pushing past him. She might be able to take on a minor demon, but not a wizard. Besides, she had to get to work.

Growls erupted from the possessed German shepherd, and with a single command from its master, the dog pounced on the boy's body. She walked away, the grisly sounds of his attack echoing off the buildings.

She was grateful that she'd skipped breakfast, because there was no way it would have stayed down. Most people avoided the scene, except a couple of onlookers who watched with vacant expressions. Hurrying down the street, she tried to block out the noise. The face of the boy flashed into her mind. Her chest tightened as she mourned the boy— not his body, but his spirit that was stolen too soon.

One more demon vanquished. Hopefully, the creator would be punished, though probably not. And the boy— just more collateral damage.

Something she'd seen all too often with city life. Still, it was better than living outside the city walls, where gangs and demons roamed free. Somehow, that didn't make the boy's death easier to swallow.

She didn't slow her pace until Nikko's building came into view, an old two-story bar with dusty floors, but clean glasses. Its dark frame appeared vacant, but there was a full house. People watched from the darkened windows around the clock. Before she could knock, the door creaked open.

"Hey, sweetie." Tyson welcomed her with a sly smile. His large frame and soft face gave him the appearance of an oversized teddy bear, but she'd seen that teddy bear break a man's neck.

"Nothing sweet here." She strode past.

"Okay," he replied, one hand rose up in defense.

As she continued on, he murmured, "Heard she knifed her last lover."

Her lips lifted in a grim smile. She'd worked hard for that kind of rep—a necessary tool in a business full of men.

The bar reeked of smoke and alcohol. One wall was decorated with a rainbow of colored bottles. Across the floor, two guys played a game of pool. An older man nursed a cup of coffee at one of the many small wooden tables. She'd have to grab a cup later.

She turned down the hallway and maneuvered to the back, to Nikko's office. After a quick knock, Nikko called her in.

He hovered over papers at his desk while a cigarette burned away in the ashtray. He played with one of the metal studs piercing his brow. She studied him while he remained deep in thought, knowing better than to interrupt.

A dark, intricate tattoo decorated one side of his face. Ancient runes she often tried to decipher. Rumors said his family came from Asia, farther away than she could imagine.

Dressed in a fitted navy suit that complimented his short, dark hair, he emanated beauty and terror all at the same time. Long ago she advised him to forget about dressing so nice, since everyone stopped at his face.

"Becca." He didn't bother to look up. "I need this out of here." He finished writing a note and sealed it in an envelope

"Who in the world needs to get high this early?" She fell into a nearby chair not quite ready to head out. Yes, she ran drugs and other things for a crime lord, but she was never dumb enough to do them. At least with Nikko, she could face the thugs head on, instead of at the factories where they lurked in the shadows.

"What we supply is in constant demand." His brown eyes glimmered with mischief. "That's why we both have jobs. Today, I need you to head out of the city to Mariah's place."

Tension shot through her and she bolted upright, hands fisted on her knees. "Not Mariah's. I'm not going there again."

"Calm down." He dismissed her objection with a wave

of his hand. "You're the only one I can trust not to get sucked into her little tricks. Last time, Tobi returned in such a state he couldn't remember how to piss straight. I can't afford that."

"Tell your guys to grow a pair. Or get them tats." She didn't remember even getting her tattoo as a child, but it had saved her hide more than once.

"That would cost more than Tobi." He finished packing the bag. "You know the deal. You want another job, you do this one."

"I may end up killing that witch." She meant it. The best kind of magician was a dead one. She also couldn't ignore the nagging voice in the back of her mind that said she might run into someone she knew, someone she didn't want to see again. The only magician she ever let get close to her, too close.

Nikko ignored her protest. "Just get me my cash first."

"I hate you," she said with no real malice. Lucky to have landed a job outside of the factories, she owed Nikko a lot. He'd helped improve her knife skills and paid her enough so she could afford her own studio apartment. However difficult the job, she'd do it. And he knew it.

"That's why we get along so well." He smiled. "Take the bike. Mariah wants this soon."

"What? Is she sacrificing small puppies?" Becca grumbled as she got to her feet. "Or her own mother this time?" A witch could stew up endless nightmares.

Nikko ignored Becca and tossed her the bag.

Catching it, she sighed. "Don't tell me. I don't want to know." Who knew what dead creatures or bones might be in there? Drugs were easy in comparison.

"I never do." He pushed keys across the table. "Just take good care of my baby. She's worth more than you."

"Telling me that every time I touch Dedra doesn't

help my self-esteem."

"Can't believe you named my Ducati like an old mare," he mumbled, standing up. "Just get it done and bring it back tonight."

"Will do." A smile lit up her face. She'd named his bike when she realized the price he paid for it. Guys only do something that stupid or expensive for a broad. With the bag on her shoulder, she turned to leave.

"And, Becca?"

She turned back. "Yeah?"

His dark eyes warmed. "Be safe." Beneath the sarcasm and crappy jobs, Nikko watched her back, maybe because she was his best runner, or maybe he considered her a friend. She never asked.

She winked. "Ain't I always?"

CHAPTER 2

After grabbing coffee, some supplies, and gas for Dedra, Becca headed out of town. The sleek black bike roared through the forest. Even the apprehension in her gut couldn't stop the smile on Becca's face as she raced through dirt roads and inhaled the smell of trees. She grew up driving a slow stubborn mule that wouldn't go over ten miles an hour, and so going fifty over small dirt mounds provided an exhilaration she rarely experienced.

Her father had once told her people used to race cars going almost two hundred miles an hour. She couldn't fathom it, the life before. Her father, who had lived through The Rising, always referred to time as "before" or "after" The Rising, when covens replaced the government and magicians ruled.

Continuing through the back roads, she kept her speed up, wanting to get this delivery over with. She avoided the main highway that wrapped around the boundary of the city and any unnecessary attention. The coven magicked the city boundaries for protection against rogue demons and stationed guards at entry points. Outside those walls, anything went. Gangs roamed the countryside and lived in the rundown buildings from before.

Another hour ticked by before she finally slowed outside of Mariah's place. The sun hung high and bright, but it wasn't enough to chase away the creeping sense of unease.

Becca rubbed the Hand of Mary tattooed on the nape of her neck, which her ponytail barely covered and prayed it would be enough. The hand shaped tattoo turned down with an eye in the palm, and colored in various shades of blue. Intricate symbols filled the fingers.

Mariah's home must have once been magnificent. Now broken shutters littered the old two-story home, faded blue paint peeled from the side, and boards were missing from the porch. The various dead rodents hanging from its roof didn't help.

Becca knocked loudly on the weathered door. She reached in the bag and pulled out the package and her knife. Mariah, herself, wasn't too dangerous. She messed with people's emotions, but without a greater coven or Soultorn to call upon, she only could harm idiots who wanted to succumb.

"My darling…" The witch purred as she opened the door. Her slurred voice indicated the celebrating had started early. Her long black hair hung in a ratty braid, her dark features highlighted by eager silver eyes.

Becca's lips curled in disgust. "Do you have payment?"

"Tsk, tsk, tsk. Always all work and no play." The witch grabbed an envelope from inside the doorway. "I wish that tall blond boy would come back to visit."

Becca's hands tightened, but she didn't trust herself to reply. Just get the money and get out.

"Do you want some side work? I know how stingy Nikko can be."

The scrape of the witch's magic against Becca skin made her neck ache. The tattoo on her neck warmed with pinpricks. "No thanks, witch." The word spewed out like a curse.

Mariah leaned against the doorway, and to Becca's annoyance, acted oblivious. "What about some gossip? People are willing to pay a lot for gossip, especially a scavenger like you."

She was a runner not a scavenger, but Becca didn't bother to correct her. She reached for the envelope, but the witch moved it just out of her grasp.

"Cut the crap, Mariah, and give me the money. You know Nikko doesn't pay for gossip. He'll only give you a cut if the deal pans out."

The witch traced a long finger down the envelope. Becca's spine stiffened. Fear shot through her body as she lost control. Her knife remained clutched in her hand, but she couldn't move her arm. She couldn't even speak. Becca shouldn't have come. Mariah had gotten stronger.

Mariah's eyes flared with haughtiness. "You need to learn some respect. You're a minion. I'm a witch. I can have my demon eat you for breakfast."

Becca hollered obscenities or tried, but she could only manage to blink. Fury built inside of her, at the feeling of helplessness under the spell.

Undeterred, the witch kept talking, "Tell Nikko there's a small farming community east of here, burned to the ground. Never cleaned out. The ashes are still smoldering. I want a cut on what he gets, and he better not try to cheat me. Hear me?"

Did this stupid witch expect her to reply? A silent moment passed where Mariah gloated like a bird with her feathered chest puffed out. In the quiet, the slow tentacles of fear crawled up Becca's back. She pushed them down. There were several farming communities that hid from the attention of the city coven. It could be any of them.

After she relished her moment of triumph, Mariah touched Becca's forehead with one long finger. Becca stumbled back, the power losing its spell.

Becca regained her footing and glared at Mariah. She wanted to fight her, but was outmatched in a head on fight against magic. "You think Nikko's going to send someone way out here for a wild goose chase? If you waste his time, he'll double your costs."

"If you blow a big deal for him, he may lower his costs in other ways," Mariah grinned, looking hideous and threw the money at Becca's feet. "Trust me."

Becca picked up the cash and thumbed through it. "Not a chance."

Tossing the package to the witch, she headed back to the bike. She knew better than to turn her back on a witch, but Mariah wanted Nikko to get this message. She wouldn't kill the messenger, not yet.

"You know you're curious," Mariah said barely loud enough for her to hear.

Becca turned the key and started Dedra with a loud roar. Speeding down the road, the witch's words spun around her mind. She was already out here and familiar with the land to the east more than she wanted to admit. Nikko would want the information as soon as he could get it. Gas may be tight, but she should be able to take a more direct path back to the city.

Besides, she'd told herself she'd go back one day, but then one day turned into eight years. She ran out of excuses. She had to go, even if she lacked the courage to knock on the front door.

☙❧☙

Caleb awoke next to his parents' grave. The reality of their death set in with the rise of the sun. He'd buried them last night, with the end of a burnt shovel. Lying against the cold earth, he lacked any desire to move, to leave their graves. Smoke permeated his clothes, his hair, and his existence as he stared at the burnt wreckage of what had been his life.

As he dug his hands into the grass, hollowness enveloped him until he couldn't feel anything at all. Dirt and soot darkened his hands. There were no more tears left as he sat in front of their graves. His world had vanished, and the embers of his family home were still warm.

He'd buried his parents under his mom's favorite bush. Its white flowers grew into tight balls and gave off a fragrance that smelled like her. The heavy green branches covered their graves, hiding them from scavengers.

He plucked a petal and crushed it in his hand. Lifting it to his nose, he could only smell smoke. The remnant of what killed his parents. He placed a clenched fist on his chest as he struggled to draw a clear breath.

Off hunting days earlier, he had seen the smoke first, dropped his kill, and taken off for the house. It had been burning for hours by the time he arrived. He was forced to watch it, unable to do anything. Now all he wanted was to lie down next to their graves and never get up.

He was disgusted with himself. What would his father think? But his father wasn't here anymore, was he?

Caleb coughed, and his throat burned as he spat out black phlegm.

"Why?" he cried to the sky. Why were his parents in the house? They should have had plenty of time to get out. What about the neighbors?

The other homesteads flashed through his mind. Though miles away, they would have noticed a fire. The flames were contained before he arrived, so someone must have been here. Who was the question?

Slowly, the pain in his chest morphed to anger. He stood with resolve and purpose, his large shadow covering their graves. He might never see his parents again, but he would make sure whoever did this would pay.

CHAPTER 3

Haunting memories appeared along the dirt path as Becca weaved through the forest. The cool wind whipped against her face, as she stared through her dark sunglasses.

She could never forget the last time she took this road. Years ago, she walked this dirt trail—more like ran. Swallowing down the guilt and shame, she pushed away the cold memories of that night, which floated like ghosts among the pine trees.

The stream that she often swam in as a girl weaved behind acres of old farmland and scattered homes. Some empty. Others full of people or families hiding out, not willing to live in the cities and play the coven's game.

Becca continued maneuvering the rugged path. Her hands ached from gripping the handles of the bike. She slowed as old fears surfaced. What would they say? She took off for a reason, but it wasn't because she didn't love her family.

In a few more miles, the smell hit her. Smoke.

Dedra roared to life as she remembered Mariah's words. The burned down homes couldn't be her family. It couldn't.

Her breath caught in her throat as she glimpsed the disaster on the other side of the river. Where her family's two story home once stood, now all that remained was blackened debris. She recognized their brick fireplace dark with soot.

No. Not her home. Her hands shook and the motorcycle skidded into a nearby bush. She barely registered the pain in her leg, probably just road rash. She untangled herself from the branches and hurried toward the rubble. She had to cross the rushing river and searched for the spot to cross. She soon found the large fallen tree that she'd helped her father carve into a makeshift bridge.

This couldn't be happening. Where were they?

After crossing the bridge, she stopped. Someone was hunched over in the midst of the wreckage, a scavenger picking over the burned remains. Her family's remains.

Blood pounded in her ears as she pulled out her knife from a sheath on her belt. She lightened her steps as she approached, scanning the area. Scavengers usually didn't work alone.

Her shoe crunched on the burnt debris. The scavenger's head snapped up, his thick frame tall even for a guy. Becca didn't think, just barreled toward him, her knife at the ready.

He spun to the side, deflecting her strike. The knife glanced off his forearm. She spun around and something hard crashed into the side of her head. She stepped back as dark spots danced in her vision. He was bigger and heavier than she'd realized, but she had the rage of a demon. She feigned an attack with her knife and then landed a solid kick to his thigh.

"Sweet Jesus," he mumbled, taking a step backward.

As the black spots finally cleared from her vision, she focused on his voice. She'd heard those words so many times and had watched her best friend get smacked by his mother for swearing.

It couldn't be. This guy stood over six feet. His face

had filled out and was now covered with a scruffy beard. His dirty blond hair held a familiar wave, though cut short, and those almond-shaped green eyes hadn't changed at all. There stood Caleb, her best friend from years ago.

She faltered.

He notched an arrow in his bow and aimed it directly at her. "Don't make me shoot you," he said with a voice, deep and full.

How did she miss his bow? She didn't compute the threat in front of her. Soot streaked his face and darkened his hair. His jaw clenched. The mischievous green eyes, she'd loved years ago, now watched her carefully. He must have recognized her, though it had been several years.

Ever so slowly, she sheathed the knife, raised her hands, and pulled back her dark hair. The tie must have fallen out at some point.

Despite her shock, her heart warmed at the sight of the friend she'd never thought to see again. "Caleb."

His eyes widened. He lowered his bow, and his breath escaped in one long rush. "Rebecca?"

She shivered with a cold chill, as if stepping over a grave. She had buried that name long ago with the rest of who she used to be.

"Is that really you?" He stepped closer and reached out, as if she might not be real. Before she could find her voice, he wrapped his large arms around her. She froze in shock. This was Caleb, her Caleb, here in front of her, holding her.

She let his strong arms hold her and, for a brief moment, they took her back to a time when his kiss was all she wished for. Yeah, they had been best friends, plus some.

It took less than a minute for her to come to her senses. She pulled away. A warm flush covered her face.

"What are you doing here?"

"I was out hunting several miles north when I saw the smoke. They burned out all the homesteads along the creek." An emptiness haunted his features that she'd never seen before.

"All of them? Are your parents okay?" She had happy memories of his parents and their kindness and humor.

He looked down and shook his head. "The Brightons too," he said, his voice tight.

She couldn't feel her legs and struggled to breathe amid the ash. "Are they all dead?"

The words felt distant as if some other person asked it, some other person whose heart hung on a precipice waiting to shatter.

His eyes ached with deep pain. "Yes."

Tears filled her vision. She dreaded the words she had to say. "My family? I need to find them," she said, biting back the sorrow and grief that threatened to explode inside of her.

The odds they survived were low, but if they didn't, they would need a proper burial before a witch like Mariah found them and used them for dark magic.

He nodded. Without speaking, he began sorting through the remains of her old life. She tied a handkerchief around her face and joined him, racing against the falling sun as they sorted through the twisted metal. They pieced together some recognizable items—a sewing machine and an old knife, but most were lost, burned beyond recognition or use. The large two-story home was reduced to a skeleton of what had been.

They approached the last back corner of the house, where her parents' bedroom had stood. She prayed as her blackened hands dug through the soot.

"I can do this if you want," Caleb offered, wiping a rag

across his forehead.

"No. I have to do this." *For my family.* She might have abandoned them years ago but not now. Guilt tore at her, like an open wound that wouldn't stop bleeding.

"I know."

She glanced at him, holding his gaze. He did know.

They searched where her parents' bedroom would have been. Under a twisted metal frame, she found the remains of her mother and father. The blackened masses were skeletal outlines of petrified bone and ash. Caleb knelt down picking up an object. He rubbed the soot off of it, and she recognized the gold misshapen band as her mother's wedding ring.

Becca stumbled back onto the grass. Turning away from the fire, she threw up. Tears poured down her face as she emptied her stomach. Pain tore at her heart, shredding it to pieces. They were dead. The words played over and over in her mind.

She stumbled farther away from the house, wanting a clean breath.

She couldn't help the most obvious question that had haunted her all day. *Would this have happened if I'd never left?* I could have prevented this. Saved them. She'd always been the strongest in the family, hunting with her father regularly.

Caleb approached from behind and held out a knife— her father's hunting knife, black and charred. "I thought you might want this."

"Thanks." She hastily wiped her eyes on her sleeve. She needed to pull herself together. "Did you find Elizabeth?" Her heart burned with the memory of her sister.

"No. No other bodies."

"Is it possible we missed her remains? Could she have

escaped?" She was scared to let herself believe it. Her chest heaved, heavy with the smoke in the air. He shrugged. "Maybe."

"Why was my dad in the bedroom with my mother? If gangs came or even a fire, they would have gone to the cellar." Her words came out slow, remembering the emergency shelter behind the house. "The cellar," she said it again, hoping Elizabeth would have been smart enough to run there.

Becca rushed to the backyard, stumbling over debris. She knelt on the burnt grass and brushed off a layer of dirt, revealing the metal door. Caleb helped her lift it open. If her family was attacked by gangs or rogue demons, Elizabeth would have been sent to the basement for safety.

Hurrying down the stairs, she called out for her sister.

"Elizabeth. Elizabeth!" There was no reply.

Her words bounced off the concrete walls lined with canned goods and emergency supplies. Becca grabbed a glass jar of peaches and threw it against the wall. The jar shattered and the smell of peaches filled the room. Peach cobbler. Her mother's favorite dessert. Becca clamped down on the flood of memories and focused instead on her heavy breath and pounding heart.

Where's Elizabeth? Could she be alive?

"I never knew you had this," Caleb said, taking stock of a nearby shelf.

"No one did." Becca wanted to scream and break everything. All of these supplies didn't help save her family.

Leaving Caleb in the basement, she took the stairs up two at a time. Elizabeth had to be here somewhere. Becca stood in the middle of the scorched remains.

Turning in a circle, she searched, hoping for a clue as to where Elizabeth was and who did this. Soot covered

Becca's shoes and dusted the rest of her body. The debris of her former life caused a sickening in her gut. She coughed repeatedly from the ash in the air.

She had to move. Get out of this hell. She jumped off what had previously been her front porch and sprinted up the worn path to the well. She welcomed the burning in her legs as she finally reached the top, gasping.

The bucket, in its usual place, hung off the back side of the pump. The twisted irony that no one even made it to the well to put out the fire, made her want to punch something.

Filling the bucket with cold water, she poured it over her head. Then she reached for the pump to fill it again, and again. She rubbed the ash, the misery, and the death off her skin and clothes. The cool water numbed her to the core.

After scrubbing her body clean, she sat down under a nearby tree, exhausted. Her breath calmed with the smell of fresh grass as she watched the sun set amid scattered clouds. She was grateful for the time alone to pull herself together.

Caleb took his time striding up the hill. His broad, muscular shoulders stretched against his jacket. He had grown in more ways than one since she'd been gone. He had a confident stride now, and a strength in his face. He sat on the ground next to her, with a familiarity that she missed.

"I searched around the house, but didn't find any sign of her," he said. "Do you think she would've run?"

"I don't know." She offered him a drink, which he took.

He finished the water and then stood to get more.

"Where would she go?" she asked. "Our only living relative was my uncle, and we never knew where he lived."

The thought of Elizabeth running to her uncle sent a cold shiver down Becca's spine. "It's a long walk to the city."

"You made it." He held her gaze. His eyes held more questions than she wanted to answer.

Caleb moved aside and dumped water on his head, shaking out his hair like a wild dog. Streaks of grime covered his muscular arms.

Turning back to the wreckage of her old home, she rubbed her neck and tried to think of some answers. "The smart thing for Elizabeth to do would be to hide along the river and wait for whoever it was to leave. Then grab food from the basement and wait out the fire. But the basement was untouched. She would have come out if she heard us."

Caleb ran a hand through his wet hair. "My mother once told me they had men in a large red truck that use to put fires out for people. Can you imagine that? Now we just have scavengers to pick through the rubble."

Becca ignored his comment. Talking about what used to be never did any good. A lot of things were better before The Rising.

"If she was scared, she could have taken off," he suggested.

"Maybe, if she's alive." The words hurt to say, but they were a reality.

The sun descended behind the trees, their shadows falling on the remains. From this distance, she could only make out a few things: the stove, fireplace, and a crumpled metal swing that sat in what used to be the front porch. Wooden beams surrounded the house in an odd pattern— almost intentionally separated or pulled back from the house. Standing, Becca headed to the tree.

"What are you doing?" Caleb asked.

"I need to get higher. Give me a sec." She grasped a familiar knot, and hoisted herself up. She winced as her leg, still fresh with road rash, rubbed against the tree. Maneuvering through the dense branches, she scaled the tree. The nearby homesteads were difficult to see, but Becca could make out the blackened remains.

How could they all burn down without spreading to the forest? And why?

Turning back around to her house, she noticed certain beams not burnt laying around the home in a distinct pattern, containing the fire. The hairs on her arms stood on end. This was more than looting or gang violence. Slowly the pieces fell into place.

The witch told her of this destruction earlier. No wonder scavengers hadn't found it yet. Only wizards could have done this. But what were they after? Maybe this was just a message from the coven, that no one was safe outside city walls.

But where did that leave Elizabeth? Dead or stolen away? Becca had to find out.

She needed to go to Mariah's. The witch had told her about the burnings, and she probably knew more. Not that getting it out of Mariah would be easy. Becca glanced down at Caleb, whose bow hung over his shoulder. She'd told Nikko she would kill that witch, and she just might.

CHAPTER 4

Elizabeth watched the scenery flash by the window on the car ride to the city. Gray buildings and dirty bricks looked dismal in the daylight. She tucked her hands under her long skirt. She could hear her mother, scolding her back at their homestead, "A lady doesn't chew her cuticles."

Mother was right. Elizabeth had nothing to be afraid of. People had traveled in cars regularly since before her parents were born. If anything, she had been waiting for this adventure, a life outside of the farm for years. But something felt...off.

She better not be getting sick from pollution. The windows of the car had been closed tight since they'd entered the city limits. The silver car's upholstery shined bright, but a sickly odor of mold or mildew permeated the car. It could be the men in the front. The driver's slicked-back hair looked greasy and the man next to him, with dark sunglasses, possessed an unsettling stillness.

It's probably just homesickness. City people are bound to be different.

She yelped as the car hit a large bump in the road.

Uncle Jeremiah patted her knee. "Just a pot hole, dear."

She pulled her sweater around her tighter. He had a sharp coldness about him. She'd never felt comfortable with him, but he offered her a future she couldn't get back on the farm. So she ignored his heavy hand.

He probably meant to be comforting, but she felt like a child instead. She was eighteen years of age, heading to meet her future husband—not a child at all.

She hated to admit it to herself, but part of her ached for her parents. They'd seemed so distant when she said goodbye. This was their idea, though, and had been planned for years. It was for the best.

Out the car window, weathered buildings and abandoned store fronts flashed by. This run down city held no attraction for Elizabeth. Why anyone would choose to stay here was a mystery. Her thoughts traveled to her sister Rebecca, who'd run away to the city years ago, only to die at the hands of some street thug.

"Rebecca was always a wild one," her father had often said.

Mother called it a rebellious spirit and warned Elizabeth against the same. "Even if it doesn't have the eyes of a demon, it can still be evil."

She worried how her parents were going to get on without both of their daughters. Once married, maybe she could live nearby her family's homestead.

"Can you tell me about my fiancé?" she asked her uncle, hoping to ease the worry knotting in her stomach.

"He's older. Wealthy, of course. His grace and influence is unmatched." With a quick glance at Elizabeth, he added, "Quite handsome, too, from what the other women say."

She tried to smile and push out the picture of a wrinkling man sitting in a mansion. Once again she had to remind herself just how lucky she was.

ⱸﯗⱸﯗ

Countless stars watched from above as Caleb and Becca finished burying her parents. They worked hard to hide the graves near the river. She rubbed her numb hands together.

All feeling had fled into the cold air, mirroring her insides. Her tears had run dry, and no words could ever make this right.

They headed back to the basement. The flashlight trembled in her hand, bouncing along the path ahead. Revenge kept her moving, urging her to get on the road quick and find answers. Luckily, no one had come to check out the fire yet. The hollow sounds of her heels echoed across the basement.

Caleb snatched a couple bottles of water off a nearby shelf. "So how far is this witch's house?"

"A couple hours." She grabbed a nearby backpack and loaded it with water and food from the cupboards for the ride back. She hadn't eaten all day and didn't feel like it now, but had to keep her strength up. "And this witch will know something about the fires?"

"How strong is she?" He had a deep edge to his voice she wasn't familiar with.

"Not terribly strong, but she does have magic. It will be difficult getting answers, especially if she doesn't want to give them." A bottomless ache resonated in her chest, and her determination to get answers, one way or another, grew. They finished packing supplies and headed back to the bike.

"Come to think of it." She stopped suddenly and turned, forcing Caleb to bump into her. "Mariah will be more talkative if I'm alone."

He started shaking his head before she finished her sentence. "You're not going in alone. It's too risky."

"I know, but I'll have a better chance by myself." That's what mattered.

"You're not the only one who lost everything." He closed the distance between them.

She lifted her chin to meet his gaze.

"It's not worth the risk," he said.

She steadied her emotions, the raw pain turning to anger at those responsible.

"Let me try," she said. "I'll keep her on the porch. And if I need help, you'll be ready with your bow." It was the best plan she could think of. "She could use you against me. You're more dangerous, where she can't see you."

He spoke through gritted teeth, "All right. But one false move, and I'll pin her to the door frame."

"I'm counting on that."

They found the bike sticking out of a nearby bush. The crash felt like an eon ago, despite the road rash burning her leg.

Caleb inspected the bike. "Will it run?"

"It better. Nikko will have my hide otherwise." She already worried about having enough gas since Mariah's place was miles out of the way for the trip back.

He picked up the bike. "Nikko?"

"My boss. Usually pretty reasonable, but he loves Dedra." She yanked a branch out from the handle bars and knew there would be hell to pay. "Longest relationship he's ever had."

Caleb swung a leg around, taking the driver's seat.

She pulled up short and frowned. "Umm, I think since it's my boss's, I better drive. This bike is worth more than my job."

His lips pulled up in a crooked smile. "We both know who the better driver is. Plus, I gave you the last argument."

It had been years, but the familiarity of their conversations, even their arguments summoned a soft comfort she didn't realize she missed.

"I beat you a couple times, you know?" She'd forgotten their makeshift racing around their property.

"Because you cheat." He turned on the engine, tuning out her rebuttal.

She rolled her eyes, threw on the backpack and his bow, and climbed on, holding on as he sped forward. Her chest tightened at the forced closeness. He wasn't a stranger, but she'd sure changed. Was it possible to repair the damage to their friendship and start anew? She would have to think about that later, for they had a witch to visit.

ᴄ◌ᴄ◌

Her raw throat burned from yelling directions for the last couple hours. The motorcycle slowed as she saw the flames shooting up amid the forest.

Her stomach clenched, in anger. It had to be Mariah's house. Their only chance for answers burned in the distance. Becca rubbed the back of her neck. What happened?

They watched from the safety of the forest. The second story had collapsed in on the house. It had been burning for a while and was another controlled burn since it wasn't spreading to the rest of the forest. Anyone who might be responsible was long gone.

Becca leaned back, putting space between them. "I shouldn't have left without more information."

"You had to," he reminded her.

"Maybe." But now the trail and any chance of answers were lost. What was the connection between her family and Mariah? The only link she could think of was herself. That wasn't good.

"You want to wait to investigate?"

"No." There would be nothing left.

"Where next?" Caleb asked. "We have less than a quarter tank of gas."

There was one person who might have answers. The only wizard she really knew. Someone she'd trusted, maybe even loved once, until he lied to her repeatedly. Darion.

"I have an old acquaintance in the city. He may have some answers." Ex-boyfriend was not something she wanted to admit, to anyone. And introducing him as such to Caleb felt even more off.

"Okay." Caleb peeled out in the dirt and shot forward.

She held on, trying to focus. The trip back would take longer as they had to enter at a city gate. While anyone could leave the city through the coven's invisible wards, entrance was only possible at certain points.

Trees thinned and night had fallen as they finally approached city limits, and Dedra sputtered to a stop.

"It went farther than I thought," she said.

They both climbed off, stretching their legs. Caleb pulled the flashlight out of the backpack.

"No light." She pushed it down. "We don't need any unwanted attention."

"Right. Right," he said putting it back. "I must be more tired than I thought."

Even in the moonlight, Becca could see his heavy eyes and slow steps. "When's the last time you slept?"

"You mean before I buried my parents?" His voice held no anger, just a numbness that tore at her heart and ignited her need for vengeance.

"It's only four or so miles to the city. We can rest at my place." Out in the open and exposed as they were, they didn't have the luxury of rest.

He pushed Dedra down the dirt path, lining the side of the road. "Your place, huh?"

"It's not much."

She scanned the area but couldn't see past the shadows of trees and bushes. She didn't like this. They were too exposed. The cloudless night offered little cover. Going through the woods wouldn't work, since pushing Dedra without a trail would be noisy.

Noticing Caleb's watchful gaze, she asked. "What is it?"

He shook his head. "Nothing."

"No, what?"

"I keep wondering if this is real, if you're real. It's been four years. But with you here—" He glanced at her again. "—I never thought I'd see you again."

"Me either." It was surreal, walking with Caleb in the forest. Yet here he was, awakening those old memories and feelings that she never thought she'd experience again. Part of her died that night when she left. The other half was scarred for life.

They continued on in silence, the bright stars shining down with unearthly promises. A disconcerting rustle sounded in the trees up ahead. Taking the bow off her back, she handed it to Caleb, more sure of his ability than hers.

"Just in case," she whispered.

She took the backpack from him and grabbed the bike's handles. He notched an arrow, and kept it low and ready. About the time she began to wonder if maybe she imagined things, something rushed out from the darkness.

CHAPTER 5

A man tackled Becca to the ground, his size overwhelming. His weight crushed her, and her breath rushed out. He pressed a large branch of some kind against her chest, trapping her on her back.

How could an elephant of this size move so quietly? She fought against the make shift staff as it inched its way to her windpipe, and wished for the knife at her side.

"Get that bike out of here," the man shouted.

She struggled and turned her head in time to see a handful of men take off with Dedra. A classic stab and grab.

Thugs. Nikko was going to kill her.

Several feet away one man lay on the ground with an arrow sticking out of him, while another man rushed Caleb. There wasn't enough time to get off a shot, so he punched him in the face. The man staggered back, and then charged forward. Caleb was strong, but these men fought dirty.

She turned back to her attacker, as anger rose bringing a sour taste to her mouth. Pressing in her heels, she pushed against his body, struggling against the man's massive size. The movement tipped him forward just enough for her to catch the scent of rotting fish. The stomach roiling stench made her gag.

Slamming her forehead into his nose, she ignored the

gushing blood and the resulting pain from the hit. Swearing, he reared back and reached for his nose, releasing the pressure on the stick at her throat. Taking advantage of his distraction, she grabbed the knife from her waist and struck repeatedly. He hollered in pain.

Rolling out from under him, she jumped to her feet ready to strike again. Caleb's bow thrummed, beating her to the punch, his arrow piercing the large man's throat. He collapsed in a gurgled heap at her feet.

She stepped back. The trees spun around her as she tried to clear her head. Dedra was long gone. Caleb stood on shaky legs as his bow was aimed on the last attacker still standing.

The small dark fellow retreated, hands raised, and then turned tail and ran. They let him. He wasn't worth chasing.

She dusted off the backpack while Caleb collected the arrows. Their movements were quiet, only the sound of their breaths mingled with the wind in the trees. She turned her head as he yanked it from the man's throat. This hadn't been her first fight, but death never settled well with her.

"Thanks," she told Caleb. This was one fight she wouldn't have survived alone.

Branches broke nearby and Becca turned, knife at the ready. *More friends?*

Something small pushed through the underbrush. A short demon scurried out and attacked the dead body. The demon wore the shape of a mongrel dog, but with a thin torso that twisted and arched unnaturally. It tore at the man she fought only moments ago. Bile rose in the back of her throat.

The twang of the bow cut through the night as Caleb released another shot, and it found its mark. He walked over, put his boot on the demon's head, and yanked out the arrow.

She quietly backed up, her limbs tingling with exhaustion.

He cleaned the gore off his arrow, but motioned to her shirt. "You okay?"

Looking down, she noticed the blood covering her chest and shuddered in disgust. "Yeah. It's not mine. I could use a shower, though. And you?"

"Nothing that can't wait till we're out of here." He started out, heading deeper into the woods, a tired rasp to his voice.

After five or ten minutes, fatigue pulled at her. Her dragging feet were making too much noise, and she struggled to soften her step. Her body ached, and she could feel that last fight. A little farther along, Caleb started favoring his right leg, which spoke more of his injuries than he would.

She slowed down. "Drink?"

He nodded and took the bottle

She checked her watch. They had a few more hours until dawn. They might make it, but without sleep and rest, if they ran into anyone else they might not fend so well. "Let's find a spot to hole up in. We both could use a couple hours of rest."

He shrugged. "Sure."

His easy agreement told Becca she made the right decision. He could still move with a hunter's step, silently among the cluster of fallen branches and leaves, but his shoulders hung heavy.

They found a cluster of oak trees that should provide some protection while they rested. She turned sideways to slide into the grouping. Branches snagged at her clothing, but there was enough room to hide. She sank down against a tree trunk. Caleb snapped off a couple branches before he lowered himself to the ground. His bow, still intact, lay across his lap.

She closed her eyes, trying to shut out the world and the last twelve hours. As the night settled quietly around them, she could hear Caleb pulling off his jacket. She scooted toward him and turned on her flashlight, pointing it at the ground. "What happened?"

"He stabbed me with something. Not a knife. Not a real one at least." Blood soaked the material.

She rolled his sleeve up. Blood smeared over his thick, muscled arm. The gaping cut bled slowly. "Probably homemade."

Grabbing her backpack, she pulled out the water bottle and some gauze and duct tape. She wished for alcohol, but that would have to wait until they got back. Dirty weapons made for infectious wounds.

He held the flashlight low while she went to work. Maybe it was the attack, or the darkness surrounding them, but she was very aware of the short distance between them. His sweet breath on her brow. Her cold hands fumbled with the tape.

The past drew her back to the warm memories of them together. Long afternoons of hiking and climbing, of summers spent playing in the trees, swimming in the river, and convincing themselves they could live off of squirrels and leaves. They'd shared their first kiss. He had known her inside and out.

Things were different now, she reminded herself, as she carefully finished binding his wound. He sat quiet, watching her work.

A quick look at his worn, beaten face told her she wasn't the only one who had changed. "That will have to do. I'll clean it again when we get back. How's the leg?"

Clearing his throat, he looked down. "Fine."

Realizing she still held his arm, she quickly let go, hoping the flashlight didn't catch her embarrassment.

"What happened to you Becca? Why did you leave?" Shadows hid his features.

She threw the tape in the backpack and zipped it up. Such a simple question, but she didn't have a simple answer.

"Last I heard," he said. "You were being shipped off to live with your uncle to find a spouse. Instead, I find you fighting like you've made it your profession." His voice held a soft-spoken agony. "You left me with nothing, Becca. I couldn't even put my foot on your land without your father using me for target practice. I thought I deserved better."

She would rather he yelled. It would give her something to fight against. His kind demeanor tore at her heart.

It was a reminder of when things began to change between them. The awkward moments and stolen glances, that slowly turned into something more. Something neither had ever experienced but both wanted to.

Then they were caught. Her uncle, who came by for a visit, found them together in the barn, making out. The last time she saw Caleb, her uncle threatened to kill him for taking away her virtue. They didn't have sex, but it was heading that way. That day Caleb was forced to leave, but that wasn't why she left him.

She took a deep breath, shame bubbling up in her throat. "I couldn't face the future my uncle and parents had planned for me." Her voice broke, unable to tell him the whole truth. She couldn't face what she let happen to her. "I took off. Headed for the city to get lost."

"By yourself? Were you possessed?" Surprise and pain colored his voice.

She actually thought she might have been. When she left that night with her father's knife, she contemplated suicide. The pain was overwhelming, but she made it to the city. As scary as the first few days were, it was better than a past where she couldn't trust herself.

"You should have come to me. You could have stayed with us."

"They would have found me. You know that." She pulled her knees up to her chest, trying to warm that cold empty spot in the middle of her chest that appeared every time she thought of that night.

"I would have gone with you." He lifted his hand as if to reach out to her, but stopped short.

"It doesn't matter." The lie felt heavy on her lips. She grabbed the flashlight and turned it off. "We better rest while we can."

CHAPTER 6

S itting in a floral armchair with cats twisting around his legs, Darion wondered what kind of hell he was in.

Lady Katherine sat across from him. Tears heavy in her eyes, she stroked a calico on her lap. "Can you tell me more about my cat, Sprinkles," she asked, motioning to the dead cat that lay on an embroidered pillow on the coffee table in between them. Her aged face struggled to keep its composure. "I think it was those damn dirty Mundanes that got her. If it wasn't for my security, they probably would have eaten her whole. If only the coven would exterminate them as promised."

Old and racist. What a peach.

He ran his fingers through his short black hair that stood on end, while keeping his expression polite. That's how he made his money: his reputation, his charm and lastly, his talent. He was the best pyromancer in the city, and charged for it. But some days, like today, he felt any good con man could pull this job off. "Exactly what are you seeking to know?"

"Talk to poor Sprinkles," Lady Katherine demanded. "Tell me what happened. Does she know who killed her? Does she miss me?"

He strove to put on his best sympathetic face. "I will need to burn her remains to find your answers. The fireplace will do." He moved to gather the deceased cat from the pillow.

"Wait? Do you have to use her whole body?" she asked. "Can you leave her head possibly?"

He covered a laugh with a cough and added several others for authenticity's sake. "The more I have, the more I can see," he answered truthfully.

What does she want to do with a head? Stuff it and mount it?

A contemplative look creased her brow as she pet the other felines meandering around the sitting room. He wondered if he should pity the rest of the cats or envy them. No one would miss him this much when he died.

"All right. Go ahead."

Before grabbing the cat, he heard a scuffle coming from the hall. Magic pulsed, like electricity running up his arms. He recognized the voice and swore silently, before turning back to Lady Katherine.

"Excuse me for one moment. I have a colleague that seems to have tracked me down."

"But what about Sprinkles?" Her voice rose to a cat like screech. "I have paid good money, you know?"

"You never want to rush something of such great importance," he said with a gentle tone. "Sprinkle's spirit will stay strong. Be with him, while you can."

She appeared placated for the moment. Ignoring the commotion outside the room, she leaned forward speaking quietly to the deceased feline.

He slipped through the door in time to find the body of her security guard falling to the floor. "I hope you didn't kill him. This is one of my better clients."

"He's alive," Peter said dismissively, while brushing something off his expensive suit. His blond hair feathered to the side with way too much hair product. Not much had changed from their school days.

Peter's Soultorn, a neatly trimmed Hispanic man, rested over Lady Katherine's guard, one foot pressed on the man's neck.

Darion had grown up around demons, but their presence unnerved him, no matter the host. He knew what dwelt deep within. The Soultorn studied him, licking its lips.

"Stop," Peter commanded. The demon sulked back against a wall lined with pictures of cats and bowed its head in mock obedience.

"Hey, Pete. I heard the Ryma finally let you have a level four Soultorn as a pet." Darion nodded to the demon standing by the wall. Ryma was the coven leader and Governor of the city "Finally got the training wheels taken off, huh?"

"Not everyone just lets magic waste away." Peter glared as he brushed his dirty blond hair out of his eyes. He was backed by a powerful Soultorn. He had the upper hand, and they both knew it. "Jeremiah wants you."

Darion leaned against a nearby coffee table. "I'm in the middle of something."

"The car is waiting outside."

Jeremiah always picked him up, as the drive uptown took a couple hours and several silver pieces in gas.

"What's this concerning?" Darion hated being treated like a second-class maid, running as soon as they said the word. But disobedience came at a cost, and he had run out of chances and excuses.

"Doesn't matter."

"You mean you're not privileged to know. And here I thought they finally trusted you, giving you your own pet and all?"

He pushed Peter more than he should, but he couldn't help it. Peter had been a prick since he was ten years old.

Peter's sneered and shoved him back up against the wall. His hands sent a tingling sensation through Darion's clothes. Darion could always get this idiot to rise to the bait, as he did now with precise timing. Peter's magic was Spirit based, great at controlling demons. But he was never top of their class, and that's why the demon stood frozen by Peter's last command, only grinning at the chance of violence.

Peter's face burned with frustration. "It's removing some girl's Hand of Mary tattoo. It's one of the few things your pathetic powers are good for."

"Of course," Darion said while pulling power from his own demon, locked in a pentagram at home. He itched to strike out, release the fiery inferno burning inside of him.

Peter let go of him, his dark eyes seething with rage. "I could finish you."

He might be right. Darion had never taken on a level four Soultorn before. "But you won't."

The coven needed him. It was probably the only reason they tolerated him.

"Just finish up and get in the car." Peter motioned for his Soultorn, and they left without another word.

Darion took several deep breaths, steadying the magic burning to get out, and replayed Peter's words in his head.

Some girl's Hand of Mary tattoo.

What are the odds that the tattooed girl is her? Becca?

CHAPTER 7

I t didn't surprise Becca when the dream returned again. It always began the same, in her family's barn with Caleb.

His arms were warm and secure around her as he playfully tackled her onto soft hay. Her light laughter filled the barn, only silenced when his lips pressed against hers. The kisses, playful and sweet, began slowly. Bliss blossomed in her chest, flowing to every part of her body.

It wasn't going to last. It never did.

The dream slowly morphed into something dark, every kiss leaving a rancid taste in her mouth. Caleb was no longer Caleb, but a black demon, twisted and evil. Its tentacles grabbed at her, consuming her. She startled awake.

"It was just a dream," Caleb murmured, rubbing her arm. "Just a dream."

Her heart raced as she struggled to breathe. She pushed Caleb's arms aside and turned away. She hoped she didn't say anything while dreaming. Could he know? She thought she'd drown in the doubt and shame of her past. She wished he would say something.

"You okay?" he finally asked.

Maybe silence was better. Becca avoided the question and checked her watch. "We need to get going."

His first night back and she was already acting like a

freak. She grabbed the backpack, ignoring Caleb's concerned looks.

Without another word, they headed toward the city. Dawn peered out over the trees by the time they crossed through the gates. The city guards, with demon dogs at their sides, nodded them through. Two ragged Mundanes were of no concern to them.

She couldn't help her slight embarrassment as she approached her apartment building. Four stories tall, most of the windows were boarded up. There was no key to enter and the elevator had been broken since she'd arrived. The manager was fair, though, and on lucky days the water ran hot.

Wood stairs moaned under their weight as they trekked up to the fourth floor. After the takeover, city maintenance had fallen apart. Magicians enjoyed the luxuries of modern electricity and appliances, and, for a price, you could have them. Magicians often spouted the doctrine of freedom and blessings of magic. But none of them had to take cold showers in the winter, or better yet, had to fight a rogue demon with their bare hands.

"This it?" Caleb asked as she paused in front of 4G.

"Home sweet home." The sarcasm in her voice sounded empty and turned to a deep sorrow for what they both had lost. This was the only home she had left. Everything else was gone. Lost in thought, she unlocked the door and stepped aside to let Caleb in first.

"I thought you said you lived alone, Becca," Caleb said.

She whipped out her knife. One of Nikko's men reclined on her bed, a book in hand.

He lowered the book and sat up. "Easy, girl."

"Get the hell off my bed, Grismo." She didn't have much, only a small studio apartment. Her only excess was a pile of paperback novels and a coffee pot that recently broke. But it was hers, and Grismo knew better than to sneak in.

He raised an eyebrow. "What? You didn't say that last time."

"There was no last time." Her hand itched to slap his ridiculous smile.

"That's right. It was in my dreams. And you were fabulous by the way. Didn't talk at all."

"Get out." She spit out between her clenched teeth. She wasn't in the mood for his jokes.

"Come on, girl," Grismo started.

"Do as she says." Caleb notched an arrow, pointing straight at him. "Grismo, is it?"

Grismo raised both hands in the air. "Whoa. No need to get testy."

An arrow flew and stuck into the wall, inches from his head. Caleb usually wasn't this short tempered, but they'd both been through hell. Grismo needed to leave.

Grismo jumped off the bed, mumbling a string of expletives. "Tell your boy toy to relax."

Caleb was no one's toy, but she enjoyed watching Grismo about to piss his pants. "What do you want?" she asked.

Grismo kept glancing at Caleb. "Nikko wouldn't like me dead, girl."

"A hole or two wouldn't hurt, especially if I told him you were in my bed."

The last words appeared to have struck Grismo. He straightened his back and smoothed out his dark shirt. "Nikko wants his money and the bike. He sent me here when you didn't make it back last night. He couldn't have one of his runners actually taking off."

She took the bag off her back and found the envelope.

"Here's the cash. I got mugged and lost the bike."

Grismo took the money and began to count it. "Mugged, really?"

"Long story. Give Nikko the money, and tell him to keep my cut to help cover the bike."

He laughed and tucked the envelope in the back of his pants. "You think your cut is going to cover it?"

"I'll work off the rest. He knows I'm good for it." Her words snipped with annoyance. She couldn't deal with the bike or Grismo right now. Her sister came first.

"Don't think you can tell Nikko how the deal is going down," Grismo said, a dark edge entering his voice. "He'll come and get you soon. I'm sure."

Caleb tensed and readied his bow.

"You should leave. Now." Becca bristled at the threat.

"I'm not sure," Caleb interrupted. "Maybe we should sell his body bit by bit, to pay for the motorcycle."

Grismo froze for a minute and laughed nervously. "I think I like you," he said to Caleb and headed for the door.

Caleb moved to the side to let him leave, the muscles in his neck still taunt.

"Maybe this guy can survive you, after all." Grismo shut the door behind him.

❦❧❦❧

Elizabeth paced the confines of her bedroom. The doorbell rang. She paused for a moment. It must be who Jeremiah was waiting for. She continued pacing, picking at her nails. She ached for her mother, someone to ease the knots in her stomach.

The sun peered through the window, framed with lace curtain. It taunted Elizabeth, who had been trapped in this floral nightmare of a room. From the roses on the wall, to the iron flowers woven in the bed frame, and dried flowers on the nightstand, either Jeremiah or his maid, Paula, had a thing for tacky flowers.

Elizabeth glanced at the unfinished letter on the desk, and the attempted letters that filled the wastepaper basket. Every time she tried to write home, the words felt inadequate. She was expected to write letters of thankfulness for this opportunity to get married, but gratitude escaped her.

She had been on a strict schedule since arriving. Even walks were supervised. And now, her tattoo? Her uncle said her parents knew about removing her tattoo, but why? What was their reasoning?

Jeremiah had told her no future husband would want her to have a tattoo. It could be hiding some evil lurking inside.

At the time, she didn't argue. Shock had overwhelmed any commonsense objections. Now, at the idea of someone burning her flesh, she could think of a million or two reasons to not go through with this. First of all, it would hurt. Second, why would her husband care if it protected his wife? She would wear her hair down for the rest of her life if she needed to keep it from him. When they discussed this arranged marriage at home, Jeremiah never said anything about removing her tattoo.

Elizabeth jumped at the sound of the door. It was Paula, carrying in the tea. The older woman had a strong beauty that was lined with slight wrinkles. Brown curly hair framed her face with never a curl out of place.

"Here, sweetie, something to calm you down and help with the pain."

I'm not your sweetie. Elizabeth bet this woman wouldn't be so eager if she was to have an iron stuck on her skin.

"I put honey in it," Paula said, coaxing her into the

chair.

Elizabeth murmured a quick thanks and took the cup. She tried to remind herself that it wasn't this woman's fault she was stuck in here like a prisoner awaiting her doom.

Paula sat across from her on the bed, watching her drink the tea.

The sweet taste of honey overwhelmed the flavor, and Elizabeth savored the warmth down her throat. Maybe she could just talk to Jeremiah, convince him to wait until she met her fiancé. She took another drink then set the cup down and closed her eyes. The room spun slightly. She pressed a finger to the bridge of her nose, fighting off what felt like a migraine.

"Paula, do you think we could do this later?" Elizabeth asked. "I'm not feeling that great."

"Of course not. The specialist, Jeremiah called, is already here."

Elizabeth fought her drowsy eyes. "I'd feel a lot better about it if I could talk to my parents first. Or write them a letter."

Every part of her felt heavy, though her heart beat quickened. Anxiety pricked at her skin. She wanted to run, but her limbs were not obeying.

Paula stood and retrieved sheets from the closet, covering the bed. "Don't worry about a thing. Jeremiah will take good care of you. He wouldn't let anything happen to you." She took Elizabeth's arm and led her to the bed. "Come on dear. Let's lie you down. They'll be here soon."

Elizabeth tried to pull back but her arm felt like rubber, as if it wasn't connected anymore to her brain. "My drink. Was there something..." Her speech slurred as her vision became hazy. Something was wrong.

"Of course sweetie. Jeremiah didn't want you to have

to be in pain during this. I told you, he'd take care of you."

"But, but—" Her screams of protest were unvoiced, muted inside her mind.

Trapped in a body with no control, she was placed face down on the bed. Paula tied something around her wrists and ankles. This was wrong. No matter what Jeremiah said, this was wrong.

Paula tugged at her hair and zipped down the back of her dress.

People entered the room. Muffled voices spoke as if they were far away, yet someone approached her. She tried to squirm away, but hands steadied her.

"Be still," Jeremiah's deep voice radiated through her body.

She couldn't fight the pull of her heavy lids and found peace in the darkness.

Without warning, a scalding pain shot through her body. Her eyes snapped open. She couldn't control the scream that erupted. The high pitched cry sounded animalistic. She arched, pulling against the restraints. Pain pierced her to the core as if severing some vital part of her soul, something that she had never known was a part of her.

CHAPTER 8

D arion closed the door on the crying girl, and a guilty relief washed over him. He leaned against the wall in the narrow corridor. *Thank God, it wasn't Becca.*

The young girl's pale hair and full face was a stark contrast to his ex-girlfriend's. The only similarity lay on the girl's back. The Hand of Mary tattoo matched Becca's exactly, down to the blue ink. He could only wonder what that meant. The powerful tattoo carried a complicated spell few knew and even less could afford.

Soft cries traveled under the door. A nauseated feeling, which had been present in his gut since he first placed a hand on the girl, threatened to overwhelm him. He hurried to the bathroom down the hall and shut the door. Bent over the sink, he repeatedly splashed cold water over his face. He didn't dare raise his face to the mirror. He loathed himself for working for the coven, especially Jeremiah.

He needed to leave the city. Get off everyone's radar if he ever wanted to be free of them. Being raised in the coven didn't spare him from the leader's influence or anger.

His parents had died before he reached eight, and his last living relative died three years ago, singing the praises of their coven leader, Ryma.

And now, with Becca gone, he had nothing holding him back. He had run before at the death of his aunt, and the coven found him. But he was younger then. Maybe he could go to the coast?

He dried his face and hands. A renewed determination gave him focus. He needed these jobs, and the money to get him far away from here. Maybe he could even sell some demon names. Wizards were always willing to pay for the names to summon demons. No. He would need those names to remain hidden. They were his last defense. He was dead without them.

He opened the door and froze.

Jeremiah stood waiting in the hall. He was tall, but it didn't hide his extra weight that came with age. His pale skin was a stark contrast to his dark eyes and hair. He peered down his sharp nose with disgust, as if he could read Darion's thoughts.

He wasn't a mind reader, Darion resolved and stood straight.

"Come have a drink." Jeremiah didn't wait for a reply, but walked down the hall.

Darion reluctantly followed. Jeremiah probably had at least five or more demons in this home, waiting eagerly to strike: two or three Soultorns were security around the building, Jeremiah's own personal Soultorn was a level five, and probably several less powerful demons lay in wait.

Not many wizards could control that many demons, and several had ended up dead in their attempts. But Jeremiah was next in line for coven leader. It took work to maneuver that high. Rumors were that Jeremiah was supposed to be the current coven leader, but he was passed over as Ryma wormed his way into power. That hurt had to last for years.

They entered Jeremiah's den. One portion of the room was filled with expected decor, bookshelves, a desk, and two leather arm chairs. The other side of the room resembled some dark wizard's torture chamber as the main stage.

Jeremiah's Soultorn, a manicured Neanderthal with strong sharp features and smooth blond hair, sat on a single wooden stool. It sat next to a pentagram that held another demon in its true form. The creature almost resembled an albino bat, with blood dripping down its chin. Its wings, shredded and crimson, unfurled and its ears grew into horns as it hissed at Darion.

He sat down and accepted a drink from Jeremiah, pushing the images out of his mind. His skin prickled with the energy radiating from the two demons. He detested the part of him that wanted to tap into that power, relish it.

Jeremiah reclined in his chair, drink in hand. Shadows from the lamplight fell over his sharp features. He looked at ease while the demon writhed soundlessly behind him.

Darion took a sip, welcoming the burn down his throat, and then set the glass down.

Jeremiah continued to work on his drink, the ice clinking softly. "I know you have chosen not to align yourself with coven politics."

Darion remained silent.

"It's of no consequence. The coven comes first. You know that."

Darion bit his tongue. He'd been lectured, punished, even persecuted in the name of service and sacrifice. The cost of disobedience was high. If he chose not to serve the coven, his power, rare and valued, would be funneled through a demon possession. He preferred to control his own body, so he submitted. "I am always willing to serve where needed."

A smile crept over the wizard's face. "That's good to hear. And your service here is of real importance. Not that the wealthy elite don't have their purposes."

Darion quickly finished his drink, hoping to rush this conversation.

"My real question is where do your loyalties lie?"

Cold tendrils of magic curled around Darion's feet. As an enchanter, Jeremiah could push him to swear loyalty to him solely. And if Darion wasn't careful, he just might. Darion drove his magic back in defense, strong and hot. If there was going to be a fight, he wouldn't go quietly.

Jeremiah smiled, acknowledging the silent exchange between them.

Darion was sick of the games. "You question my loyalty?"

Jeremiah's hand appeared to brush imaginary lint off the chair. "I just want to make sure your devotion is to the coven, and not to a particular person. We all want what's best for our kind."

For the first time, Darion's interest piqued. This girl, without her tattoo, was more than he thought. Would Jeremiah be brave enough or stupid enough to make a move against the coven leader, Ryma?

"I have always been loyal and have never made oaths or vows to any other," Darion said.

Magicians often swore loyalty to stronger wizards or witches, hoping to gain power, favor, and protection. But his loyalty always remained to himself. And magically binding himself to another never appealed to him.

"I know. But you may soon be requested to do so." Jeremiah set his drink down, and leaned forward. "Unrest and rebellion spreads like a sickness. Magicians with too long a leash need to be reined in for the safety of us all."

"Is that what the girl is for?"

"She's just an interest of mine," he said, leaning back in the chair. "The real question is what side will you fall on when the fire starts?"

A sense of dread sat in his stomach as Darion considered the implications. There had been recent rumors of rebellion. Darion needed to leave town before the rumors became something more. A takeover at that scale would leave countless bodies.

"I'll always stand faithfully by the coven, like my parents did before me." He stared Jeremiah in the eyes as the lie slipped easily from his mouth. Darion said it often enough that he almost bought it himself. But he wasn't naïve enough to think the path his parents took would end any differently for him.

"Good." Jeremiah scrutinized Darion as if dissecting his every word. "Just remember that."

"Trust me. That is something I never forget."

CHAPTER 9

Dressed and anxious, Becca drummed her fingers against her jeans, waiting for Caleb to finish in the shower. She'd showered earlier, before going out to grab lunch for both of them.

They had to wait until night to head to the magician's district to find answers. They needed the crowd that nightfall brought, to hopefully blend in. Sticking out as a stranger or possibly a Mundane wasn't a good idea.

The district was a strip of bars frequented by the magical kind and their best hope to find Darion. He no longer lived in his old place. She'd checked earlier.

Caleb stepped out of the bathroom, and she forgot what she was thinking about. She couldn't help but stare. His snug shirt showed off his toned body and tanned skin. He shrugged on his green jacket covering the white bandage wrapped around his bicep.

"Ready?" He caught her staring, and his face lit up in a smile.

She turned toward the door. It had been a long time since she had a man in her apartment. "Yeah."

"Right behind you."

With weapons hidden within reach, they headed down stairs and into the dark night. Shadows lay long in the street from lamp posts dotting the sidewalk. As they traveled through town, people shut themselves up in their apartments, and a discord of night creatures came out to roam. Mostly stray animals, rats and the random dog.

After a couple of blocks of rundown buildings and makeshift shelters, an uneasy silence settled in. Old warehouses and vacant stores loomed over them, dark shadows buried within.

Their steps were careful as they traveled the dark road scattered with potholes and loose gravel. No lights or electricity ran in this area. Abandoned after the takeover, it remained a home to minor demons, usually unleashed, hiding their existence from this world to which they were summoned.

"Welcome to the demon's playground," Becca warned. "Where all good ghost stories begin."

He pulled his bow off his back and kept it ready at his side. "Should we have come during the daylight?"

"Doesn't matter too much, except for our nerves. They lurk around searching for food day or night."

"Comforting."

"Just shoot them if they notice us before they call other demons." She was grateful to have him near. And maybe together, they would have a chance to find the answers they searched for.

A nervous tick crept up her back. A deep breath steadied her hand, and she scanned the street.

An animal screeched overhead. Caleb readied an arrow, but Becca yanked him to the shadows before he could let it fly.

Not expecting it, he stumbled into her. He pressed her up against the nearby wall, one hand holding his bow and arrow, the other holding onto her waist. His touch sent heat curling into her body.

"It hasn't seen us yet," she whispered, his face only inches away. She released her grip on his jacket. "We don't want any undue attention."

He didn't move his hand that rested on her hip. "Is that a vulture or a demon?"

"There's a difference?" she asked.

He glanced through a dirty window next to them. "I suppose one is much harder to kill"

Becca turned upward as the large bird flew out of sight.

"It's gone."

Caleb dropped his arms and slowly stepped back, waiting for Becca to take the lead. They continued down the street, hiding in the shadows of buildings. For the next several blocks only the cries of distant demons kept them company.

Finally, the lights of the magicians' district shone ahead, going from one kind of monsters to another. Unfortunately these blocks were much harder to maneuver.

The magician's district was lined with the neon light of clubs, restaurants, and upscale condos. People flowed through the streets, the murmur of voices filling the air. An upbeat energy, carried on the air, felt almost alive, even electric.

She sheathed her knife, not wanting to draw attention. Caleb swung the bow over his shoulder. Demons were everywhere, whether trapped in a black eyed dog or cat, sitting obediently next to a wizard, or a pretty dark-eyed Soultorn woman trailing beside. It was the magicians holding those invisible leashes she worried about.

"Here." Becca turned the corner, heading toward Studio Z, known best for its alcohol, gaming, and information. She'd come a couple times before with Nikko.

A cool breeze, laced with the sharp smell of burning

salts, welcomed them to Studio Z. The salts protected the bar and relaxed the clientele. She focused on her surroundings, fighting the magic in the air.

Heads turned as they crossed the crowded floor. Gazes raked them up and down, measuring their worth. She ignored them and focused on the task ahead. As much as they needed to find Darion, her stomach turned at the idea of seeing him again.

She'd dated Darion for close to a year before finding out his secret. Despite her tattoo and her line of work, she never guessed he was a wizard. He was the first person she really opened up to and dared to care for since moving to the city. And he lied to her, every single day.

"Try not to breathe too deep," she told Caleb.

He moved closer. "I'll try. But breathing is sort of a necessity."

"It's a relaxant. Keeps the fighting to a minimum. It'll make you feel like you've had a couple of drinks."

He looked uncomfortable, constantly scanning the room. "Remind me again, who we're looking for?"

"Darion, a pyro with black hair and fair skin." She left out the part that he might be just as likely to set them on fire as to help. She recalled words like "liar" and "I wish I never met you" coming from her mouth. Not great when looking for a favor.

They approached the bar, which looked more fitted to serve some sort of flamboyant royalty. Its large marble counter was accented with gold trim. Behind the bar were huge golden frames, filled with different colored liquors. Three dimensional flowers, that appeared alive, covered the ceiling.

"Is this for real?" Caleb asked.

"With magicians, nothing ever is." She raised a hand.

A barista approached. Her tanned skin was smooth,

and her bright emerald hair wound around into a bun on top of her head. Her sunken in cheeks and thin frame gave her the look of an addict, whether drugs, alcohol, or magic. Whatever the substance, the results were the same.

"What do you want to drink?" Her voice was rich, almost a purr.

"I need to find someone."

"I serve drinks, not information." Long nails that matched her pale purple eyes clicked on the counter.

Becca leaned forward in attempts to keep the conversation private. "I'm looking for Darion."

The woman's face remained bored.

"The pyro," Becca added.

"Let me know when you're ready to spend some money." The woman turned to a more profitable customer.

Becca sat back in the stool, contemplating her next move.

Caleb brushed up against her, sending a tingling sensation up her arm. "Was it supposed to be this easy?"

"I'm going to ask around."

"With this crowd?"

"It'll be fine." She thought working solo might be for the best on this one. People might be willing to talk more.

His brows creased, and he looked around the bar again. "Don't go out of sight."

"I won't." She wasn't careless, and didn't want to be somebody's follower. There were Mundanes that were desperate enough to latch onto whatever magician they could, despite the cost.

He took her seat at the bar. She brushed her hand through her hair, looking for someone to approach.

Several rejections later and after almost getting in a fight with a smarmy old man, she headed back to the bar.

Nobody wanted to talk for free. Caleb sat at the bar, drink in hand, talking to the same barista. Her mouth curved into a welcoming smile as she leaned over the bar, most of her chest falling onto the counter.

Becca stood next to Caleb, waiting for the woman to finish a joke involving three demons walking into a bar. Becca feigned laughter.

Caleb turned, finally noticing her. "Any luck?"

She shook her head, attempting to keep the annoyance off her face.

"Kimmy here may be able to help us."

Becca arched an eyebrow in doubt. "Kimmy?"

"It's going to cost you." The sneer from before reappeared on Kimmy's face.

Figures. Between Becca and Caleb, a couple of beers were all they could afford.

"I can work something out for you," Kimmy told Caleb. "How about a couple cups of your blood?"

"Blood?" he asked as if considering the implications.

"Fresh." Her light pink lips pressed together as if she would taste it herself. The cost of blood made it an expensive high, but worth it to some magicians.

"You're not giving this woman your blood." Becca didn't know if they could trace him later or use it against him somehow. Giving a magician any part of yourself was always a bad idea. "Let's try a couple places."

He agreed. Not that it did any good. Everyone on the damn block stonewalled them, unless they were willing to give part of themselves. Kimmy's offer was looking pretty good. They headed back to Studio Z.

"We need the info right?" Caleb asked.

She couldn't deny that. Darion was her only contact in the wizarding world.

Kimmy's face lit up as they approached. "I knew you'd

be back. I'll be in the back room when you're ready." She motioned to a door past the bar.

"Let me. I have my tattoo to protect me." Becca offered.

He shook his head and headed to the back. "No chance."

"This is more than just blood. Magicians can use this to trace you." She'd just found Caleb and wasn't ready to put him at risk.

"In some twisted way, I think Kimmy wants my blood for herself." He pulled off his jacket as a blush grew on his cheeks. "It was getting a bit uncomfortable—so I didn't press."

Becca wasn't sure whether to be disgusted, or grateful. If it stayed with Kimmy, Caleb might be safe. The sour taste in her mouth told her it was disgust.

They pushed through the door. The room was void of the exuberance in the main bar.

"Glad to see you won the argument," Kimmy told Caleb as she crossed her long tan legs. She sat alone in the sparsely furnished room, next to a metal tray holding medical supplies.

"Where do you want me?" Caleb said, stepping forward.

Kimmy's violet lips curled in a mischievous grin. "Come have a seat by me, cutie. I won't bite, unless you want me to."

Becca couldn't refrain from rolling her eyes. She might have to ask Nikko sometime what witches could do with blood. She wasn't sure she wanted the answer, though. Caleb took a seat and rolled up his sleeve.

As Kimmy reached forward with a needle, Becca stopped the woman and motioned to the knife in her hand. "We're using my knife."

"It's easier with a needle. Less intrusive." Her wide smile did nothing to calm Becca's fears.

Becca knew enough of germs and infections. She wouldn't trust this witch, even if she cleaned it herself.

Kimmy shrugged. "Fine have it your way. Scar up your boyfriend here."

Caleb nodded, and Becca pulled the knife across his forearm. Blood dripped down his arm in a glass jar.

Becca was not negotiating. "One cup will be enough."

The witch milked his arm like some farm animal. As the glass filled, the woman spoke. "Darion is rumored to live a mile north of here in a tall gold building. He frequents Pepper's place a couple blocks west of here. I have a friend who works there."

"Anything else?" Becca had to try.

"Not for a cup."

As the woman tied a bandage around Caleb's arm, several men entered behind them.

Becca spun around and swore. "The deal was fair."

The woman shrugged, but didn't look too concerned.

"They aren't with me."

And they weren't. Grismo stepped out from behind the other men. His sly smile told her this wasn't a courtesy call.

When did Nikko hire these other guys?

The one with slicked black hair and a long nose was first to speak. "Nikko wants to speak with you."

"I don't know who you are, but just let him know that I'm close to getting his bike. I'm paying for info as we speak." Becca repositioned her feet slowly and had her knife already out. It didn't take long to feel Caleb's presence at her back.

"Name's Marco. I've been instructed to retrieve you."

Becca wondered when Nikko hired a new guy. He had

the rough chin and confident stature of a seasoned man.

"I understand," Becca said her muscles coiling to spring.

"I just can't lose this lead—on the bike."

Grismo's smile contorted his already ugly face. "I'm glad you want to do this the hard way."

"Shut up," Marco snapped at Grismo. He turned to Becca. "We were told to bring you back alive. Not necessarily conscious. We don't have to hurt you."

Yeah. Nikko usually saves that for himself. Nikko had always been fair to her, but who knew what Grismo told him? Maybe Nikko did think she took off on him. She didn't have time to explain herself, though.

She scanned the room briefly. There was only one small window. The girl, holding her bloody payment, silently slid around the group and out the only door. Becca couldn't see a way of out of this one. She cursed herself for bringing Caleb into this mess.

Marco approached slowly, Grismo and the other two at his side. "Don't make this any worse."

"Not sure that's possible."

Marco took another step. Between one breath and the next, Caleb strung his bow behind her just as two of the men pulled out guns. She pulled her knife and aimed straight at Grismo.

For a moment no one spoke. The tension in the air grew heavy as each side assessed the situation. For the first time, a growing knot in her stomach told her this might be about more than an expensive motorcycle.

Caleb finally broke the silence, speaking to Marco. "You'll be the first to go down. I always hit my target."

"I understand." Marco replied then turned his attention to Becca. "Our instructions were to bring you in alive. These men will shoot him first. My life and his—"

He nodded briefly at Caleb. "—will be wasted if you do this."

She understood his threat. The two guns pointed directly at Caleb. That was why there were so many men. Nikko only needed one gun to put her down. He wanted her alive.

"Put it down," she said to Caleb, lowering her knife. "If Nikko wants to talk, we'll talk."

"You know, I might be dead either way."

It might be true, but she couldn't watch it happen. Not now. She'd worked for Nikko for two years. He killed when he had to, but out of necessity, not pleasure. If they were going to have a chance, it would be with him.

CHAPTER 10

One of Elizabeth's long blond strands of hair kept slipping into her face during dinner. Her mother would have been appalled, but Elizabeth couldn't figure how to pin it back. She struggled with the simple task until tears threatened to spill down her face. Her emotions were taking her on a roller coaster ride she never signed up for. They said it was the pain medication for her burn. *Get a hold of yourself.*

"Paula," Jeremiah requested of the woman sitting across from Elizabeth. "Assist Elizabeth."

Paula stood from her seat, her mouth set in a stern smile, and walked around the table.

Elizabeth lowered her face, warmed with embarrassment, while Paula secured the stray lock of hair.

"I'm sorry, Uncle," Elizabeth murmured.

"Please, there is no reason to be ashamed." He put a finger under her chin lifting her porcelain face. "And what have I said about calling me Uncle."

"I apologize—Jeremiah." It felt odd in her mouth after the years of etiquette her mother had instilled in her.

"Thank you." He nodded and then reached for his wine.

She turned back to her dessert and found it already cleared from the table. *Did I already finish it?*

"I wanted to talk to you about something." He waved a hand at a servant and soon tea was placed before both of them.

"Yes?" She hoped it was about her fiancé, or maybe a word from home. She sipped warm mint tea.

"It's bad news. Very unfortunate indeed." He ignored his tea and drank from the wine glass. "There was an incident at your parents' homestead. Gangs, they presume."

Cold dread seeped down into her bones. The cup in her hand began to shake, rattling the saucer as she placed in down. Gangs were a threat, a dangerous one at that, but her father was prepared. He hid guns, against mother's wishes, and the family dog was great at sounding the warning.

Jeremiah reached over and took her hand. A sickly calm ran over her skin. It didn't ease the tremors in her stomach.

Why hasn't he spoken yet? She searched his face for any inkling of comfort. But found none. "What is it?"

"They didn't survive. There was a fire. It consumed everything."

Time froze. She waited for him to continue, to explain what happened, to tell her they may be injured but would be fine. They had to be fine. She must not be understanding this correctly. She began to shake her head in confusion. "No. You're wrong."

"They died."

Those two words consumed her whole world. Elizabeth stared into the tea cup, a dark endless abyss of nothing.

Someone came and spoke to her uncle. Standing, he spoke to her, but his words washed over her numb skin. Her life, everything and everyone she loved was dead. There was no more going back. She imagined sitting at the bottom of that tea cup in a well of darkness.

There was no more mother or father. No home. No Pixy. Only empty memories of what once was. How could her heart continue beating when the rest of her felt dead?

⌘⌘⌘

Grismo shoved Becca, and she stumbled over the threshold, falling onto Nikko's entry way. Hands tied behind her back, she landed on her knee and cheek. She shook off Grismo's hand as he tried to pull her up.

"Big man that can hurt a girl," Caleb said from behind.

Grismo turned and pulled back to punch him, but Marco raised a hand. "You'll have time later. We don't want to keep them waiting."

Becca wasn't sure if it was the "later" or "them waiting" that scared her more. Becca was pulled to her feet and struggled to see Caleb behind her. Every vein in his neck bulged as his arms strained against the binds. He'd wanted to shoot these men earlier, and she stopped him. She'd hear it from him later. Or she hoped she would.

They continued to the back. Two days ago she was here, and now she entered with her hands cuffed behind her, stripped of her weapons.

She tried to jerk out of her captors grasp. "I know the way." It's not like they could run anywhere. Nikko's men guarded the building. Several smiled at her as if they enjoyed watching her walk to her doom—which they probably did. Grismo just smiled and kept his hands tight.

She'd always been straight with Nikko, and he'd treated her right. She was one of his best runners. She rarely drank and ran jobs on time. He had to know she would pay him back. Why wouldn't her heart stop racing then?

With a single knock, they entered. The room was filled

with smoke, a fog in an already dim room.

Grismo pushed Caleb and Becca forward. Becca attempted a reassuring look, but Caleb stayed focused on the threat ahead.

Nikko sat at his desk with one light on. He didn't look happy. "Shut the door and leave."

Grismo opened his mouth to argue, but Nikko silenced him with a hand. The men left. An uncomfortable chill crept up her back.

"Nikko," Becca said, "I was just about to track down the men that stole the bike. I was this close when your guys grabbed me. I—"

"Shut up!" He stared at her hard. A bruise was forming over his left brow. And his bloodshot eyes held an anger and sadness that she struggled to believe was over a bike. "I'm sorry Becca, but…" He trailed off.

She couldn't let him finish. "Let Caleb go. He had nothing to do with it except for trying to help me get your bike back. The scavengers would have probably even got the backpack if it wasn't for him."

"No," Caleb shouted.

Of course she could count on Caleb not to just keep his mouth shut.

"I'll find you the money," he continued. "Let Rebecca go. She's not worth it."

Nikko shook his head.

A voice emerged from a dark corner with a power and familiarity that made Becca automatically take a step backward. "Oh, I think we both know that Rebecca's actually worth quite a bit."

Nikko focused on something behind Becca. "This has nothing to do with the bike. There was nothing I could do."

She turned to the darkened corner of the room. A

man stepped out of the shadows. He had gained a bit of weight in his face, but Becca would never forget his sharp nose and imposing presence.

"Uncle…" The word trailed off in confusion as she struggled to put the pieces together.

"Rebecca." Her name curled around his mouth with a sickening air.

Before Rebecca could reply, or figure out what the hell was happening. Her uncle raised his hand and spoke words she didn't understand. Caleb collapsed in a pile on the floor.

Becca fell to her knees, hands still tied behind her back. "What did you do to him?"

His breath was even, his eyes rolled into the back of his head.

"He should have known better than to find you again," Jeremiah scolded.

She crouched next to Caleb, her heart racing. If he died, it would be her fault. His chest continued to rise and fall slowly. A rush of relief turned to bewilderment.

"What are you?" She stood, her mind spinning in a million directions.

"My dear." Jeremiah approached, speaking down to her. "I was hoping I wouldn't have to drag you out of here unconscious."

Memories of the last time she saw her uncle flashed through her mind. Revulsion tasted sour in her mouth. She searched the room for a weapon, anything to fight with. There had to be something.

Foreign words filled her mind. Laced with magic, they carried a tingly sensation that encompassed her. Before she could attack, he placed a heavy hand on her shoulder that she couldn't shrug off. She wanted to scream and fight. Instead her body fell into an abyss full of empty quietness.

CHAPTER 11

Becca's screams tore through the ugly peach room. Yanking at her restraints, she shook the metal bed frame that she was tied face down on. Her throat ached, but she couldn't help the obscenities pouring from her mouth. The door opened behind her. She twisted her head back to find Jeremiah.

He shook his head and took a seat in a nearby white wicker chair. "Time in the city hasn't been good for you, Rebecca. Not with that mouth."

She wanted to tell him where he could shove his disapproval. But before she could talk, he moved his hand, and it felt like a long finger brushed up her spine.

"What are you doing?" she demanded, struggling to keep the hysteria out of her voice. "Untie me."

Jeremiah leaned a bit closer. His musky scent made her sick. "It's for your protection."

She jerked back and noticed the huge Soultorn who stood quietly by the door. Black eyes stood out against his blond hair and fair skin.

Becca had known what Jeremiah was since he took down Caleb. Her uncle had been lying to her and maybe her whole family for years, hiding his magic behind a mask of religious piety.

"You're a bloody wizard," she said.

His pinched mouth remained closed.

"Where's Caleb?" She last saw him in an unconscious heap on Nikko's floor.

"I was hoping you'd cooperate."

Really? Tied spread eagle on a bed? "Where. Is. Caleb?" Every muscle was flexed, wanting to tear into her uncle.

"I took care of him."

"If you hurt him, I swear I will kill you," she screamed at him, limbs straining to break free.

Then with a single touch from Jeremiah, her body went slack. The shock stunned her into silence. Her tattoo protected against minor magic, but what he had scared the hell out of her.

"We can do this the hard way, or a harder way." He knelt by the bed. "This won't be easy. I won't lie. But it will be done."

He stroked her back. An unnatural calm weighed her down, her body slow and sluggish. Disgust turned her stomach. A scream echoed in her mind, but never made it past her lips. This wasn't happening. Not again. The familiar fear from her nightmares, flooded her body. She couldn't do this again.

Amid the web of lies that clouded her reason, she searched for answers. "What happened to my family? To Caleb?" Her voice came out in a whisper, as she struggled to speak. What was he doing to her?

She hated the tears that betrayed her. It was as if she was walking on paper thin ice, waiting for her world to shatter, to be swallowed by the dark truth below.

"So you went home, did you?" A brief look of surprise crossed his face. "I'm sorry you had to see that."

She wanted to scream at him, curse him for whatever role he played in their deaths. But she needed answers.

"What did you do? Light the match yourself?"

"You were always so spirited." A smug smile plastered his face as he avoided the question.

Rage built up inside of her, pushing her over the edge. She snapped at his hand. Ready to tear him apart however she could. "You killed them."

He pulled his hand back, and chuckled. "It doesn't matter."

Her body arched back, straining to be free. He placed a hand on her ankle, and against her will, her body went slack on the bed again. No longer in control, she felt her breath came out in short desperate gasps. This man, who her parents had welcomed into their home, burned it to the ground, killing everyone inside. Almost everyone.

"Elizabeth. What happened to her?" Her sister had been her last spark of hope in this disaster.

He stood up, brushing his suit jacket. After a moment of quiet, he looked her in the eyes. "She's dead."

⁓∽⁓

Darion shook out his wet coat in the greeting room, hoping to ruin the rug under his feet. It was supposedly morning, but someone hadn't told the weather that. Heavy clouds kept up a constant drizzle. His body wasn't in much better shape after having too much to drink with Cynthia last night. One drink, turned into several. Avoiding going home had never used to hurt his head this much.

"You took your time, Darion. He isn't going to be happy," the housekeeper said in a shrill voice that clawed at his brain like nails on a chalkboard.

He nodded, not trusting himself to keep his tongue in check.

"Go straight up. He's waiting."

He climbed the stairs, feet heavy, dreading the task ahead of him. Kip stood outside the door, clothes wet from the rain, waiting for him. His closely shaved head and tattooed arms made his bark definitely worse than his bite.

"What's going on? Been playing in the rain?" Darion asked looking at Kip's drenched clothes and muddy boots.

"Had to deliver a boy to the Moondance Festival. The dude was big. Dropped him like three times." Kip chuckled at himself.

Darion wished he hadn't asked. "What does Jeremiah need me for today?"

"Same as last time."

"What's with these girls?"

Kip's lips pulled into a smile. "Not sure. But this one's feisty."

"Want me to burn your tats off next?" Darion doubted this big guy could keep it together any better than these girls.

Kip broke into laughter. "You'd have to catch me first."

A tingle of magic pulsed from inside the room. Darion rubbed his arms, cold under his damp coat.

"Better head in," Kip said, stepping to the side.

Darion's stomach sank, though he kept his features smooth. Part of the job, he reminded himself. A few more jobs like this and he would be out of here.

☙❧❧

A heavy silence filled the room as Jeremiah's word sank in. Dead? Becca struggled to breathe. A heavy pressure crushed her chest. Elizabeth couldn't be dead. That meant Caleb was lost for nothing.

"How?" she asked, straining to keep her voice under

control.

"She was injured in the fire. I did my best to save her."

How could she believe him? His whole life he spewed out lies to her family. But why lie about this? Becca was trapped and at his mercy.

She didn't want to believe it. She couldn't. The one thing she'd needed to do to make up for the past, for running out on her family years ago and she failed. She failed.

She pressed her head against the mattress, squeezed her eyes tight, and struggled to keep all the pieces of herself together. She crammed the tears, the pain, and the memories back into that tight black box where she had hid so much.

"You killed them." It didn't matter if he threw the match or not, he let this happen. "Your kind killed them all."

"I didn't start the fires. I tried to save them."

She laughed, a sick cackle. It sounded as if she was losing her mind. Maybe she was. "And I'm supposed to believe you? Tied to this bed?"

"You took off, abandoning your family. I couldn't take that chance. I can't have you roaming free here until I remove your Hand of Mary tattoo. Then I can ensure your safety."

"My safety?" She thought he had to be high or something. "You have a Soultorn here. You're a wizard. You're not concerned about my safety."

"I looked for you for over a year. However my sister chose to raise you, wizards are not the problem. They're the solution to what ails mankind."

She glared at him. He couldn't be serious. Her family was dead, and he really thought she was going to side with him. He might have forgotten what happened in the barn that night. She hadn't. Her shame and regret grew into something dark and angry. Her nails dug into her palms, and she ached to claw herself out of this room.

"He's here," the Soultorn said in a deep voice.

Jeremiah nodded to the demon. The door opened and someone entered. "I don't like to be kept waiting," Jeremiah scolded and went to the door.

"I came as soon as I could," the man replied.

Her stomach dropped. The familiar voice struck Becca like a cold glass of water. She whipped her head to the side. It was Darion.

She'd been looking for him, hoping he could provide a clue to what happened to her family. Now he stood in her uncle's house a black bag under one arm. Whatever Darion claimed when they were dating, he obviously worked with the devil himself.

Darion's face went slack as he saw her, an incredulous look frozen on his face. He hadn't changed much. His black hair had a messy look to it, as it was almost long enough to get in his eyes. Rough stubble now covered his jaw, and those brown eyes hurt to look at.

"Get to work." Jeremiah headed to the door to talk to the Soultorn.

Darion approached her with hesitation in his step, like one would a wounded animal. "How?" he silently mouthed to her

"Help me." It came out as a whisper, a quiet pleading.

Darion was a good guy. He might be a liar, but he couldn't do this to her. Could he? He once claimed to love her. That couldn't be for nothing.

"What's the hold up?" Jeremiah returned, standing next to Darion.

"Nothing, sir." All surprise had vanished from Darion's face. The familiar poker face showed no emotion.

"I can take care of this if you have work to attend to."

Jeremiah shook his head. "This one can be a handful. I'll make sure she doesn't cause you trouble."

Darion slowly swallowed, but didn't object.

Did that mean he was going through with it? She didn't dare let her uncle realize she knew Darion. As much as she loathed him at the moment, Darion was her only chance out of this thing.

"Please," she pleaded to both men as they approached.

Jeremiah placed a hand on her leg, and, with a word, a sick languid feeling enveloped her body. She waited for Darion. Any second he would attack Jeremiah, knock him out, and use his magic to save her.

Instead, Darion pulled up a stool and moved her hair out of the way, exposing her tattoo. Her breath came in short gasps. Her pleas for them to stop were rejected, and her body ignored her requests. She was helpless. Darion was going to do it.

"Begin," her uncle commanded.

A light powder fell on her neck, cold at first. Then it grew warm, slowly building to a searing pain. She clawed at the sheet on the mattress and clenched her jaw to keep from crying out. Darion spoke in a foreign tongue, and the agony struck her to the core.

A scream escaped her lips, and she bit down on the bedding. Silent tears spilled down her face. Darion wasn't going to be her savior. Not after she'd walked out on him almost a year ago.

She wasn't sure what hurt more, the flame burning on her neck, or Darion, who she'd loved at one time, betraying her so easily.

The fragile ice that held her up shattered. She lost her only protection against magic. Her family was dead, and who knew what happened to Caleb. As she tumbled into the dark waters of pain and grief, she wished she could join her lost loved ones.

CHAPTER 12

S he needs something for the pain," Darion struggled to keep his façade in check. "She's twitching."

Jeremiah kept a firm hand on her ankle. "It's fine. She's already calmer."

The tattoo sizzled under Darion's flame. He could feel the pulse of Jeremiah's power on Becca. Darion remembered to relax his hands. He needed to keep his anger in check if he was going to get her out of this alive.

He wanted to push this flame onto Jeremiah, burn him alive where he stood, but Darion would never survive the level-five demon looming in the doorway. And if Jeremiah discovered the truth between Becca and him, things would only worsen for both of them. He needed to wait. Jeremiah wouldn't be at her bedside forever.

Darion placed ointment around the tattoo to contain the fire. The blue flames gradually died and a light sulfuric smell permeated the room. Her shoulders were still tense as the last remains of ink began to fade.

He lightly pushed at the flames, smothering them. He had dreamed of touching Becca's skin again, but never like this. Never hurting her. He had done that enough already, pretending he wasn't a magician at the bidding of the coven.

She finally relaxed against his touch. Her eyes were closed, but her pulse was steady. Losing consciousness would be blessing for her at this point.

He'd questioned Becca about her tattoo before, on a hot summer day. She'd claimed not to know much about it. She'd never talked about her past much, though. He'd assumed she had rich or connected parents before coming to the city.

"What are you doing with the girl?" he asked, before thinking.

"What concern is it of yours?" Jeremiah snarled.

"Nothing," Darion said too fast. "Just wondering if she needs a bandage, or if she'll stay on her stomach." There was no nurse maid or cold rag awaiting Becca like with the other girl.

"Finish your work and bandage her. Kip will be outside with your money." Jeremiah headed out the door without a second glance.

"I'm almost done," he said to Becca, grateful to finally be alone with her. He applied a compress of aloe and lavender to the wound before bandaging it. It wasn't the first time he wished he had more knowledge of healing.

She didn't stir. Her eyes were closed, but he doubted she slept. Her face held too much tension. He had missed that freckled nose, and her lips, soft and pink.

He finished placing the bandage on her skin. He couldn't leave her here. Not to this fate. Taking her away, meant defying Jeremiah, a powerful member of the coven. He wouldn't let Darion get away with it. Darion's only choices would be to leave the city or beg for mercy from Ryma.

He couldn't think about the repercussions. Not with Becca so close to him. He brushed back a stray hair from her face. Her eyes opened, confused and frantic, scanning her surroundings. He wanted to comfort her, to touch her and tell her it would be all right. But he wasn't sure of that himself.

She wet her lips and finally focused in on Darion. "I'm going to kill you."

ↄↄↄↄ

Anger boiled inside of Becca, and she itched to claw that sympathetic smile off Darion's face. He looked concerned. He didn't have the right.

"You can kill me once we get out of here," he offered.

Could she believe him? "Untie me" she demanded. Her back burned like hell, her world had crumpled around her, and she wanted to kill him.

He hesitated for a moment, as if weighing the consequences, then began to untie her. Blinking back the tears, she forced herself to focus. She had to get out of here. She wouldn't stay put to be at her uncle's command. Pulling off the last of the ropes, her hands shaking hard, she fisted one and then swung at Darion.

He grabbed her hand, easily blocking her punch. Something in the air, slowed her movements, made it hard to think. Maybe the salts?

"Let go," she ordered. "I'm leaving."

"Not like this," Darion pleaded. "I'll get you out of here. Just trust me."

She almost laughed. "Trust you? You're kidding right? You lie about being a magician. Then you tie me to a bed and burn me." Her voice cracked. Rage threatened to break out. "Did you burn down my parents' house, too?"

Confusion flashed in his eyes. He reached out to her. "I didn't burn anyone's house down."

She pulled back.

"I couldn't fight Jeremiah. He would have killed me and you would still be here. I needed him to leave. Now we have a chance."

"Why?"

"Do you really have to ask?"

She wanted to believe him. She had wanted to trust him for months. But he lied. Still, although she'd vowed to never let him close again, he was her only chance to escape.

She took a deep breath, trying to collect all the scattered pieces of herself. She had to pull it together if she was to be free and find Caleb. "Do you know what happened to Caleb?"

"Caleb?"

"A friend." She rubbed her wrists gently. Rope burns circled both of them. "I'm not leaving without him."

"Big guy?" he asked. "I think one of Jeremiah's guys dropped him off for auction at Moondance."

"The market. Damn." She turned away and placed a fisted hand on her forehead. It was another hit, threatening to bring her down. Moondance was a human market, where bodies dead and alive were sold to the highest bidder for dark magic. Its location was unknown to most Mundanes like herself. She didn't have a clue how to get there. She noticed her jacket on the desk and shrugged it on. They needed to get out of here.

"I see you kept it," Darion said.

Heat raced to her face. He'd given her the jacket for her birthday last year. "It's a good jacket." She wished the words didn't sound so lame.

"True," Darion agreed.

Her fist curled, ready to smack the pleasant look off his face. She needed to get out of here first. There was a reason Jeremiah wanted her tattoo off. "Let's go."

He headed toward the door, while buttoning up his jacket. "Follow me."

"Are we going to just stroll out?"

He attempted a smile, probably meant to be reassuring. "A long as Jeremiah is busy. We have a chance."

She scowled.

He opened the door. A guard stood there just beginning to turn around. Darion grabbed the guard's neck and spoke a few words. A warm breeze blew into the room, and the guard collapsed. Darion pulled him into the room with some effort. The man had to weigh at least twice as much as Becca.

"That was…" She was at a loss for words. She'd never seen him use magic before. A tingle of fear, or maybe amazement, raised the hair on her arms.

"He's more brawn than brains, or magic really. The rest of the household won't be so weak." Darion picked up some coins from the man's hand. "My payment."

Becca held out her hand. She wasn't so quick to forget the past hour of her life. Her neck still ached fiercely. "Then, I guess it really belongs to me. Since without my tattoo, you wouldn't have had a job to perform."

He dropped the money into her hand. "If I had any other option of getting you out alive, I would have taken it."

Logically, it might have made sense, but she wasn't ready to accept any apologies yet. The rope burns were still visible on her wrists.

They didn't run into anyone as they walked down the hall. Her head slowly cleared but her steps remained cautious. She searched the walls for any clues as to where they were at. Did Jeremiah live here? She'd detested Jeremiah ever since she left home years ago, but she never suspected magic ran in his veins.

They hurried down the large staircase with an

antiquated chandelier hanging from the ceiling. She followed Darion and wondered how he fit into this puzzle with her uncle. It made her sick to think of a connection between the two of them.

They turned a corner and ran into a young serving girl. Before she could speak, Darion covered her mouth and grabbed her from behind. He whispered into the girl's ear. It might have been mistaken for an intimate embrace, but soon the girl's legs collapsed under her, and Darion carefully laid her on the ground.

"We need to hurry," he said, turning another corner.

"There should only be one guard on duty out this way. Hopefully, he's distracted."

Becca couldn't believe their escape plan included hoping someone had a short attention span.

They turned into a large kitchen. Pots, bowls, and cutting boards littered the counters as breakfast was in full swing. Behind them a wooden pantry door creaked open.

"Darion, you better not be begging for scraps this morning. You know how I hate—"

He slammed a black skillet against her head. She fell to the floor, her faded flower dress in a crumpled heap.

"Beating up old ladies?" Becca asked. This woman would have stopped them, but seeing her gray hair and wrinkled face made guilt prick at Becca. "Why not the same as the other girl?"

"She's too strong and well protected against magic." He reached down and yanked an amulet from her neck, tossing it to Becca. "She doesn't deserve your sympathy. She's gutted Mundanes smaller than you."

The grim twist of his mouth told her, he was serious. This granny was as dangerous as anyone else, Becca reminded herself. All magicians were, including the one in front of her.

He grabbed a kitchen towel and rummaged through a couple drawers. She turned to the counter. Next to an onion was a carving knife. She picked it up, feeling the balancing point in her hand.

"You always liked your knives," he whispered over her shoulder, his breath tickling her neck.

"We can't all be bloody pyros, can we?" He should feel lucky she wasn't using the knife on him.

He glanced at the knife, as if the same thought had crossed his mind. Then, turning his head, he peered out the back kitchen window. "If anything happens, run for the woods. We're in the north part of the city, the coven's estates. Go south and you should see the city by nightfall."

"Okay."

She ignored the snippet of guilt in her gut. She'd question Darion's loyalty, and now he was putting her safety first. Jeremiah would make him pay for this. "Make sure you get out too."

"I will," he said, heading to the back door. "Stay behind me until I grab the guard then run."

She nodded and gripped the knife. She was a bit put off that he found her so weak in a fight. The pain on her neck reminded her she didn't have the same protection she once had. Her pulse picked up, her body finally waking up from whatever magic Jeremiah used on her.

Outside, a gray drizzling sky hung heavy. She wondered if it would interfere with Darion's magic. Rain couldn't be good for a pyro.

A guard, a good two hundred yards from the house, didn't notice them on the porch at first. He leaned against a large tree, cigarette in hand, with his back to them. Farther past the guard, dense trees filled a beautiful forest. Only the dark haired guard, and who knew what other magic, stood in their way.

Darion had a casual gait as he headed toward the guard. An uneasy feeling settled in the pit of Becca's gut. Darion stayed in front of her, blocking the guard from her view. He stepped off the back porch, leaves crunching underfoot.

"Hey, Marco, got an extra smoke?"

The heavy guard briefly glanced over his shoulder, cigarette in his mouth. He looked twice, before realizing Becca was behind Darion. Becca started to curse the stupidity of the simple plan when the guard's cigarette exploded.

He yelled in surprise and began cursing in a foreign tongue. The air felt electric as Darion closed the distance between the two men in the blink of an eye. But something stopped Darion short of making contact. They stood a foot apart, an invisible barrier separating them. The fire was gone as quick as it appeared.

Becca stepped off the porch. Leaves swirled around her ankles, the air carrying a live current to it.

Darion's jaw tightened as he softly cursed the wizard. His hands opened, palms up.

The guard snapped his head up in her direction. Something tossed Becca against the porch railing. She struggled to move against magical bindings. Each move was like slugging through drying concrete. Her arms hung heavy, too heavy for an effective throw. Her knife would do little against the power at play here. Pulling on the wet railing, she slowly moved down the length of the house.

Darion spoke in a strong voice, containing a power, both frightening and amazing, that she'd never seen before. The green leaves on the trees began to burn, a dark smoke that traveled through the magical barrier. The smoke crept over the dampened earth throughout the clearing, stinging her eyes.

The man struggled to breathe, his lips unable to continue the steady stream of words. He fell to his knees, coughing and gasping for air.

"Run," Darion ordered through gritted teeth.

She jolted awake, rain splattering down on her. Whatever magic that held her back, disappeared. She could run. But what about Darion? She couldn't leave him to Jeremiah. A scream sounded from inside the house. They had to get out of there.

"Darion, come on." She almost could hear the commotion in the house, people sounding the alarm.

"I'll be right behind you." He focused on the man in front of him. "Go. Now!"

Run, she told herself. Run.

CHAPTER 13

"Hold still," Paula demanded as she pulled Elizabeth's hair into a braid.

Hard to hold still while you're yanking my hair out. Elizabeth bit her tongue. Arguing with Paula was pointless. At least the pain in her scalp kept her thoughts from overwhelming her.

Paula had lectured repeatedly about how lucky she was to be in Jeremiah's household, blessed not to be living like the scavengers in the slums. Elizabeth's bedroom shone with an opulence she'd never seen at home. Lush carpet, lavender scented sheets, and maids that Elizabeth had thought only ever existed in books. Even now, her reflection was surrounded by a large golden frame.

The luxury didn't ease the gnawing sensation eating at her. She missed her mother's soft hands combing through her hair, and her father's big hugs and woodsy smell. Tears blurred her vision at the thought of never seeing her parents again. It didn't feel real.

She was sure, if she went back home, they would be there. Mom would be singing in the kitchen, and Dad teasing her as she did the dishes.

Staring at her reflection, with every hair in place, Elizabeth didn't feel lucky.

There was a quick knock on the door. Paula finished the braid in a huff and answered it, hands on hips.

One of the guards stood in the doorway, the tall one with a cute smile. "Jeremiah needs you in his office," he said.

"Fine. I guess breakfast can be late." Paula left with a swish of her long skirt.

Alone, Elizabeth's stomach growled at the news about breakfast. She reached for the water pitcher, only to find it empty. She stood with slight hesitation.

They wouldn't mind if I get water, would they? It's not like they want me starving and dehydrated.

They had never strictly forbidden her to be out of her room. She had left several times—never alone, though. Paula, with those stern set of lips, claimed her uncle had company for work, and it would be inappropriate for a young woman to be roaming the house. Elizabeth wasn't a mangy mutt. She planned to slip to the kitchen and back before anyone would notice.

She opened the door to the hall, glad to find it empty. Padding down the stairs, she silently cursed her nerves for being on edge. She was soon to be a bride. She could get herself a drink of water and stop acting like a child sneaking a cookie.

She crossed a hallway and opened the door to the kitchen. The smell of baking bread floated down the hall, and Elizabeth realized just how hungry she was. Maybe she could convince that mean old cook to let her have a slice.

A scream erupted from the kitchen. Elizabeth ran toward it, running into one of the serving girls, Julia.

"What's wrong?" Elizabeth asked.

Julia just pushed past Elizabeth, yelling for security. She stopped for a moment. Should she hurry back to her room? What if someone was in trouble? Growing up on a farm, she had seen her share of emergencies. Her heart picked up its pace as she continued forward.

She found the kitchen empty, just breakfast cooking in the oven. A moan erupted from behind the pantry door. "Tulla." Elizabeth raced over to the cook, who was struggling to sit up. She lent an arm to the woman. "Are you okay?"

"What do you think?" Tulla sniped. Her hand clutched the side of her head. "Get me a drink. I'm going to be sick."

Elizabeth paused, questions ready on her lips. Tulla scowled, and Elizabeth turned to get that drink. She grabbed a glass in the cupboard and turned on the cold faucet.

As the water rushed into the cup, she stared out the window. Smoke filled her view. The large ash tree was on fire. Two people ran toward the woods. From this distance, she couldn't make them out. The water in the cup overflowed down her hand. Startled, she reached to turn off the faucet.

"Water, child," Tulla called from the floor.

Ignoring Tulla, Elizabeth peered closer. Smoke twirled from the branches. A cold chill crept up her back. The smoke's movement, unnatural and snake-like, had a mind of its own. The vapors wrapped around a body. Two feet jutted out of the smoke, men's shoes, dark and still.

The glass in her hand shattered in the bottom of the sink.

☙

Becca sprinted into the woods, legs burning. She slowed her pace once she found the shelter of the trees. Fall leaves were scattered on the ground, and she couldn't afford to leave a trail. Her step was light and swift. She turned her head, checking for any followers.

Darion approached, with no one behind him, for now. "We need to head east," he said, motioning deeper into the woods. With the overcast sky, it was hard to sense direction. They kept up a steady pace, jumping over random rocks and branches.

She focused on her steps so as to not leave a trail or break an ankle. "I thought the city was south."

"It is. I can cover our tracks to some extent, but not hide us completely." Darion's words came out between rushed breaths. "Jeremiah isn't going to be traipsing through the woods. He'll send others to find us."

Darion then turned and spoke a spell, ruffling the leaves behind them. A ripple passed through the air, as if she could almost watch the magic. Her imagination was going overboard. On a second look, she realized it was water drizzling through the canopy of leaves.

Without a word, they both kept moving under the gray sky. They traveled for hours, slowing to a brisk walk when she needed the break. The only sounds were the crunch of the leaves and their breath. Sweat dampened her shirt, the wound on her back screaming with every step. Her legs went from burning, to numb, to feeling like useless appendages.

She didn't mind the pain, though. It pulled her mind away from the recurring thoughts of her family, Caleb, and her uncle. Pictures of her beautiful sister, dead at the hands of magicians, swam through her mind. Then she worried what Caleb's fate would be.

One foot in front of the other. She had to keep moving. Caleb was out there, and she would do whatever was needed to get him back.

c∕⁀ɔC⁀ɔ

Cold hard concrete pressed into Caleb's cheek. He blinked several times, clearing his vision. Metal bars filled his view as his last conscious moments came flooding back.

"Rebecca." He bolted upright, searching for any sign of her.

He resided in one of many cages, barely big enough to stand in, with only an orange bucket for company. He scanned the other cell, hoping for a glimpse of Rebecca.

They were housed in some type of warehouse, with tall ceilings and yellow industrial lights. Rebecca was nowhere to be found.

He called her name again. Some of the occupants stirred slightly. Others used quiet, but colorful, language to tell him to shut up.

He tensed and fought the urge to yell. The door of the cage held a heavy lock which he couldn't budge. There was no way out.

"Rebecca!" he screamed in frustration.

"Hey, muscles, quiet down before you get us all in trouble. You came in here alone," said a thin young woman in the cage next him. Her blonde hair was knotted in a bun on top of her head. Her dress—short and tight—didn't leave much to the imagination.

He ignored the hot blonde and continued pulling on the barred door. He prayed for something, anything, to give. He couldn't just sit here. A panic deep inside threatened to explode. He had to get out.

"Maybe muscles, but not brains," a short older man said from the cage on other side of the girl. "Don't make too much noise or the guards will come back."

"I have to get out of here," Caleb said.

Last he remembered her boss had kidnapped them at gun point and turned them over to Rebecca's uncle,

Jeremiah. Caleb had never trusted that man and couldn't fathom the role he played in all of this. Caleb had lost everything. His family. His home.

Rebecca was the last piece of himself he remembered. He couldn't lose her too. He lay on his side and tried to kick the lock lose.

The blonde twisted a piece of hair around her finger. "It won't help, muscles. Not unless you have a demon up your sleeve."

He couldn't believe that. There had to be something. He couldn't lie down and die, trapped like an animal. He continued kicking at the lock.

A loud scratching sound echoed off the bare walls as a large sliding door opened. He froze, hoping to glimpse something outside this hell. Beyond the door, was nothing remarkable. A cloudy sky and dirt field with nothing else in sight.

"Thanks, buddy," the old man scoffed a few cages down.

People scampered to the back of their cages. The hair on Caleb's arm stood straight up. A change in temperature sent a slight chill creeping up his spine. He stood tensed and ready to fight.

A couple approached. The man reminded him of a rodent, with short spiked hair and a tight shirt. But Caleb was drawn to the beautiful Soultorn on his arm in a black dress.

Tall and thin, it moved with a dancer's grace. Its light hair framed pink lips, pristine skin, and pitch black eyes. Neither the man nor Soultorn spoke, but continued on a straight course for Caleb.

They smiled, stopping a few feet from his cage. "Welcome to my establishment. I hoped your neighbors informed you of the rules."

"What happened to the girl that was with me? She had—"

The man lifted a hand, and Caleb was forced to his knees. His muscles strained against the magic, like tight cords ready to burst.

"Let's remember our manners, shall we?" The man slowly dropped his hand, and the pressure on Caleb released.

"I'm Pove. The manager here. If you follow the rules, you'll leave here soon enough. If you don't, you'll wish you were dead."

Caleb knelt on the floor, not ready to move until he thought he could get away with it. He focused on this little man, hoping he'd step closer to the cage. If only he could reach him.

"The rules are simple. Be quiet. Be obedient. Be kind, especially to customers. And don't try to escape."

"That's all?" Caleb asked. Did Pove think he would actually comply so easily?

"For now."

"What about the girl?"

Pove shook his head slightly. "Questions are not part of this game."

Caleb stood, gripping the bars. He had to find Rebecca. "The girl, Rebecca, has dark hair. I need to know if she's here?"

Pove ignored his questions and nodded to the Soultorn on his arm. It opened its mouth. A buzzing noise erupted out of the Soultorn and crawled into Caleb head, devouring reason. Searing pain brought him down on all fours, head pressed into the hard concrete.

A brief glance showed that the other people were in similar positions—hands over ears, crouched on the floor. The wretched noise continued on until he wasn't sure when it began or how it ever was going to end. He struggled to think outside this pain.

It took several moments for him to realize the noise had finally ended. The echo of the pain ached in his bones and swam in his head. He remained crouched on the floor, uncertain if he could sit up or move without being sick. When he looked up, those perfect pink lips smiled wide.

The man squatted low in front of the bars, his voice rough. "There's nothing outside this cage. No one. You can live with or without this beauty in your head. Sometimes I like to feed her just to make her happy. Isn't she so pretty when she's happy?"

Pove didn't wait for a response, but rose, took the Soultorn's hand under his arm, and walked out. Caleb was left with only the memories of his past to haunt him.

CHAPTER 14

Becca's feet screamed in protest when they stepped out of the rundown cab. Darion had flagged it down when they first entered the city. They got out a few blocks before their destination. Even though she didn't see any of Jeremiah's men, it didn't mean he couldn't follow their trail.

"We're going back to your place?" she asked.

"No, too dangerous."

They weaved between darkened buildings uptown in the magicians' district. As they approached a street, he lifted a hand, holding her back. A group of guys walked down the street, loud and probably drunk. Not until they turned the corner did Darion step into the street.

"Why do you even bother hiding?" she asked in hushed tones. "You're a magician. You can burn them alive."

"Sorry to disappoint, but I'm not invincible. And I usually try to avoid trouble where I can."

As much as magicians disgusted her, she wanted to know who or what Darion really was. When she'd first learned about his lies, her anger and rage pushed out everything else. She didn't stick around to listen to any explanations. But now, his powers were necessary to her survival and, possibly, Caleb's.

Darion moved to a dark doorway halfway down the

alley. "My friend owns a bar we can crash at."

"He'll be fine with you bringing a friend?" Becca was tired, but the uncertainty of a new place, new people, possibly tied to magicians, put her on edge.

"He's a she," he informed her and knocked on the door.

Becca wasn't sure if that was better or worse.

A dim yellow bulb hung over the worn green door. It flickered for several seconds before a small window opened in the top.

"Tell Cynthia, it's Darion," he said to someone behind the door. The wood slat returned to its original position. After another minute, the door opened.

A look of relief crossed the woman's face as she pulled Darion into a hug. "I've been worried. Come in."

Becca had no claim on Darion and didn't want one, but she couldn't help but wonder who this woman was. The woman looked older, maybe in her thirties, and was utterly gorgeous. Her long wavy black hair shimmered with dark purple and blue highlights. Her clothes fit perfectly, accenting every curve. All of a sudden, the dirt, grime, and sweat weighed Becca down. She ignored the urge to adjust her clothing and followed them inside. They entered a hallway, stacked with random supplies. It looked like a back office or storage.

"Jeremiah's put a summons out for you," Cynthia told Darion. "What did you do?"

He smirked, part of a smile tugging up. "Nothing you wouldn't have done."

"That isn't reassuring." She looked him up and down, as if making sure he was all right. "Need a place to stay?"

"We do." Then he motioned to Becca, "Cynthia this is Becca."

As Cynthia turned her attention to Becca, all the

warmth left her face.

"In the flesh," Becca joked. She couldn't find the energy to smile, though. After the last twenty four hours, she didn't have it in her.

"Great," Cynthia said without feeling. "Go upstairs and get cleaned up. I'll find you some food."

Becca followed Darion through the hallway and up a flight of worn stairs.

"Who's Cynthia?" she finally asked as they reached the second floor, forcing a casual tone.

"I told you." He reached a door, holding it open. "A friend. An old one."

She didn't look that old to me, she thought as she followed him inside.

Darion flipped a switch behind her, and lights bathed the room in an artificial glow. The large room held a king sized bed, a dresser, and small table with two chairs. The light blue walls and a chic bed cover spoke of refined money that unsettled Becca. She picked up a heavy marble ashtray off the table. It could probably pay her rent for a month.

Darion always had money while dating her, but nothing this elaborate. He'd claimed he worked for the black market. She wondered how he really lived. The Darion she thought she knew drifted farther and farther away.

She set down the ashtray. "So...only one bed."

"I can take the floor." Six months ago, Darion would make some joke about them wrestling for it. Instead, an awkward silence settled in between them—two strangers with a complicated past. "Why don't you go take a hot shower, and I'll get you a change of clothes? Then we can get a bite to eat and figure out our next step."

She nodded. Shower first, everything else could wait

until the stink and pain of the past couple of days was washed down the drain. The bathroom was nice, clean, and with soft toilet paper. It took work for her to not like Cynthia.

Becca stripped and climbed into the shower, hissing as the water hit the burn over her back. After a few minutes, she began to relax, letting the warm water work out the knots in her aching body. After several minutes, she turned off the water and wrapped herself in a thick towel.

Darion spoke from the other side of the door. "I'll put the clothes just outside here. Let me treat your burn before you finish dressing."

"Okay," she mumbled and then reached outside the door for clothes. She pulled on a low cut tank top and jeans which were both a bit big on her. She wiped the foggy mirror and met a tired and worn reflection. Nothing she could do about that now.

Though they'd spent the last several hours together, Becca shivered at the idea of going out there. She tied up her wet hair and, with a long sleeved shirt in one hand, headed outside.

He sat at the table, which held a plate of white powder and several small bottles.

"You have a lot of drugs there." She wasn't sure what she was looking at, but they reminded her of Nikko's stash.

He glanced at her and then averted his gaze. "It's my job."

"Selling drugs for wizards?" she asked.

"No. Magic. Séances. Readings. Whatever I can do to make money. Short of killing my neighbor's dog."

"It's good to draw the line somewhere." The words were met to be a joke, but they fell flat. She didn't know what to say to Darion. *Thank you for the help? I hate that you lied to me for years and hurt me for my uncle's sake?*

He pulled out another bandage and avoided her gaze, motioning to the chair front of him. "Take a seat."

She sat down in the chair, water still dripping down her neck from her wet hair. The thin tank top left her back and neck exposed.

"I'm sorry about this." He removed the bandage on her neck. "I didn't have a choice if I was going to get you out alive."

She swallowed the tight knot in her throat and focused on a spot on the tile floor. She was grateful to be out of her uncle's house, but she struggled with everything that had happened.

A light sent of lavender filled the air as a sense of relief washed through the wound. His gentle touch sent a familiar warmth through her. While his touch might be familiar, the rest was a mystery. He taped a new bandage over the wound.

Becca slipped on the long sleeve shirt. She hadn't forgotten about Caleb. "When is the next festival at Moondance?"

He hesitated before asking. "Is he worth it?"

"Yes." She didn't hesitate. She had to get Caleb. He was the closest thing she had left to family. She left him years ago, but not again.

"I'm not even sure it's possible. You'll need money, and we'll be jumping into a den of snakes."

"You don't understand." She turned around. The hollowness of what she lost burned inside her chest. "He's from my past. And the only reason he even got caught was because of me."

"Explain."

"My uncle Jeremiah hated him for years, for what we did—" Her throat tightened at the thought of that night.

"Your uncle?" Darion's dropped the roll of bandages in his hand. "You never told me he was your uncle."

She bristled at his accusing tone. "Sorry, I forgot while we were running for our lives."

He stood, running his hands through his hair as he paced across the room. "He's not going to let you just go."

"I'm not giving him a choice about it."

He turned, worry etching line in his forehead. "You don't understand. He might have forgotten about a girl, there are several on the black market. But if you're his niece, he will hunt us down. Going to Moondance will be out of question. He normally doesn't go there, but he'll have people there."

Fear rose up her spine, but she clamped it down. Jeremiah had haunted her life for long enough. "It doesn't matter. I have to go. Caleb would do the same for me."

He moved toward her, a silent pleading in his face. "If that's true, if he really cares for you, he wouldn't want you to do this."

"You don't have to come. You have risked enough so far. You don't know Caleb or have any reason to help him. I was the one who dragged him into this mess."

"I don't have a reason?" Darion pulled back, his shoulders tightening. "We're all in this mess, Becca."

All of a sudden, the distance between them was too close. A hint of smoke clung to his clothes. The smell had never bothered her before, but now it reminded her of what he was. The room was closing in on her.

She headed for the door. Despite the aching in her bones, she couldn't stay in here and fight over what she had to do. "Don't worry about it, Darion. I'll be out of your hair soon enough."

"You're just going to leave again?" His words struck.

Yes, she was good at leaving. Sometimes it hurt less

than staying. Becca stomped down the stairs in her old boots. She itched to hit something, anything. She needed to get out of here and find Caleb. Reality, though, like a brick wall, brought more problems than solutions.

She'd lost all the cash from her last job. Jeremiah made going to her apartment out of the question. And all she'd heard about the Moondance was most humans, like herself, weren't on the guest list but the menu.

Darion did mention this place had a bar. Maybe she could strum up a job or information about how to get to Moondance. Only a couple days to find cash meant dangerous work outside of her usual connections. Murder was out, which usually only left jobs where she was the one likely to get killed.

An employee in the hallway downstairs pointed her in the direction of the bar. She passed through a busy kitchen, mouth watering at the smell of food, and swiped a roll. She almost made it out the door.

"What are you doing here?" Cynthia stood tall, exuding a confidant beauty.

"Just needed some air."

Her brow creased, as if knowing what getting air usually meant. She glanced at the roll tucked in Becca's hand.

"Sorry. I was hungry."

"Darion should have fed you. Go to the end of the bar.

I'll send food your way."

Guilt pricked at her empty stomach. "I can't pay." "Of course," Cynthia said in exasperation. "Don't worry. I'll put it on Darion's tab."

"Thanks," Becca said then, before she could stop herself, added, "How do you know Darion?" Darion wasn't her boyfriend anymore. She didn't care what he did, she told herself. But she wanted to know how they were connected and how much she could trust this woman.

Cynthia laughed. "You don't want to go there. You might not like what you find." She caught the arm of a waiter passing by and left in a rush before Becca could say anything else.

A low murmur of conversations welcomed Becca as she entered the restaurant. Smooth wooden floors held intimate tables, mostly full. It had an earthy smell mixed of cooked meat and alcohol.

The darkened bar near the back beckoned her. A dim blue light lit a variety of liquor bottles shining like Christmas in September. She didn't drink often, but tonight—she had plenty of demons to chase away.

CHAPTER 15

"Muscles," called the blonde in the cage next to Caleb.

He stared at her beauty, framed by dingy bars, and wondered if he'd strayed into some kind of sick circus.

"Do you have anything to smoke?" she asked with slight agitation, pacing in her cage. She was small enough to actually stand up straight.

"No," he replied. He sat on the floor, his back to the bars, staring out at the surrounding cages. He forced himself to breathe through his mouth, trying to block out the smell of dirty bodies and waste.

"Didn't think so. You look too clean cut. First-timer for sure."

His head snapped up. "You've been here more than once?" He wasn't sure if that was a good or bad thing.

"Yeah. Third time in." She spoke with such bravado, while her hands fidgeted with the hem on her dress.

"What is this place?"

"Don't you know?" She grinned. Her arms spread wide as if showing off a grand hall. "You're at Moondance. The Magicians' Market. From talismans and amulets, to potions and people. You can find everything you need for dark magic, all in one place. Even people."

"Moondance?" He'd heard rumors of a human market, but never thought he'd be a part of one. A heavy feeling weighed him down.

"An auction for people." Bitterness laced her words.

"Sold to the highest bidder."

"Sold?" His breath hitched in this throat.

"Are you always this slow? It might make it easier for you, come auction time."

He stared at his empty hands, contemplating his escape. He had to get out. Find Rebecca. A wave of heat washed over him as he tightened his hands. "How do we get out?"

"You met our beautiful captor." Ice entered her voice. "We don't."

He remembered the lithe and graceful demon, whose voice drove spikes into his brain. He didn't know how to get around it. "What about after? There has to be a way. You did it? How did you get out?"

She barked a laugh. "You think I escaped? My owners got tired of me and are trading me in. Upgrading, if you will."

She stood and approached the front of the cage, bare feet slapping the concrete floor. The dress, tight and short, showed off thin legs scattered with scratches and bruises. Despite it all, the sway to her hips held confidence and allure. Her beauty was a weapon, one nicely honed.

His thoughts traveled to Rebecca, whose natural beauty lingered in his dreams. He prayed she was all right. He had to get out of here.

He turned back to the only person that could give him any information. "What's your name?" he asked.

"Candy."

"Really?" He doubted any parent was that cruel.

She bit her lower lip. "How about Cinnamon?"

His disbelief must have shown.

"Are you more of a Tiffany type of guy? Or Emily?

Meredith?"

"I'm Caleb," he interrupted, frustration clipping his words short. "I'm not sure what game you're playing, but I have to get out of here."

"Look here, muscles." Her fingers with their chipped red nails gripped the bars. She spoke slowly, as if to a child. "You can only wish they'll kill you here. The wizards know how to restrain people. They've been practicing on demons for years. See that kid over there?"

He craned his neck to look down the row she pointed. It took only a second to see him—a boy, no older than fourteen, laying on his side. Even from his cage, Caleb could see thin shoulder blades jutting through the threadbare jacket.

"He's a wizard. Or at least some form of one. So he'll be unconscious till auction time. They don't take chances. They have people here who read powers and plan accordingly. Our kind, Mundanes, we're no threat. Just regular folk, with a little fire in them. Easily put out."

"I won't give in that easy." Unsure whether to pity her or shake her, he banged his fist on the gritty floor.

"Like I said, I've been to this pony show before." She slumped down against the bars. Her dress hiked higher, revealing most of her thigh.

Caleb turned his head, giving her privacy, even if she didn't care to have it.

"Best to keep your head down," she said. "Maybe a poor old widow will want some eye-candy. Too strong, and you'll be demon fodder."

He didn't reply. His breath hissed out between clenched teeth. He'd spent his life strong and able. His thoughts traveled to his father, quiet and unyielding, and his mother, feisty, yet sweet. Their absence left a pain in his chest he could never replace. But he wouldn't disgrace them.

He had to find a way out, locate Rebecca, and flee. Go south. His mother always told stories about her relatives down south. People who played on white sandy beaches. He'd never seen a beach before. He imagined this other world, one with water that never ended.

He slowly uncurled his hands. He needed to think, not rage. He wasn't ready to play dead just yet.

❧❦❧

Darion took a long shower, scrubbing his skin as if he could wash away his frustrations currently called Becca. Did he make the right choice, letting her leave? A gnawing sensation grew in his stomach, thinking of her alone in the magicians' district. He didn't think she would go far, but he never knew with Becca.

Even if he'd made her stay, he couldn't force her to let him help. Her stubbornness often overruled logic. Why couldn't she see, that he would be willing to go to hell and back to make things right? To atone for what he did, the lies he told.

There might not be a chance for a future with her. Lying had destroyed that when she found out the truth about his magic. But he could try to make it right.

He couldn't help but care about Becca, even if she didn't return the feeling. She reminded him of another life, another way to live, outside city walls and coven influence. He admired her strength and unselfishness in searching for her friend, even if jealousy reared its ugly head.

Climbing out of the shower, he noticed Becca's torn shirt on the floor. He questioned his decision again of letting her go so easily.

In the tall dresser, he grabbed the spare set of clothes

he kept there. On the occasions he stayed here, he helped Cynthia with the business and, in return, received free room and board. The business arrangement suited both parties. Cynthia and Darion had a brief history together, but both decided they would have a longer relationship in the future if they were only friends.

Dressed, he combed his fingers through his wet hair. On the table, warm food awaited him. "Thank you, Cynthia," he said aloud to an empty room. She was a life saver.

He brushed his hair out of his eyes and devoured a small steak with mashed potatoes—his favorite. After he ate, he distracted himself by organizing his supplies, and reorganizing them. He even tried to read an old paperback he found in the closet. After reading the first page three times, he set it down.

He was determined not to go after Becca. He'd quit that chase. Yet, the ulcer growing in his stomach was because of her.

Someone stumbled outside their room.

"I can take care of myself," Becca said loudly out in the hall.

He swore. That was how things were. He cursed when she was here and cursed when she wasn't. "Just doing my job," replied a man's voice.

Darion opened the door. One of Cynthia's employee's, Greg, was escorting Becca to their room. "Cynthia said I could leave her with you."

Darion couldn't help the laugh that bubbled up. "Thanks."

Greg headed off, while Becca's brow creased in indignation. "I was doing just fine, on my own, ya know?" A wave of alcohol floated on her breath.

Darion held the door open for her. "Really?"

"Yeah. I even had a couple jobs lined up." She sat on the bed and started pulling at her boots.

"You probably shouldn't be looking for work while drunk." He owed Cynthia for watching out for her downstairs.

"I'm not drunk." She glared at him, daring him to challenge it. She continued tugging at the laces on her boots, creating a knotted mess.

Sitting down next to her, he lifted her boots onto his lap. She might not be drunk, but totally sober Becca knew how to untie her boots.

"I'm not really drunk." A softer edge entered her voice, a dangerous edge.

He glimpsed at her face, smiling for the first time since he found her. Returning to the boots, he worked on the laces. She leaned forward and began playing with his hair. A slight tingling sensation followed her touch.

"I love your hair." She let her hand trail down his cheek and onto his arm.

He focused on the boot, pulled one off, and worked on the other.

Her hand traveled down his neck. "I missed you."

"No, you didn't," he said, ready to cut the damn laces off.

"Yeah, I did. But every time I almost made it out my door, I'd remembered what a lying bastard you are."

"That sounds more like you." He pulled the other shoe off and set it on the floor. "You should rest."

As he reached up to pull down the comforter, her hands locked around the back of his neck, pulling him down. With his hands on either side of her, he barely prevented himself from collapsing against her. He studied her soft lips and sincere gaze. Becca always held a soft strength in her features that amazed him—a natural beauty he never got tired of. Was this a drunken impulse, or was there some part of Becca that had moved beyond his past mistakes?

"What are you doing, Becca?" he asked, wary of breaking whatever this moment was.

"What I want." Her words were clear as she stared straight at him.

He chuckled, imagining a completely sober Becca wanting to slap this girl silly. Becca was always so reserved, so private. It had taken him months before she would open up to him this easily.

She pushed up against him. A shudder went through his body, threatening to unravel his self-control. Becca might just be the end of him.

He'd missed her. As much as he hated to admit it, he craved her touch. Her hand grazed the skin under his shirt, and then her nails dragged down his stomach. His muscles tightened, and willpower crumbled.

"Damn you, Becca," he mumbled, falling onto her warm body.

He brushed her lips, soft and light. She wrapped her arms around his neck and returned his kisses with greater force. A current passed between them that lit him with a desire that he'd repressed.

His hand trailed down her neck, over her shoulder. Tightening his hold, he wrapped his arm around her waist, not ever wanting to let her go. He cared for Becca more than he'd ever admitted and couldn't stand for her to leave again.

She bit his lower lip. A soft moan escaped him. His lips traced down her neck, savoring the taste of her skin. She gasped under his touch.

"You're beautiful and stubborn," he told her in between kisses. "Every inch."

She grabbed the bottom of his shirt and yanked it over his head. Her hands caressed his body, starting at his shoulders and traveling all the way down his chest, as if seeing him for the first time. "You look pretty good yourself."

He leaned down, wrapped an arm around her, and pulled her close. The kisses turned urgent and hungry.

Her fingers played along the top of his jeans, and he closed his eyes, knowing if he started down some paths, he couldn't stop.

He grabbed her hands, some sense returning. "You're drunk, Becca." Somewhere there better be an angel blessing him for this.

"I'm not that drunk." Her lips were swollen from kissing. "I want this. You want this."

"No, not like this." He wanted her. But he wanted her sober, safe, and happy. They couldn't just jump into their relationship like the last few months had never happened. He wouldn't be a distraction for her.

Grabbing his shirt, he headed out the door.

Something crashed against the door as he closed it. Becca never did like being told no. He didn't have the energy to smile at the irony of dreaming of Becca for months, and now he was the one walking away.

Outside the room, he banged his head on a nearby wall. He wasn't ready to leave her alone. He stayed in the hall for a while, making sure she didn't try to leave.

After several minutes of annoyed grumblings, Becca settled down. Assuming she finally nodded off, he headed down the stairs, searching for a distraction or a cold shower.

CHAPTER16

T he rush of the river and smell of budding trees was a balm to Becca's soul. She rested at the river's edge, dangling her feet in the cool water. Her family home stood tall and whole, a comforting presence behind her back. In the distance, her mother hung laundry on the clothesline.

Part of her consciousness realized it was a dream, and she savored every second.

"Be careful near the river," her mom hollered. Her long blonde hair was wrapped up in a messy bun. The white sheet in her hands flapped in the wind.

"Sure," Becca replied. She picked a long blade of grass, placed it in her mouth, and lay back, eyes closed. The heat of the sun warmed her straight through.

She was home.

I wonder if Caleb wants to go fishing this afternoon if his chores are done. Or maybe I can convince Elizabeth to go. A cool breeze brushed over her body as a shadow fell over her.

"I'm okay, Mom," Becca said, eyes closed.

"Becca?" The voice shook with a youthful uncertainty. It wasn't Mom.

Becca's eyes flew open, and she bolted upright. The young woman in front of her had long light honey hair like her mother, and bright blue eyes. Could this be her sister, Little Lizzy? The last Becca saw her, four years ago, she was fourteen years old. Now there stood a woman.

"Elizabeth?" Becca asked. "Is it you?"

Elizabeth nodded slowly. "Rebecca?"

Becca stood, examining every feature and facet of her sister. Elizabeth nearly reached Becca's height. Her face was thinner and a light scattering of freckles covered her nose. A dull ache swelled in Becca's chest at how her sister had changed and what she had missed.

"I'm sorry, Elizabeth. I should have saved you." A silent tear fell on Becca's cheek. There weren't enough tears to shed to show the regret in her heart.

Elizabeth's brow furrowed in confusion. "From what?"

"The magicians. The fire. For leaving you." The list could have gone on.

Between one breath and the next, the landscape changed drastically. Clouds darkened the sky, and the once large home was reduced to ashes. Even the clothesline resembled a skeleton, lone wires slack in the wind. The mirage of happiness turned into the nightmare of her reality.

"The magicians?" Elizabeth retreated backward, as if the word itself struck fear in her. She noticed the home and staggered for a moment. When she finally spoke, her voice broke, "What happened?"

"Elizabeth, I came back for you. I tried." Becca reached for her hand. A pleading entered her voice.

Elizabeth pulled back, clutching her chest. "You left. You died."

Becca's legs shook, panic rising in her throat. Is that what my parents told her? And for a moment, Becca almost wished those words were real. "I didn't want to leave you." Tears spilled onto Becca's cheeks. The image of her sister faded in front of her. "I never wanted to leave you."

ↄ/ↄↄ/ↄ

The slam of the door woke Becca. She buried her head, trying to compose herself, and swiped at the tears on her cheeks. As much as she hated the overwhelming guilt, she savored the image of Elizabeth as a woman.

She dared to peek and found Darion standing at the table, dressed in dark pants, a blue button up shirt, and a jacket. She wished he didn't look so good. He dropped a bag onto the table.

She closed her eyes again, as a wave of nausea rolled over her and the events of last night came back to her with vivid detail. Warm embarrassment flooded her face, and she prayed her hair, which felt like a hay stack and probably looked worse, covered most of it. How could she have been so forward? Yes, part of her still wanted Darion, but she wasn't quite ready to tackle their past or forgive him. Taking a deep breath, she decided on the best course of action: avoidance.

She headed to the bathroom, not gutsy enough to glance in his direction again. She'd slept in her clothes and needed to pull herself together before talking to Darion, especially with what happened last night.

She splashed water on her face and drank straight from the faucet. It tasted as if a cat vomited in her mouth. She found an old tube of toothpaste and used her finger to brush her teeth. She looked like hell. Dark circles ringed red eyes. She found a large comb and began working on the knots in her hair.

She swore at the small tangles, pissed not only at her hair, but at herself for acting like such an idiot last night. Not for the first time, she swore off alcohol. But she couldn't blame her behavior on a few drinks.

She'd missed Darion. She could admit that. His lies had forced her to leave him, but her heart didn't always get the memos her brain sent.

She had to trust him. She needed his help to get Caleb back, but it didn't change their relationship.

She finally emerged from the bathroom, and found Darion making the bed and beating the pillows with an unnatural furor.

"What's wrong?"

He pulled up the comforter and tucked it in tightly, not answering her question.

"Darion." She crossed her arms, waiting for an answer. She could be patient when she had to be.

After finishing the bed, he turned to face her. "Cynthia told me how eager you were to start working again. You approached some heavy players last night."

"You said we needed money," she snapped back. Okay, maybe patience wasn't her strong suit.

He ran a hand through his hair, looking as if he wanted to pull it out. "Becca, you're not stupid. You can get yourself killed that way."

"My options are limited. I'm not some bloody magician." Heat rose up her face. "I need money to buy Caleb. I'll get money."

"Did it not occur to you that Jeremiah wants both of our heads on a platter? It's a bar. People talk." He grabbed his bag and jerked the zipper closed. "We need to leave before people come looking for us. It'll be bad for Cynthia."

She bit her lip. "Right. Cynthia."

Plopping down in the chair, he let out a frustrated sigh.

"You don't understand Jeremiah's power and influence in the city."

"I get it." She grabbed her boots by the bed and shoved them on, her fingers trembling with anger and embarrassment. He must have thought her a drunken idiot, searching for jobs and throwing herself at him.

"About last night—" he began.

"I'm sorry about last night." She forced herself to meet his gaze, a heavy coldness settling in her chest. "It was a mistake, nothing more."

"Right." His blank stare gave nothing away. "A mistake."

"Look, I'm grateful for your help and for saving me yesterday." Pushing away her disappointment at how things passed between them this morning, she concentrated on what needed to be done. "I know we need money. I'll do whatever I can to get it, but I need your help in getting into Moondance."

She'd heard enough of the market to know it required magic to enter. And Mundanes who were not leashed by a magician, didn't go.

"You'll need more than just locating it."

She dug her nails into her hand. She couldn't be more vulnerable if she stood naked in front of him. She had to ask so much of Darion, when all she wanted to do was hate him. She couldn't hate him anymore, though. It wasn't forgiveness, but it was something.

At the thought of Caleb vulnerable in the hands of magicians, her pride shattered. "I hate to ask you to put your neck on the line. I'll do whatever it takes to get him back."

Darion's features turned to stone. She wondered for a moment, if he would say no. He would have every reason to turn her away, and she half expected it.

"I'll help," he replied. "And, with me, you always have a right to ask."

Neither spoke for a minute. Only a few feet separated them, but emotionally it felt like miles.

"Thank you," she said. She wanted to hug him, thank him for his help. But she'd made the boundaries clear and didn't trust herself not to cross them.

"Okay." He stood, breaking the awkward tension. "Let's go find a car."

"A car?" she asked skeptically. She didn't know anyone who owned a car in the city.

"Yeah. I'll have to call in a few favors, but I can pull it off. Then I have an old friend I used to work with we need to go visit."

"What kind of work?" Becca followed him out, wondering just how much she'd learn about Darion.

"Don't worry. It's nothing respectable."

CHAPTER 17

Lady Katherine's house remained quiet as Darion wondered the best way to enter it without detection.

Standing next to him, Becca shifted her stance. "Is this part of the magician's code? Steal from old ladies who have too many cats?"

Darion bristled at the insult. His patience waned thin after spending a good chuck of their morning finding a car and then talking the man down for the piece of junk. He couldn't chance retrieving his bike at his apartment. So instead, he now owned an ugly green four door sedan that cost double what it should.

"After working for Nikko, you're getting picky about work?" he asked. "If you knew how many Mundanes this lady killed during The Rising, you wouldn't feel guilty. Plus, her money will go to the governing coven when she dies." He turned his attention back to the house.

An unfriendly current settled between them. Becca zipped up her jacket against the chill. Maybe it was the heavy clouds threatening rain, but the outside guard hadn't done his rounds for the last fifteen minutes. The outside barriers, a light shimmer around the house, appeared to be in working order.

Could it be she wasn't home? Darion wondered. Lady Katherine rarely left home, but maybe. There would be a house maid and another security guard he would have to deal with, but that shouldn't be difficult.

"It looks like Lady Katherine may be gone."

"We could use a break." Becca gripped the knife he bought her. It was nothing near what she needed to protect herself, but all he could find on short notice. "Let's go."

"There's still the outside ward to break, a couple servants, and a dozen or so cats," he reminded her.

"Not bad. I can manage cats." Becca's mouth remained impassive, but she couldn't keep the smile from her eyes.

"The servants usually stay downstairs. Upstairs is Lady Katherine's personal rooms. That's where you'll find the money." After much discussion, they agreed to split up. It wasn't what he wanted, but it was probably the best choice.

"Will the upstairs windows have alarms?" she asked.

"Not after I break the shield." Darion straightened. "Ready?"

She nodded, and they left the cover of the shed. Before stepping on the manicured grass, he put a hand out to stop Becca. He whispered the Latin words to disable the first shield. Magic brushed his skin and the power of the shield dissipated like popping a balloon filled with invisible glitter. That was the easy one, as it was there to keep out wild animals or Mundanes.

Becca bounced on the balls of her feet, her energy almost palpable. He nodded to give her the go ahead. Between one step and the next, a draining blow threatened to pull him under. He swore.

Someone had killed his demon. Instead of having a Soultorn, an idea he never liked, he hid a level-four demon in his apartment and pulled from it regularly for power. He had enough precautions that if anyone else besides him entered, the small apartment detonated. Whatever wizard Jeremiah had sent had just been blown to pieces.

"Are you okay?" Becca asked, close enough to touch.

"Fine," he said, recovering his step. Darion could only imagine her disgust at the idea of him being tied to a demon.

They approached the next shield, the main protection over the house. He had helped set these wards up, but disabling it without a demon would drain him. He pulled out a knife. "Keep watch. This will take a minute."

She crinkled her nose as if an unsettling smell crossed her path and shifted her feet. "Just remember, we're sitting ducks."

Could she actually sense the magic in front of her? He had heard of Mundanes who could sense magic. He didn't have time to consider it. They were too exposed on the lawn.

He pricked his finger to offer a blood sacrifice, gathering what magic he could find, and began the incantation. It only took a minute, maybe two, but sweat crossed his brow by the time he finished.

"Won't that leave a trace?" she asked, referring to his blood.

"They won't be able to trace me. Maybe identify me, but we'll be gone by then."

They approached the house. Lace curtains lined the windows. A large wood porch wrapped around the house complete with a white trim.

"Maybe we should go together," Darion offered again. He was hesitant to let Becca go alone when facing magicians, even if it was just a maid with limited magic. "It might be safer."

"Stick to the plan. Secure the first floor. Then meet

me upstairs." Becca's hands were tight, anxious.

He agreed. She climbed on top of the porch railing and then hoisted herself up onto the roof with a lithe strength that amazed him. There was no sign of security around the house, yet his stomach churned with anxiety. He reminded himself how strong and able she was, and the best way to protect her would be to eliminate the threats as fast as possible.

He approached the front door and noticed it hung slightly ajar. Something was off. Lady Katherine was diligent in keeping her house in order, and her employees had to toe a very straight line. He pushed through the door to find the entry room empty.

"Where's the welcoming party?" Darion whispered, heading straight into her sitting room. Something crashed to the floor. Darion's heart raced as he took in the bloody scene in front of him.

Lady Katherine lay in the center of the room on the mahogany coffee table, her white hair unpinned, spilling around her shoulders. A dark pool of blood spread from the wound at her throat, staining her hair crimson and pooling on the carpet.

A familiar Soultorn, leaned over the body, knife in hand and blood staining its lips. The Soultorn, inhabiting a short stocky man, radiated with sick happiness. Its pitch black eyes matched his short dark hair. A short beard covered his chin, painted with blood. It wore all black, which hid the stains of his deeds.

"The prodigal son returns." Peter's face was flushed with excitement as he stood on the far side of the room. He probably didn't want to dirty his perfect gray pinstripe suit, or smooth blond hair.

Darion couldn't help but wonder about Peter's relationship with Jeremiah, since he'd first came calling for

Darion at Lady Katherine's house days ago. He thought Peter was Ryma's lackey, but who knows how deep that loyalty went? So many butts to kiss, so little time.

Peter must have passed the wards on official coven business and then murdered Lady Katherine. Was her death ordered by Ryma? Or just for fun.

A heavy rose potpourri scent, mixed with the scent of blood, turned his stomach. A broken candy dish lay in colored glass pieces at Peter's feet.

Darion swallowed and smoothed out his features. *Get control of yourself. Who cares that you lost your demon, and here's Peter with his recently fed Soultorn?* Not one of his better pep talks.

"You know there are easier ways to get my attention," Darion said. "Some people send cards, flowers—I like chocolates."

He sauntered in, taking a seat in a nearby armchair. Crossing his legs, he plastered on a smile. A tabby cat jumped on his lap, and he buried his hand in its soft fur. Peter didn't know Darion's demon was gone yet. He couldn't. Could he?

"Jeremiah wants the girl."

"And, here, I thought you missed me."

"He wants you, too, though not necessarily in the same condition." The edges of Peter's lips curled up.

"That's a slight problem. You see I had a date with dear Katherine here. Services I intend to provide." Darion tried to prolong the inevitable. If he could distract these two, it'd give Becca more time to find the money and escape.

Peter's Soultorn licked the edge of the knife and, catching Darion's eye, it winked.

"Why kill Lady Katherine?" Darion continued. "Because she employed me? I thought she was a great contributor to Ryma?"

"I didn't kill her. You did," Peter lied effortlessly. "I tried to bring you in, but you took her as hostage."

"Amazing, I didn't even get my hands bloody."

Peter smirked. "You don't have to. You'll be dead soon, along with this grandma of yours."

"Your parents must be so proud. You've grown up to kill little old ladies." Despite Lady Katherine's dark past, no one deserved to be a demon's meal.

"Ha. Ha." Sarcasm laced his words and he nodded slightly, giving Darion barely enough time to react.

The Soultorn hurled the knife as Darion lunged behind the couch. He shot an easy spell, sending the blaze soaring into the fireplace as a distraction.

No matter how weak Darion was, fire would always bend to his will. But he wasn't completely fire proof, and this Soultorn wouldn't let him go that easy.

The Soultorn leaped over Lady Katherine's dead body and landed on top of the couch, knife in hand. Darion raced toward the fire, but wasn't quick enough. The Soultorn slashed out. Pain shot up Darion's arm.

Turning to face him, Darion raised his forearms in defense. The Soultorn licked the blade, obviously not in any hurry to kill him. Out of the corner of his eye, Darion saw Peter smile, the sick bastard.

Stepping back, Darion rubbed his hand over the wound, pulling power from the sacrifice. He threw his power, sending the drapes behind Peter ablaze, and strengthened his magical shield.

The Soultorn struck out at Darion again and again. Darion dodged the blows, blocking and retreating with every hit. His movements gradually slowed, his arms heavy, as Peter attacked his defenses from across the room.

Darion swung and missed, opening himself up as the Soultorn slammed into his chest, sending him flying back. Crashing into the wall, he slid to the floor, struggling to clear his eyes. Smoke filled his vision. Mere feet from the fireplace, the carpet and old wallpaper carried the flames.

The Soultorn pressed forward, blade in hand. In a last ditch effort, Darion shot a hot current through the blade.

It dropped the knife, probably due to surprise. It shrugged, not bothering to pick it up. It didn't think it needed it anymore. And it probably was right.

Darion attempted to stand, but a flood of magic pinned him down. Peter, damn him. This would not be a short or clean death.

Darion remembered Becca upstairs and gathered his courage. Feeling the heat next to him, Darion stuck his arm into the blaze. It might be suicide, but it was all he had.

Clenching his jaw, he muffled a scream as the fire burned his hand. The Soultorn lunged at him. Darion gathered his remaining strength to free himself from Peter's restraint and embraced the Soultorn.

The flame raced up Darion's arm as he clung to the Soultorn, focusing his energy on protecting his body as the Soultorn rained hits on his torso. A couple ribs cracked under the pressure, and its teeth bit through his jacket.

Darion screamed and pinned its head between his arms. The possessed body in Darion's arms convulsed uncontrollably. Darion couldn't see past the smoke engulfing them both, and he struggled to remain conscious from lack of oxygen.

His grip loosened, unable to hold on any longer. The Soultorn lost consciousness, sagging lifeless on the carpet. Darion rolled away from the body, letting the fire consume the Soultorn and send it back to whatever realm in hell it came from.

Extinguishing the controlled flames on his arms, he sucked in a lungful of air. Oxygen was great. Being alive was better, especially after a hand-to-hand fight with a Soultorn. Something he'd never done before. His hands burned like they were still on fire, but there wasn't time to pull the heat out of them.

Hacking and coughing, he struggled to his feet. The fire had spread to the coffee table and Lady Katherine. Peter held a cloth over his mouth, standing next to the door with a gun leveled at Darion's chest.

Isn't that my luck? Peter never did play by the rules. Darion drew on the blaze and destruction to fuel his magic. But if magic was a car, he would be on the big E with the gas light flashing.

"You always did hate to dirty your hands." Darion coughed at the surrounding smoke. He'd been too distracted to control the blaze.

"Where's the girl?" Peter shouted.

"Dead," Darion lied.

He felt the spirit of Lady Katherine trapped in the fire. Not noticing it before, he realized the Soultorn hadn't finished sucking her dry.

A new power surged through his veins. The power of death was a high that he hadn't experienced for a long time, a high that he loathed himself for but he would use.

"The girl, or you die." Peter's face was red with rage. "And I won't shoot to kill."

It didn't matter. Darion had killed his Soultorn. Peter would not let him walk away. With his increase in power, Darion threw a curse, and Peter's gun exploded in his hand. He dropped the gun and cradled his hand, glaring at Darion.

Only what stepped out of the fire could have kept the

two men from attacking each other. It was Lady Katherine, whose corpse was covered in flames. Darion's stomach dropped. Even as a pyro, it wasn't something he'd seen before.

"My babies. Where are my babies?" she cried, searching the room for the missing cats that had been chased away by the fighting.

She approached Peter, screaming for answers. He fought back, but it was too late. Power from Lady Katherine surged through the room, like an oppressive heat that wanted to smother them both.

Sparks shot from her body, and Darion retreated to the front door. He could no longer contain the power in the room—just ignite it.

A searing blast roared in his ears as he flew out the front door. He tumbled onto the lawn, the heat chasing him out. On his hands and knees in the grass, he gulped in fresh air.

He coughed, holding his ribs gently as adrenaline wore off and the pain from the Soultorn's punches sank in. He turned to the fire that crawled up the side of the house. A single thought flew through his head, one that made him panic.

Becca.

CHAPTER 18

S moke covered Caleb's dream, in dense sheets. He pushed through the heavy smoke, stumbling over something, a wooden horse from when he was a child. His home was on fire. He kept moving forward, searching for his parents. Terror gripped his heart. He had to find them before they burned. Where were they?

A scream pierced the night. Loud and clear. At first, he thought it was his mother. He ran forward, banging his legs against furniture. Maybe she was in her room. Smoke flooded his senses, blinding him. He had to save her. The cry sounded again. Loud enough to wake him from his dream.

Frantic, he pushed himself up, crouching in his steel cage. His heart raced. *It wasn't real. The dream wasn't real.*

The pretty girl in the cage next to his cried out again, thrashing in her sleep.

"Shush," an older inmate said in low tones. "Want to wake it up?"

"Hey…" Caleb didn't even know her name. Just the several fake ones she told him. "Candy, was it? Candy, wake up please. Cinnamon? Meredith?" he said, guessing different names.

Her eyes flashed open, scared and panicked.

"It was just a nightmare," he told her. Unfortunately,

with waking up in a cage, reality didn't look much better.

"You okay?"

She nodded briefly. It took her a good minute to calm her breath and collect herself.

"You want to talk about it?" he asked.

She blew out her breath. "I think going through that once tonight is enough."

"Dreaming about what will happen to us?" He'd been going through the possibilities himself. Not great thoughts. She shook her head and rolled to her back. "No. Just nightmares about my past. Or a nightmare about being named Meredith," she added sarcastically.

Guess her name isn't Meredith. He couldn't imagine what this girl had gone through and wasn't about to pry. He had lost a great life, while this girl had been forced to live a tortured one for years.

"So, muscles, where did Pove find you? You look fresh off the farm."

"Almost. Magicians burned down our farmhouse, with both of my parents inside." Caleb picked at his pants. "I came to the city for answers, but didn't get far."

She gasped slightly. "A real farm? Are you serious?"

"Yeah. It wasn't very big. But it was beautiful, with a small stream running behind the house." A wistful air entered his voice, longing for what once was.

"You are serious." He could hear the smile in her voice.

"Tell me about this farm, muscles."

He looked over to see if she was sincere. "Really? It's probably boring."

"Please. I love boring." Then, in a softer voice, she added, "Take me away from this hell hole for little while."

Why not? "Where to start?"

"Cookies," she quickly answered. "Did your mom ever

make cookies?"

"Oh, sure. Usually for Christmas in different shapes—stars, trees, and hearts…"

He continued talking, telling her about the frosting, and other Christmas decor. The rest of the warehouse fell quiet.

Caleb's smooth voice traveled softly around the room.

He spoke of the farm. The day their dog had puppies, and how hard he cried when he realized that the Christmas ham came from their sow Sally.

He turned his head once, to see if the blonde next to him was awake. She was on her back staring straight ahead, with silent tears streaming down her face. He turned back and started the story of learning to ride his horse bareback in the rain. He even heard a couple chuckles in the warehouse on that one.

He was glad to talk of home. He wanted to savor every memory. Capture it if possible. If he could remember all those good times, then maybe they weren't really dead.

☙☙☙

Becca shimmied through the small window and lowered herself into the bathroom, landing gracefully in a box of kitty litter. Potpourri and the stale odor of ammonia assaulted her senses.

Gotta love cat pee. She wiped her feet on the pink bath mat and eased out into the hallway. Knife in hand, she tread lightly on the plush carpet, wary of any nearby noise. Several cats ran down the hall and disappeared into one of the many rooms.

The first two bedrooms were painted in pastels. No cats. The next room held a small office. Only one cat hid under a table, but nothing like Darion described.

Becca paused. Noise from the first floor traveled up the stairs at the end of the hallway. Someone was arguing. She hurried and opened the next door, something hissed.

She backed up just in time to avoid a paw swiping at her. A white cat, one of many cats, glared at her with its tail raised.

"Relax," Becca said, not sure if it was to the cat or herself.

This had to be the room. It was covered in everything cats—live ones, stuffed ones, pictures of cats, cats on throw pillows, and even sewn into a blanket hanging over the end of the bed.

The stale musty odor and numerous sets of watchful eyes unsettled Becca. This was its own kind of twisted magic.

She began her search with the closet and the dresser. She got a few protests from the occupants as she moved through the room, but she didn't find anything.

There were some coins in the antique desk, which she quickly pocketed, but they nowhere near enough. A touch of guilt gnawed at her, until she reminded herself that most of this money came from Mundanes they killed during The Rising.

On her elbows and knees, Becca hunted under the dusty bed. With barely any light from the window, she couldn't see anything.

A cat screeched. Becca yanked her hand out, but not quick enough. Angry red lines streaked across her skin.

"Damn cat," she muttered. She repositioned herself and used her leg to sweep the cat from under the bed.

"Well, well, well. What do we have here? A naughty kitty?" A large man loomed in the doorway. Ugly tattoos, that he must have received while drunk, covered his thick neck.

Becca scrambled out from under the bed, a flush of adrenaline restarting her heart, which had stopped when she heard his voice. She gripped the knife at her side.

He loomed in the doorway with a sick eagerness stretching his face—a thug with a shaved head, but his dark suit spoke of money. His hulking frame barely made it through the door.

"I didn't realize how easy this job would be," he rumbled. "But here you are. Almost gift wrapped for Jeremiah."

"I'm never easy," she said with a false bravado, squelching the urge to flee.

Nowhere to run. He blocked the door. She'd never make it through the window.

Whispers stirred the air as he began a spell. Dodging closer, she slashed at his thick throat. He grabbed her wrist inches from his neck and jerked her to the side. Bending into the spin, she used the force to slam her other fist into his throat.

He gasped in pain. The muscles in his neck tightened. He couldn't speak at the moment, though, and that leveled the playing field—a bit. He shoved her backward, slamming her into a small desk.

Grabbing the desk lamp, she swung it at the thug's head. He knocked the lamp aside and sent it crashing against the wall. A cat streaked from the closet and sprinted out of the room.

He rubbed his throat, his nostrils flaring in anger. He mouthed something, Becca could only guess it wasn't a compliment. His arms clenched, muscles bulging in his fitted suit.

She widened her stance. She wouldn't go back. Not with Caleb at the slave market.

He surged forward, lashing out with a meaty fist. She parried the heavy blows that pushed her back. The sharp edge of the desk dug into her lower back. She lashed out with her knife, making contact with his forearm. But as her knife struck, he slammed a fist into the side of her head. She flew to the floor. The knife tumbled out of her hand.

The room tipped around her. Blinking away the starbursts that filled her vision, she pulled herself upright, using the closet door for support. The smell of smoke wafted into the room. What was happening down stairs? Pushing panic aside, she focused on the threat in front of her.

He pulled a knife from his boot, steadily approaching.

"I'm done playing, kitten," he whispered, his voice rough. "Maybe, I'll do this without magic. Just for fun."

"If you let me go, we can share the money."

The mention of money caught his attention. "What money?" his voice rasped.

"This old lady's loaded. I'm sure it's more than what Jeremiah's paying you."

"No one crosses Jeremiah." His words were fierce, but his face lit up a second later. "But there's no reason, I can't have both."

Then he charged. She spun to the side and at the same time an explosion rocked the house.

They both stumbled. Quickly regaining her footing, she slammed her boot into the side of his knee. A sick crunch echoed around the room, and the man roared with pain. He leaned against the desk.

She grabbed her knife off the floor. Before she could attack, something threw her back. Magic. She struck the wall and collapsed on the floor.

Pain radiated through her body as if she had been run over, by a truck—a really big one. She blinked away tears and breathed through the pain. Then she realized another threat, possibly greater.

Fire.

Smoke trailed into the room. She began coughing, the smell overcoming her.

One problem at a time.

The man rested against the table, swearing at Becca. She stood slowly, muscles screaming in protest. She didn't know how to counter this magic, but she had to try.

A warm hand came down on her shoulder. "Let me."

Relief coursed through her at the sight of Darion.

He spoke a curse as he approached the man. Lifting a fallen lamp off the floor, Darion bashed him in the head. No fair. It took magic to make that move work.

Becca regained her footing, resting a hand on the bed.

Darion searched her body, seeing the blood that covered her. "Where are you hurt?"

"Everywhere." She meant it to come out sarcastic, but instead it sounded beaten. Numb from the fight, a coldness settled in her bones.

"Where's the blood coming from?" His voice frantic.

She shook her head before she remembered her voice. "It's his."

Darion caught his breath but he didn't release her. "We need to go. The house is on fire."

"Figured. You did this?" she asked, her head pounding.

"Sort of." He smirked. "We'll have to head out the window."

He opened the window and a fresh breeze entered. The pain in Becca's head cleared a bit and she focused on their original goal—finding the money. She scanned the room searching for some nook or cranny where it could be.

On top of the thick bedspread, a gray cat sat upright with dark eyes. It posed like a sphinx, perfectly tranquil, statuesque, despite the fight or the smoke that crept into the room. The rest of the cats sprinted out the open window.

Becca didn't know many felines, but she guessed that this wasn't normal. When searching a witch's house, anything was possible with magic. "One second."

Darion grabbed her hand. "Come on."

This cat had to be magicked or some type of demon. Who knew with those dark eyes? "Wait. The money."

"No time."

She shook free of his hand. "Just a sec."

A picture of a young girl stood on the nightstand next to the bed. Becca scratched the cat on its neck and felt a deep purr. "Help me out, sweetie." She picked up the cat, and found a thick throw pillow behind it.

Could it be that easy? Was the money in the pillow? Hiding in plain sight and guarded by a magicked cat?

"Come on. I can't control this anymore. We have to jump." Urgency and anger laced Darion's words.

She grabbed the pillow and the cat and crawled through the window out onto the roof. Smoke carried up from the first floor. The roof warmed beneath her feet. Climbing down the way she came was out of the question. And having a pyromancer next to her didn't resolve the fear that she might burn to death.

Darion pulled her close. His hair was dark and wild, and he had a fierce determination on his face.

Before she could ask his plan, he pulled her hand and yelled, "Jump."

CHAPTER 19

T he small pink roses on the wallpaper blurred in and out of focus. Elizabeth couldn't have said how long she'd sat at the antique desk, staring at the intricate flower pattern. In moments of clarity, she would pace the confines of the bedroom or pick up a book. She could never finish one, though. Staring at the words for hours, she'd close the book in frustration. Something wasn't right, but how could it be?

Her family was dead. The only home she'd ever known burned to ash. Her future…unknown. Days, fogged in depression and loss, grew in darkness until they threatened to swallow her entirely.

The dreams, though, burned bright. Her fingers tingled from where Becca had grabbed her last night. Elizabeth had dreamed of her lost sister for years, desperately chasing what she could never catch. In last night's dream, Becca had talked to her.

It had taken Elizabeth a moment to recognize Becca. Her face had held harsh lines, and her body was thin, yet strong. Her sister's earnest pleas had struck fear in her bones. Then Becca crumpled to ash, like the rest of her family.

Elizabeth's heart had shattered as she'd stared at the debris of her past life. Pain had washed over a body that no longer felt like hers. Part of herself lay in those ashes with her mother and father.

Out of the ruins had emerged a dark set of eyes. Pitch black, they'd pierced right through her. Her pulse had raced, and her scream had torn through her nightmare.

Even now, awake in her room, the dream haunted her. Elizabeth rubbed her arms absently, trying to chase the chill and her nightmares away. She focused on the small red roses, memorizing each petal, itching to tear them from the wall, so perfect and small. She picked at the paper until her nail ripped, red gathering along the cuticle. She continued until she finally tore a piece from the wall, and a warm relief washed over her. Holding it up to her nose, she could almost smell the sweet fragrance that reminded her of the garden at home.

"Elizabeth. What are you doing?" Paula's stern voice was brisk.

Elizabeth hadn't noticed her entering the room. "Nothing." Her quick response sounded guilty, even to her ears. She placed her hands in her lap, wondering how long Paula had been standing there, watching her.

Paula sighed and smoothed out her perfectly pressed dress, with the matching cardigan and necklace. Everything was so perfect, sometimes Elizabeth wanted to scream. "Jeremiah would like you to call on him in his study," Paula informed her.

"Okay." Elizabeth bolted up, a bit unsteady but excited to be getting out.

"Ladies don't wish to seem overeager, dear."

Someone should tell her bosom that. Ignoring Paula's comment, Elizabeth hurried out of her room. The familiar scent of burnt rosemary lingered in the air as she maneuvered down the hall.

"Elizabeth," Paula reprimanded from behind.

Elizabeth struggled to slow her step, but her legs

stretched with welcomed freedom. She paused in front of the door, her hand poised and ready to knock, when voices spoke from inside the study. Her uncle's voice was a recognizable murmur, but the other voice was boisterous and haunting.

A quick laugh carried into the hall. "Your offer is insulting. So little to rise—"

Her uncle's voice rose in anger. "Yet, here you are, the grand duke, at my mercy."

Paula yanked Elizabeth back down the hall. "Ladies don't go lurking in doorways."

"I wasn't. I just didn't want to interrupt." Uncertainty flooded Elizabeth's words.

"I see." Paula pushed back a wave of hair as a worried look crossed her face. "It seems I misunderstood. He must have company."

"A duke—" Elizabeth began to say.

"Hush, child," Paula scolded.

Elizabeth shrank against the wall. Part of her wanted to argue, wanted to defend her actions, but this wasn't home. She was lucky to be taken in by her uncle at all. A gnawing sensation ate at her, as if there was a game going on in the house, and she was the only one without the rules.

Paula smoothed her dress again. "We will return to our rooms until summoned."

They didn't make it to the end of the hall before a bell rang from his study. Despite her obvious annoyance, Paula turned around and escorted Elizabeth to the study.

Elizabeth was soon tucked into one of the leather armchairs, a cup of tea in her hand, and her skirts spread over her lap. She'd never worn so many skirts in her life. But she owned nothing herself, and relied on what Paula provided her.

This so called duke wasn't in the room. Was Jeremiah on the phone? Elizabeth hadn't thought royalty existed anymore. Not since The Rising. Dukes and princes had only ever existed in the fairy tales that her mother had read to her.

She couldn't find any trace of another guest. No food or extra drink was set out on the dark coffee table. She couldn't imagine this den was used much for entertaining. Old rugs covered a concrete floor. The familiar security guard in dark glasses sat tucked away in the corner.

Her head pounded. A peculiar scent permeated the room, despite open windows.

"Thank you for your patience, dear." Her uncle sat in the chair across from her, dabbing his brow with a white handkerchief. He pasted a generous smile on his face then picked up the cup of tea.

An uneasy feeling swirled around her, raising goose bumps along her arms. Her stomach turned with disgust. She should be grateful for the generosity of her uncle, she reminded herself.

He set the tea down without taking a drink. "We need to discuss your future."

She placed the tea cup on the coffee table, not sure she could trust her hands.

"There's no room here for a bright, energetic girl like yourself." His face remained void of all emotion.

She bit her tongue to hold in the laugh that threatened to erupt. No one would describe her using either of those words. Like a ghost, she was a shadow of who she once was.

"Don't worry. I'll take care of you." His gaze felt tangible, heavy and controlling.

She should be grateful to have family that could take her in. Instead, his face unsettled her. It reminded her of what she use to have, and how he differed greatly from the warm kindness of her mother and constant comfort of her father. Her uncle gave her neither. Yet, it was all she had.

He crossed his legs and continued to watch her. "Given your parents' deaths, I think it's important to have family and be connected. I decided to move up your wedding."

Elizabeth choked and covered her mouth. A sea of surprise crashed upon her. As pragmatic as marriage might be, did her uncle honestly think she should talk about marriage, days after learning about her parents' death?

He reached across the coffee table, lifting her chin with a finger. His cold touch startled her.

As she got lost in his gaze, the tumult of emotions soothed to a rocking wave. A slow mist of understanding prevailed. She had no future, and her uncle was giving her one. Who knew, maybe the duke even had a hand in it?

"Okay, Jeremiah." The words flowed out with conscious decision.

She tasted blood and realized she'd bitten the inside of her mouth. Traveling deeper into the fog and confusion, she didn't know up from down. She only knew that Jeremiah had the answer.

౿⁄ᴐᴄ⁄౨

It took Becca a moment before she registered the small tongue and wretched breath. A cry sounded, and she snapped awake to a fuzzy face demanding attention.

"Go catch a mouse," she told the gray cat in front of her, the one she brought home from the fire.

Given the state of the room, she'd bet there was plenty of vermin nearby. Through the tattered curtains, shards of light illuminated the rundown bedroom filled with several cats.

She shifted slightly, and Darion tightened his hold around her waist. Becca's blood raced at the warmth of his touch.

When they'd fallen asleep on the tattered blanket in the abandoned house, there was a considerable space between them. Somehow during the night, she must have ended up in his arms. She'd allowed herself that peace and security through the night, but couldn't let herself go there now. She had a job to do, which involved saving Caleb.

Slowly lifting Darion's arm, she attempted to extricate herself carefully without hurting him. He was in bad shape last night. They'd taped up his ribs and bandaged his arms. The burns on his hand already appeared somewhat healed, from his ointment or his magic.

"Good morning to you, too." His rough voice brushed her neck.

She stood, heat rushing to her face as she struggled to find something to say.

He sat up carefully and rubbed his face. He looked like hell. Dried blood clotted on a gash above his brow, surrounded by a deep bruise. "Don't hurt yourself there," he said. "I understand. You only want me near if you're inebriated or too exhausted to know better."

"It's not that." She swallowed hard, knowing she hadn't slept so soundly in a long time. But she couldn't get attached to him, not again. It had taken too long to get over him the first time. She needed to focus on saving Caleb. Her stomach turned at the thought of him left in the hands of magicians.

"I know you have the farm boy," he said, as if he could sense her thoughts. His aloof smile and indifferent air put more space between them. The gray cat nuzzled his way under Darion's hand, and he stroked its fur.

Traitor. She was the one to pull it from the fire.

"Caleb. His name is Caleb," she said barely above a whisper, unable to meet his gaze.

"Caleb. Who you're willing to die for?" His words were seeped in anger.

She didn't answer. He set the cat aside and stood. He smelled of smoke, his clothes charred rags. He moved closer to her, making her lift her chin to meet his gaze. She fought the impulse to step back. His body radiated an energy she could almost feel, tangible and intense.

"Then help me connect the dots," he said. His steel eyes narrowed. "If we die or, worse, are captured, then what good will it be?"

She struggled to put it in words. How could he understand the missing pieces of her life she lost the day she walked out on her family, her life? They'd been better off without her, but a small nugget of hope had remained that one day she might return. That was crushed. Caleb was the only part of that life left. He'd been her best friend and more. He was the promise of what once was.

Becca ignored his question, wanting to avoid the fight, and reached for the bag on the floor. It had taken Darion some time to unlock the spell on the statuesque cat. Once he did, the pillow opened, full of gems and coins, and the cat returned to normal.

"Will it be enough?" she asked. The backpack didn't feel heavy enough to hold the worth of a man, especially Caleb.

"Should be." He walked to the window and peered outside. "A couple thousand dollars. You could start a new life with that. Far from here." He pulled the curtain closed, and the fabric tore in his hand. He cursed a steady stream that spoke of more than torn cloth. He paced the room, agitation evident in his tight shoulders.

"I can go alone." She wanted to give him an out if that was what he was looking for. "Get me in, and I can do the rest. I've never been. I'll be harder to recognize."

"It's more than going to a regular market and bartering for a cheap weapon. The politics alone will eat you alive. People question new faces."

"Okay…" Nothing could be simple with witches, could it?

"And even though Jeremiah doesn't usually go there. He will have men there and a price on my head."

Guilt sank, heavy and cold, in her gut. As much as she needed to save Caleb, could she sacrifice Darion in the process? She wasn't ready to give one life for another. "You've helped me more than I could expect."

He grabbed her arm, demanding her whole attention. "You wouldn't make it."

"But—" she started to protest.

He tightened his grip. "You. Won't. Survive. Alone." He forced the words through a clenched jaw. "You'll need to change everything about yourself just to get through the door. That will take quite a bit of money. Then maybe, just maybe, if you can listen to me, you might survive the auction. Trust me."

She bit her tongue, not trusting the anger and fear boiling under her skin. If it was so dangerous, why was he doing this? Guilt from their past relationship? Part of her didn't completely trust him yet. Hell, she didn't trust herself around him. But any feelings she might had have were pushed to the back burner, because, when she thought of the danger she was putting him in, it was all too much.

"I have to do this." She wished there was another way.

"Then I have to go with you. Guess we both have things we can't live without." He dropped her arm and turned away. "We better get moving. We have a lot to do before the auction tomorrow." He didn't wait for a reply before leaving the room.

Alone, Becca ignored the tingling where his hand had been and the warmth in her stomach. The gray cat rubbed against her leg. "What the hell am I doing?"

Thoughts of leaving him crossed her mind, but Darion didn't bluff. She was out of her league. She didn't know anything about Moondance. Sitting on the sidelines wasn't an option, though. Neither was losing Caleb or Darion.

Her hand trembled as she stroked the cat. She had run before. She had left those she loved because she couldn't face herself and regretted that more than anything. She would never see her family again. That fact ate at her heart, but built up her resolve.

She pushed down any reservations. They would only hinder what she had to do next. "Sorry, kitty. Gotta go." She stood and followed Darion out the door.

CHAPTER 20

The clouds parted enough for the sun to peak out. Becca welcomed the warmth as she accompanied Darion to his friend's place. They had parked a couple blocks away and walked through the rundown buildings and vacant lots littered with trash. The streets were empty, only a random person now and again who kept to themselves. Becca had never traveled to this part of the city before.

They approached a small two-story complex, complete with rotting wood, peeling paint, and a very large rat that scurried across their path. It reminded Becca of her first apartment—she still had nightmares about the roaches in that place.

In the foyer, the carpet was stained blood red like a bad start to a horror story. Gratefully they avoided the stairs and maneuvered down the hall, which appeared patched together with super glue. He stopped in front of a green door, One E. The E hung askew by a rusty nail.

"Are you sure about this?" Becca scanned the hall, waiting for some type of demon to jump out at them. "Soultorns live better than this."

One side of Darion's mouth lifted in a smile. "You'll see."

How could she love and hate that same stupid smile?

Before he could knock on the door, it opened. It only

took a few steps to see they were entering not just a rundown apartment, but a whole different world.

Light aquamarine walls, appeared in constant motion, like the surface of water on a windy day. Unique pieces of furniture were arranged to perfection and highlighted with bright blasts of exotic flowers. Even the salty tropical scent had to be fabricated. A deep purple flower with blue neon strips swayed as if alive—but it wasn't alive or even real. None of this was real.

Magic. Amazingly beautiful and terrifying at the same time.

The door shut with a loud click. Stepping farther inside, she imagined the walls closing in on her and wished to be back with the rats.

All of this was born from demon energy. All magic was. When the portal to the demon dimension opened, powers grew. Wizards fed off demons, demons fed off people, usually Mundanes—that was the new circle of life.

Scanning the hallway, she followed Darion farther into a room. Her steps were thick and heavy, as if drifting through dense fog. She must be imagining things. This was the product of an illusionist twisting reality, or one's perception of it. She had never witnessed anything like it. Becca's back straightened, her hand lingering by the knife at her side.

A man emerged from behind the wall, as if parting the sea, with all the showmanship of a practiced performer. His gold scarf and white suit shone bright against his caramel skin. His open arms and wide smile were welcoming. He looked young maybe twenty, with bright eyes and flawless skin, despite Darion telling her he was older. Magicians— you never know what you'd get.

"Darion. So good to see you again." Nevada said, hugging his old friend. "Drab as ever."

"You never were one for sugar coating, Nevada." Amusement colored Darion's words.

"Why bother?" The wizard shrugged and brushed his dark feathered hair across his brow while his lips shimmered pink. "So what did you bring me?"

He turned his bright emerald eyes on Becca. They shined with a youth that surprised her, but maybe that was an illusion too.

"Nevada, this is Becca. We are need of your services." Nevada reached forward, grabbing Becca's hand. Against her better judgment, she let him. She kept her knife hand free.

"It'll be my pleasure," he purred. Nevada led them into an adjourning room, while Darion explained what was needed.

"I've been dying to get my hands on you for some time," he told Darion. Exuberance twinkled in his eyes.

"I'm not here for a makeover."

"Yes, yes. I know." Then turning his attention back to Becca, Nevada added, "Darion is still angry from when I gave him breasts during one of our lessons."

"What?" she choked out. "I'm sorry I missed that."

"Nevada," Darion warned.

Lessons? Darion had never mentioned magical lessons. But then they rarely spoke of magic. Only what she needed to know. She couldn't imagine his life filled with magical lessons or school.

"He was busty." Nevada's laugh bounced as they entered a room.

The ocean blue walls continued, dotted with long mirrors and the ceiling imitated the sky, with clouds floating by. Dark furniture littered the room with several dressers, and a small bar.

"Please have a seat," Nevada offered.

Becca sat down in a black suede chair with an elaborate high back, while the other two sat across a coffee table that looked like a miniature tree with a flat top. She brushed her hand over the soft material of her chair in awe, while her gaze continued around the room.

"It's been too long," Nevada told Darion.

Becca couldn't concentrate on the conversation. In a corner of the room, amid all of the opulence, something studied Becca. A demon. Her muscles tensed as she gripped her chair.

The demon leered with blood red eyes, set deep within its arachnid shape. Dark brown hair covered its body and all eight legs, which ended in a type of claw. It crossed its legs in front with an unsettling human quality. It hissed at her, displaying a long row of pointed teeth. Her instincts told her to run. Instead, she turned her head away and released a jagged breath.

"You know how it is," Darion said, undisturbed. "Trying to get lost from the coven's radar is a full time job."

"Oh, I know it," Nevada replied.

She needed this wizard and, if necessary, his demon to disguise herself for the market. She was supposed to be a wealthy witch, while Darion posed as her security. With Jeremiah searching for them, it was their only option. *Sometimes you have to dance with the devil to get what you want.*

Neither of the guys appeared bothered by the demon's presence. Becca continued to feel its eyes bearing down on her, treating her like a meal that was just out of reach.

"Becca." Darion dragged her back into the conversation. "Ready?"

She nodded, and Nevada sat on the coffee table facing her. He leaned forward, brushing her hair behind her shoulder. She flinched. It was instinct.

"Stop acting like I'm about to cut off your nose," Nevada chided. "If anything, I'm going to improve it."

The demon in the corner didn't help her nerves. "So how does this work?"

"Don't tell me you're unschooled—"

Darion coughed, interrupting.

"I'm not a witch," Becca informed him.

Nevada was a friend of Darion's so she didn't think it would hurt to state the obvious. Nevada raised an eyebrow and glanced at Darion. Darion shook his head. It felt as if a silent conversation passed between them.

"Okay. Just hold still," Nevada ordered.

Her stomach continued its nervous churning, despite the necessity of the task and Darion's reassurances of the procedure.

Darion had warned her that a demon's presence would be necessary to pull power for the magic. The demon in the corner was only part of it. For the first time ever, Becca was willing to let a magician curse her—not only willing, but paying for it.

Becca shot Darion a skeptical look, as he sat in a lounge chair across the room, practically beaming with, what Becca imagined, was a sort of grim satisfaction.

Darion laughed briefly. "You're making more of a fuss than when you were stabbed by a mugger."

"I'd take a mugger any day."

"I bet."

"This can be undone right, right?"

"Undone?" Nevada choked, as if the insult physically hurt. "Do you know how much people pay for my work? You don't deserve my discount."

"Don't insult the illusionist, before he works on you," Darion warned, as he struggled to contain a laugh.

"Shush you two." Nevada began a series of

incantations or spells, most of which Becca didn't understand.

Her skin prickled and crawled. The skin on the back of her hands darkened ever so slightly as the fingers lengthened, the nails turning a light pink shade. She closed her eyes, not willing to watch the rest. Seconds ticked by slowly, as magic, like a heavy blanket, covered her skin.

"So how's blonde for you Darion?" Nevada asked as a wave of frigid air poured down Becca's head. Goose bumps ran up her arms.

Darion choked on something and, after a second, asked,

"Do you have a sister?"

Her breath left in a rush as if someone sucker punched her. She refused to pull up memories of her sister, not in front of others. She had never told Darion about her family. No one talked about their past in this city. It was safer that way. So she told him the truth, "No." *Not anymore.*

"Whatever." Nevada broke the uncomfortable silence. "I think it's overdone anyways." He finished working, a tingling sensation pouring over her head.

"Open your eyes." Nevada still sat in front of her, uncomfortably close and focused on her face.

"What eye color do you think, Darion?"

"Whatever is popular."

"Pity. That's one of the few things I like about her old look."

Becca tried not to take offense. She liked her hazel eyes too, with specks of blue and green that popped out with what she wore.

"They're recognizable. Change them." Darion's firm voice left no room for questions.

"I do so love the pale lilac that's in fashion."

Becca opened her mouth to protest, but was immediately shushed while Nevada finished his work. She could only wonder who in the world had lilac eyes and realized probably the same type of people who named their son Nevada.

"Am I done?"

Darion stood beside Nevada. He studied her face closely, searching for a piece of her former self. They both ignored the demon, now smaller, writhing in pain in the corner, its mouth open in soundless screams.

Nevada reached for her hand and pulled her in front of the mirror. "Come on. Tell me I'm a genius. I'm not modest."

Full, plum-colored lips hung ajar. A slender hand touched her face. She ran her fingers through the sleek black curtain of hair that fell past her shoulders. When the light hit right, deep purple hues emerged. The vision of this woman, who must be of Asian descent, was breathtakingly beautiful.

Amazement and fear coursed through her veins. This gorgeous mirage was a great disguise, but would she be able to find herself again? She had to remind herself: this was only an illusion. A smokescreen. There was no true transformation, just a magical hallucination surrounding her.

"Close your mouth," Nevada chided. "If I were you, I'd think about keeping it."

Nevada opened one of the large closets. "There are several dresses for you to try on. Here are some of my favorites." He set a few on a chair. "We'll figure out accessories in a little bit."

She touched her face, but nothing felt different. Her fingers trailed down her arm. It looked flawless, but there on her palm she felt her familiar scar. "So how does this work? I don't feel any different physically."

"It's a mirage," Nevada responded, as if stating the obvious.

"But are there any limits, anything I shouldn't do?"

"Not really. Be careful with fighting. You'll feel a hit, but your body won't show a bruise or cut. Hard for first aid." He pulled out two more dresses. "Others will sense your illusion, but no one will remove it. If they start that, think of how many uggos would be revealed." He laughed and took out one more bright orange dress. "I could do a dress but it wouldn't have the same feel or texture as the real thing—" The pile of dresses was as unique as his apartment.

"You ready for me?" Darion interrupted.

"Let me grab a drink and refuel." Nevada stretched out his neck. He glanced at the demon in the corner, writhing on the floor with it fangs bared. "We'll probably need my other demon upstairs."

Another pet? Becca turned away, struggling to hide her disgust.

"I'll meet you upstairs," Darion said.

Becca looked into the mirror again. Purple eyes blinked with unnaturally long eyelashes that matched in color. She wasn't ever going to get used to this reflection.

"Is this what you people find attractive?" she asked, curious.

Darion stopped abruptly. "You people?"

"You know, magicians. Do they just make up whatever fantasy they want and create it?" She didn't mean to be offensive by the question.

"If you're rich enough, sure. Personally, I stay away from illusions. When I was a kid, I once saw a hot blonde turn into an eighty year old man." He grabbed a bottle of water behind the bar. "Who would want to accidentally wake up to that in the morning?"

Becca sifted through the dresses. "True."

"When you try them on, make sure you can fight, or run in it. Nevada can get carried away sometimes."

"You don't say?" She picked up a light green dress, heavy with crystals.

"If anyone knows what people want to see, it's Nevada."

She touched this elaborate dress, and doubt overwhelmed her. She'd never worn anything like this. Could she really pull off a wealthy witch going to an auction? Her other options were to storm the place or to try to steal Caleb as he was leaving with his new owners. The first one was definitely out, and there was no way she could watch every exit to the market, even with Darion. There were too many things that could go wrong.

Darion approached slowly, as if sensing her apprehension. She tensed, not wanting to hear a lecture about how she was going to get everyone killed.

He touched her shoulder lightly, his fingers hot on her bare skin. "Don't worry. Original Becca will always be my favorite." He turned, leaving her alone in the room.

She could feel where his hand had been, as she stared at the stranger in the mirror. She wasn't completely alone, though. Demon eyes continued to watch her from the corner, reminding her of where all of this came from.

CHAPTER 21

The clanging of metal woke Caleb. He squinted at the fluorescent lights that constantly burned and blocked out any sense of time.

"Inspection," a voice growled. "Get up." A large redhaired guard unlocked the cage and threw the door wide open.

Caleb's body ached as he pushed up to a sitting position. Noise echoed through the warehouse, and the smell of bleach stung his nose.

He purposely slowed his movements as his mind raced. Was this his chance to escape? The warehouse was covered with guards but an open lock was one step closer.

"Time to clean up," the guard bellowed.

Caleb crawled out of the opening and stood next to his cage, scanning for any possible opportunity. His prospects for escape were crushed when he saw the beautiful Soultorn a few cages down. The Soultorn, in black leather pants and wavy long hair, stood next to the manager, Pove, in obvious contrast. Prisoners lined up in front of their cells while Pove inspected them like livestock.

Caleb glanced at the young woman standing in front of the cage next to him, Bubblegum, she said her name was the last time he asked. She shook her head as if she knew what he was thinking. He turned away, focusing on the guards by the front gate. He couldn't resign himself to this fate.

The Soultorn licked its perfect lips while perusing the inmates. If only it would come closer. He wondered if its neck would snap as easily as a turkey's.

The older inmate in front of Pove backed up against the bars of his cage. He acted as if he would rather be back inside. Then, with a wave of Pove's hand, the guards escorted the man off toward the back of the warehouse.

After several minutes, Pove and the Soultorn approached Caleb. The redheaded guard stood between Caleb and Bubblegum, awaiting orders.

"What do I have here?" Pove asked.

"Not much," the guard said. "A whore and possible guard. No traces of magic."

Caleb smoothed his features and tried to slow his racing heart. Just like hunting. He needed to stay calm and be smart, in order to make it out of here. He focused on the small ridge on the guard's nose and imagined breaking it for a second time.

Pove moved closer to inspect the girl. "Oh, come on. With a little cleanup, the right whore can make a good pull." He turned his gaze to Caleb and looked him up and down, as if mentally checking off a shopping list. "Let's clean up this one too. He may pull in a fair sum as a pet or Soultorn."

Caleb bit the inside of his cheek, trying to keep his rage in check. He wanted to attack this creature and didn't care if he was killed in the process. Anything would be better than being a caged pet for the rest of his life.

He remembered Rebecca. If there was even a slim chance of escape, he had to take it to find her. He registered the taste of blood and focused on keeping his mask in place.

"I'll take them to wardrobe, sir," the guard answered, standing up straight and gripping Caleb's arm.

Before he could escort them off, another man, dark and lean, approached. "Excuse me, sir?"

Pove's lip lifted in a sneer. "Yes."

"Jeremiah has sent a man to discuss security."

"Again? I told him on the phone I had it handled."

The man lowered his eyes. "Do you want me to escort him out?"

"And get hell from the coven?" Pove turned, heading back down the aisle. "No. I'll deal with him." His frustrated curses faded down the row.

Could this be the same Jeremiah who landed him in this place? Rebecca's uncle?

The guard grabbed Caleb's arm and motioned for Bubblegum to head down the row, away from the other cages. After a minute, only boxes and crates surrounded them. There was a guard and inmate up ahead, but Caleb could barely make them out.

Bubblegum walked ahead of the men with a slow and purposeful sway to her hips, stealing all of the guard's attention. He focused on her figure with a disturbing quiet. They soon found themselves alone, deep in the warehouse.

Without hesitation, Caleb punched the guard in the nose. The guard didn't have a chance to respond before Caleb's next hit. He continued raining hits on the man, releasing the anger that had been building for days. His fist bled, or maybe that was the man. It didn't matter. Caleb hoisted the guard up and slammed him into a wooded crate, his forearm pressed firm against the guard's throat.

Caleb ignored the bloody mess in front of him. "How do we get out of here? Which way?"

The guard attempted to shake his head, but Caleb pressed harder. "There has to be a way."

"Caleb," Bubblegum whispered his name in warning. "There's no way out. Outside this building is an illusion with magical barriers we can't even see. This isn't a fight you're going to win. Trust me. I've tried."

Caleb swore and kneed the man in the gut, letting him crumble to the ground. Anger poured out of Caleb, alive and burning to devour every wizard in the warehouse. Before he could kick the guard again, Caleb's body froze.

He fell onto the concrete with a sickening crack. The only thing he could see was a wooden crate. He tried to scream, to fight against the magic, but he couldn't even move a finger.

The clicking sound of high heels slowly approached.

"What do we have here?" Pove reprimanded with a joyous overtone. "Looks like someone has forgotten the rules. Go ahead my pet."

The buzzing pain entered Caleb's head. He arched back against his will, his screams echoing through the warehouse.

Agony enveloped him while everything else faded away.

❧❦❧

Darion stared at the thick pale hand gripping a mysterious blue cocktail Nevada had mixed for him. Nevada's gift was impressive. Darion appeared as a tall man with short brown hair and massive muscles. Life was never dull around Nevada.

"I guess I should be grateful I don't have red hair, or six fingers." Darion sipped his drink, which was surprisingly good, and remembered Nevada's many pranks as a teenager. Even the simple ones of adding a couple inches on the waist line of their crotchety tutor, so she would pass on sweets at every meal.

Nevada had been on the run for a couple years, staying just ahead of the coven's grasp. Sometimes, Darion helped by passing along rumors and information. It was Nevada's isolation and his detest of the coven which made Darion trust him.

"So who's the girl?" Nevada asked.

Becca was downstairs, sleeping in an extra bedroom. Darion wished he could trap her there for a couple weeks while this all blew over. But he wasn't the crazy kidnapping type, even if it meant her safety.

"An old friend," he replied.

"Really?" Nevada didn't try to conceal his disbelief. "Because I've known you for some time."

Darion lifted the glass to drink, avoiding an answer.

"Where did she come from? I would remember someone with her power."

"You felt it?" Darion wasn't sure if relief or surprise hit him first. He had felt something from Becca ever since they were at Lady Katherine's home.

"Of course. It's strong." Nevada was great at sensing other people's power, not a true Profeo, but close.

Part of the illusions, Darion always assumed. Those who created illusions could often see through them, perceiving others' magic.

"I wondered but was never sure." It made sense, especially if her uncle was Jeremiah. Magic ran in families. He couldn't have confronted Becca with his suspicions, though. She was the type to run, before stopping to figure things out.

But now that he knew for sure, he had to tell her. "I don't think she'd believe me, even if I told her."

"I thought you two were old friends."

"Things are complicated." *To say the least.* Their

relationship was teetering precariously. He had to be honest with her, but he wasn't going to shove her off the edge. "Her powers were sealed until recently."

"Is she as naive as she sounds? That may pose problems at the market."

"Her power will tell others she's as strong as she looks. I'll be there to help." A few magicians might confront Becca, push her even. But he could protect her. If he didn't believe that, he would tie her up and go alone.

Nevada smirked. "If you're not careful, you'll both be up for sale at the next market."

"You wouldn't bid on me?" Darion asked.

"Like I've said—" Nevada reached for another drink. "I've known you for a while."

CHAPTER 22

C aleb squinted against the morning sun.

The sun.

With a shot of adrenaline, he bolted up. His heart flushed with joy at the smell of damp leaves and rich earth. But the comfort of familiarity fled as silver bars came into focus. He was still in a cage, albeit much cleaner. They'd moved the cages outside to a clearing in the forest.

Shock and anger flooded him at the stunning realization someone had cleaned him and changed his clothes. He wore only a fitted pair of leather pants, his chest bare.

He stood, as his last conscious moments came rushing back to him: the fight with the guard and Soultorn's painful screech. His body ached a bit, mostly his hand. He flexed his fingers but couldn't find a scratch on them or anywhere on his body. He searched for answers outside of his cage.

"Don't touch the bars. They magicked them," Bubblegum said from the cage next to him. "Don't want us biting the customers." She snapped her teeth.

They'd changed and groomed her as well. She wore a dark green dress that hugged every curve of her body. Her light hair was pulled back. Her face, now clean, glimmered with a hint of makeup and pink full lips. She was dressed to sell.

"Thanks for the heads up," he said, grateful for her sarcasm and company, something consistent in the madness that threatened to overtake him.

Twenty or so cages ran in a of couple rows. Behind him, thick autumn trees stood with their branches twisting to the sky. Brightly colored leaves fell to the forest floor as if on schedule.

The perfection lacked soul and reality, a twisted fairy tale waiting to happen, something that could have only been produced by magic. He could smell meat roasting and caught glimpses of fantastical shops and entertainers dressed in bright colors.

"So this is it?" he asked.

"Don't fight," the girl said with sincerity. "It'll be worse if you do."

"I can't willingly submit." He had to try, even if he didn't have a chance.

"Then don't. But they'll make you go, and make you be quiet. Be smart. Kiss up to a rich old lady and avoid pissing off a wizard. Maybe they'll value our lovely personalities, or they'll give us a new one."

He swallowed hard. She was right. He couldn't give up, but maybe now wasn't the time to be stupid. He needed to bide his time until the right moment.

"What's your name?" He'd lost count of how many times he'd asked the question.

"Buttercup—"

"No." He was tired of the nicknames, the false bravado, and wanted something real from her. He spat on the ground, trying to rid the metallic taste in his mouth. "I'm not a customer, and you're not a whore."

"Not yet," she said, almost too soft to hear. She looked down, picking at her nails, a light pink that matched her lips.

She lifted her chin and met his gaze. "Grace. My birth name is Grace."

He grinned, delighted in the gift of her name. He couldn't say why one name meant so much. Her sincere expression brought a soft glow to her face. It was a beautiful name for a beautiful girl.

"I haven't heard that name for a long time," she continued. "I always thought it cruel irony."

"It's nice to meet you, Grace." He wanted to offer his hand.

"You too. Wish it was somewhere else. Somewhere far from here." Her features were stripped of their usual jovial pretense. A youthful appearance beamed from sky-blue eyes. She couldn't be older than nineteen, but he guessed she'd lived through enough for a few lifetimes.

They stared at each other for a moment. Words of regret, of injustice, and what ifs were better left unsaid—for they'd do nothing to change their predicament.

Wizards began flooding into the market, distant voices growing to a dull roar. A few meandered around the cages. Taking a deep breath, Grace straightened her shoulders. She pinched her cheeks and smoothed her dress as an older man, impeccably dressed, approached. With a flip of her hair and a coy smile, it was as if the set of steel bars separating them vanished.

Fighting the impulse to throttle the man, Caleb turned away. Grace was a survivor, stronger than he ever would be.

Could he do this? Play this role, turn into a slave, when every fiber in his body wanted to fight? He wasn't sure he could roll over and play a lap dog to any of these people. His gut tightened at the idea that he might have to if he wanted to survive the day.

A beautiful woman, with eyes the rich amber of an

animal, approached him.

He was about to find out just what he would do to survive.

∽∾∽

"You could be some sort of legendary mountain yeti, you know that?" Becca glanced over her shoulder at Darion who lagged a few feet behind. Nevada gave him the classic bodyguard look, muscles on top of muscles and short buzzed hair. His eyes were so dark brown, people might consider him a Soultorn at first sight.

She felt just as foolish, dressed up, strolling along in an old parking lot that smelled of oil and dirt.

A ridiculous grin covered his face. "Admit it. You think I'm hot."

"I'll try to contain myself," she joked, trying to ease the tension in her chest. It was better when she didn't look at Darion anyways. His new look unnerved her.

A couple of bored drivers stood out next to their cars, smoking. She shifted, unsteady under their gaze.

"To your left," Darion murmured behind her.

A small rundown office building stood in the center of the parking lot, the remains of a car dealership. Shards of broken glass hung from windowpanes. The front door swayed back and forth in a light breeze. One strong wind may take the whole thing down.

There was an eerie feeling that more than dusty furniture peered out of those vacant windows. She itched to tug down her dress. She fought instinct and ignored the slit that almost reached her hip. It wasn't *her* body anyone would see. It was Nevada's creation—a difficult one at that.

It had taken over an hour for Nevada and her to agree

on the dark silver dress that hugged her body. One sleeve traveled down to her wrist, the other completely absent, leaving her shoulder bare. At least the flexible material let her move.

Nevada had left her long black hair strait as a board. Becca missed her ponytail. But she had to admit, she'd fallen in love with her new boots that conveniently hid a knife.

"It's through the door." Darion's voice wavered slightly.

"We don't have to go."

"Yes. I do." There was no going back emptyhanded. As she crossed the threshold, a slight tingling sensation ran down her spine. In a heartbeat, her world spun, dizzying colors that morphed into something new.

Gone was the stained carpet and fallen chairs. Instead, a large dark tree trunk filled her view. The brightly colored red and orange leaves continued up to the sky. A lightheaded sensation forced her to look back down.

She wanted to bottle this smell of fresh air and fallen leaves. It reminded her of home. Not of the pain or loss, but the peace of the wild.

A squirrel scurried by, rustling through the underbrush and then continuing up the path as if leading them. The trees lined a path ahead, while the roots formed into steps, ascending under the canopy of colored leaves. It was perfection. Darion cleared his throat.

Right. Don't gawk at the magic. This demon-fueled illusion was hard not to be drawn into. Fall at its finest.

She climbed the steps as the leaves played in the wind, blowing over their feet. And though the path appeared long, they reached the top in a minute. The smell of savory foods greeted her first.

Then the trees opened up to a clearing full of

hundreds of shops, restaurants, entertainers in the street, and so many people. Wizards, she corrected herself. Magicians who wouldn't hesitate to string her up for sale, given the opportunity.

A large man dressed in black appeared out of thin air. She stepped back, startled, not expecting to be challenged so early in the game.

Darion brushed by her and approached the man. Her hand tapped her leg, inches from the knife in her boot.

"Your name?" the man asked, his thick goatee hiding his lips. "When have names been required for entry?" Darion demanded.

"When I say they are."

"Chima," Becca answered, hoping to avoid confrontation.

"From…"

Darion stood in front of her, his bulky frame filling her view. Heat radiated off of him like she was standing next to a furnace. Had he always been this way? His magic almost tangible? Or had he held back before? She'd never been close enough to other magicians to notice.

"We're meeting the Stevensons," Darion said. "Relatives from the north."

The guard narrowed his gaze in evident disbelief. The sensation of magic magnified, rising the hairs on her arms.

Becca couldn't handle the testosterone. She broke the silence, annoyance heavy in her voice. "Are you two pups done here? I have shopping to do."

She didn't wait for a response, but strode away, praying it would work. She'd counted to ten when Darion caught up. "About time," she said, grateful for their luck.

"I forgot how much pretty girls get away with," he muttered, remaining close behind.

She normally would have replied with a snarky

comment, but her attention was drawn to the astonishing sights before her.

Each stall held a shop or restaurant and contained a tiny world with its own flavor. People filled the street, perusing the stores or stopping to watch the entertainers. One bald man in a tight multicolored suit breathed fire into the sky. Another couple in animal prints performed acrobatics six feet in the air. Tilting her head to the side, she couldn't figure out where one started and the other ended and struggled to keep her focus in front of her.

They passed a stall that held a variety of creatures, including dogs, rabbits, and birds. She had a pang of sympathy for the small trapped creatures.

She entered the next shop, lined with small objects. She assumed jewelry at first, but upon closer look they were amulets, bits of hair, and even small vials of blood.

Despite her urge to locate Caleb, she perused the shop. She had time until the auction began and wanted something to help their escape. Darion assured her they had enough to buy Caleb and to live on for a bit.

Darion leaned in. His unfamiliar form raising the air on her neck. He spoke quietly. "The more powerful or rich magicians never need these. There will be jewelry farther down for a distraction."

She waved him off. This was more than a distraction. A blue stained-glass amulet glimmered in the light. These talismans and amulets had to hold more power than what was in the street markets. She and Caleb would need as much protection as she could get.

A wizard came over to attend to her. His burnt orange blazer mirrored a sunset. "If it's protection you're looking for, the lady should also look at the Mohammedan Circle of Protection."

Next to her, Darion tensed.

"But the blue matches my cat's eyes perfectly." Her voice was high, in the best pampered attitude she could manage. "Maybe I'll buy my Snowflake both, just in case."

A wide smile crossed the merchant's face as he estimated the depths of her pocketbook. "It's important to protect your loved ones."

"So true." She kept her features serious and pleasant.

With a nod, he went to wrap up her packages. This was indeed a different world. She pulled out a couple of silver coins, stamped by the coven, and paid the man.

With her package paid for and tucked into her sleek black purse, they continued through the market. She passed by the food, not trusting herself to keep anything down.

In the busy crowd, a couple of men stopped her, asking for her name in a weak attempt to flirt. Darion quickly discouraged them with a gruff, "She's not interested."

With his arms as thick as her thighs, he played the part of bodyguard well. She couldn't get use to the meaty face and shaved head he wore, though.

Becca continued forward, searching for what she wanted to buy most.

Darion leaned over her shoulder. "I think you'll find what you're looking for to your left."

She found Caleb immediately, standing several feet down in one of many silver cages. He stood tall, shirtless with no obvious injury. Leather pants clung to his muscular legs.

He was alive. Thank God. She wanted to run to him, talk to him, make sure he was unhurt. She wanted to apologize for bringing him into this crazy world of hers. A lump formed in her throat. She should be in that cage, not him.

Darion placed a careful hand under her elbow. "Do you require assistance?" His voice was oddly formal.

She blinked several times. She knew better. This was a job, just like any other. And if she lost her head, she'd lose everything. "I'm fine." She counted her steps, slow and purposeful, to the cages.

The first cage held a thin boy who appeared invisibly bound. He sat with his arms held stiffly at his side, his mouth pressed tightly together. A bitter taste flooded her mouth.

A tall woman handed Becca a paper. "Information on the merchandise," she said then continued to the next potential buyer. It took a moment before Becca found the listing on Caleb.

Thirteen. Strong virile male. No previous owner. Great physical shape. Ideal for demon hosting for the ultimate security. Starting bid: one hundred silver pieces.

Her hands shook as she fought the urge to tear the paper. She'd expected this, but the sight of Caleb with a price tag on him made it real. She had to keep it together, for Caleb. They continued down the row of cages, stopping periodically to feign interest. She repeatedly glanced down the row.

Up close, she scrutinized every inch of Caleb. His arms were folded across his chest, while the muscles in his neck strained. She couldn't find any sign of his previous injury from their attack in the woods. Not even a scar.

He stared ahead at nothing. His stoic features discouraged many wizards from talking to him, but the stares and conversations nearby showed obvious interest. Becca ached to reach out to him, to tell him she didn't forget him.

A short flashy man blocked her view. She scowled. He smiled in return.

"This must be the beautiful Chima." He took her hand to kiss. She fought the instinct to cringe. How did this man know her name?

Darion had warned her to not let people touch her. Some magicians could sense much from touching another. She couldn't figure a way around it, especially with the Soultorn on his arm.

Its pitch black eyes were a sacrilege to the beautiful body it inhabited. Blond hair cascaded around its shoulders. Its thin frame hid strength in those taunt muscles.

"And you are?" Becca replied.

He laughed and squeezed her hand before letting go. "Pove, my dear. Manager here at Moondance." He spread his arms, and his numerous rings glinted in the sun. "What can I help you find in my prize stock?"

"Just browsing," she replied. Darion's arm brushed hers, a steadying presence. It wasn't customary for security or servants to address the higher ranking magicians unless called upon.

"There's always a gem to be found. Take this man, for instance." He turned to Caleb, waving Becca to follow. "Come, boy."

Caleb slowly dropped his arms and approached the bars. He flexed his hands, the muscles in his arms bulging. Meeting Becca's gaze, he grinned—a frightening contradiction to his cold eyes that held so much malice.

She had never seen that look on him before, but there was nothing she could say, not in front of Pove. Clamping down the nerves rattling inside of her, she tried to act as if she was shopping for a new pet. The fact that Pove had picked Caleb to show to her didn't go without notice. What were the odds?

"He could be one of our best sellers." Pove's smile

widened. "Strong. Strapping. Great for security or any of your needs. I'll leave you to finish perusing the merchandise. See you at auction." He left and started a conversation with another buyer.

She approached the cage, aware of the others wizards within earshot. "Are you able to care for horses, boy? I have a stallion, Duncan, who needs a firm hand. Do you have experience?"

A flash of confusion, recognition maybe, crossed Caleb's face for a moment, but he remained silent.

Duncan had been his horse years ago. The horse had thrown Becca, and she had always hated him. Caleb would tease her relentlessly about it. He had to remember. She wished he could see past the illusion, past the lie she'd created to be here. If things went south, they needed his trust.

"I can manage horses," he said carefully, while his face gave nothing away.

"Good." She clasped her hands to keep them from reaching through the bars.

Darion cleared his throat. A couple approached from behind.

The two feet that separated Becca and Caleb might as well have been two hundred miles.

CHAPTER 23

While the market continued to buzz with excitement, Caleb's mind raced with how and why Rebecca was here. He ignored the perspective buyers passing in front of his cage and tried to follow the long, pitch-black hair weaving between the crowds. It had to be. Who was with her? The man looked like security, but from where? Was this some sort of twisted magic or a game?

As the spaced cleared, he found her standing next to that same man with an auction paddle in her hand.

"Muscles," Grace said. "I never figured you to be suckered in by a pretty face. She was impressive."

"It's not that." How could Becca be here, transformed into someone else? He had heard of magicians transforming themselves, but she wasn't a witch.

"Then what?" Grace asked.

He lost Rebecca, or the woman who he thought was Rebecca, in the crowd. He turned to Grace in attempts to make sense of his own jumbled thoughts. He didn't want to say anything yet, to give her false hope or endanger Rebecca. "I don't know."

"Did that lady work some type of magic on you already? It's forbidden to play with the merchandise before they purchase." A serious tone laced her words. "I can tell the manager."

"No, no. It's just—It's a long story." He searched for

her again, but drawing attention to Rebecca wouldn't help. He turned away from the crowd, worried his face may give something away.

"What are ya thinking, muscles? Better not be thinking about running again. I still have a damn headache from the last time." Her voice was light, but her brow was tight with worry.

"Don't you want to be free?" he asked. "Wouldn't you take a chance if you got one?" He couldn't believe she was reconciled to this unknown fate. He would fight to his dying breath.

He remembered the last time he'd tried to escape. It didn't matter. He would try again and again, no matter what the cost.

It took Grace a minute to answer with eyes lowered, her expression icy. "You're naive to believe this all ends happily ever after. I can only wish for the lesser of these evil bastards." She plastered a forced smile on her face and turned back toward the crowd. "You're not on the farm anymore, muscles."

❧❧❧

Time slowed as Becca waited for the auction to start. She sat in the back of the outdoor theater, on a chair created of twisting branches and twigs, surprisingly more comfortable than it looked. She leaned back, legs crossed. The large wooden clock on the top of the stage ticked the minutes by.

Enormous trees formed the sides of the stage, the branches twisting to frame the raised platform. Fall leaves and flowers, growing on the branches, dotted the stage with color. A beautiful stage to house a human atrocity.

Wizards slowly filled in the seats as the seconds ticked

away. The seat beside her was empty, waiting for Darion to return. He'd left to get the market gossip from the servants' bar. Something unsuitable for a lady of her supposed position.

It took several minutes to convince him that she would be all right sitting here alone. A few people had said hello, but for the most part she enjoyed the few minutes to herself to think.

"Excuse me," an old magician said to her, startling her out of her thoughts. "Found anyone in particular, dear?"

She looked up at one of the oldest people she'd ever seen. His light blue eyes were surrounded by heavy wrinkles and a huge nose. Minty breath wafted toward her as he waited for an answer.

"No. No one in particular."

"Really? And I thought you were eying that muscular boy. One of the few healthy ones here."

She swallowed, cursing herself for being obvious. "He was healthy, as you say."

"Yes. You don't want to be infested with bugs or sickness." He stood straighter. "What did you say your name was?" He held his hand out, spotted and wrinkled. His predatory look set every nerve on edge.

She ignored his hand. "I didn't."

He chuckled. "Good girl. Maybe you'll be more competition than I expected. These things can be a terrible bore."

She glared and forced a smile with the idea of smacking some sense into this revolting man. People were being sold, and he found it boring.

"Good luck," he said with a slight nod and continued down the aisle to the closer seats.

She rubbed her bare arm, trying to shake off the chill.

Darion slid in beside her. His warmth was welcome.

He handed her a tall glass.

She sniffed at the drink. "Is this safe?"

"It's just iced tea."

"Thanks." She took a drink, not realizing how thirsty she was. "By the way, who's the old wizard in the front row?"

"Abel. The oldest wizard in this city. I'm surprised he's here."

"Why doesn't he change himself? He's so old." She had seen pictures of her great-grandparents who'd lived that long, but that was before The Rising, when medicine and hospitals were easier to find and cheaper to afford.

"He likes people to know how old he really is. It takes a lot of magic to still be alive in this shark pit at his age."

"Creepy." She set her drink down. It wasn't his age that bothered her. Something was a bit off about him.

"I won't disagree. He stays out of politics, and Ryma leaves him alone. There's a reason for that."

The crowd quieted as the man she'd met earlier, Pove, took the stage. His Soultorn remained a couple feet behind him. His words of welcome were lost on Becca. She tapped her foot, anxiously awaiting Caleb.

The auction began with an older woman, beaten down with age. Bidding began at fifty silver coins. A man in the back won the bid at a hundred.

Next a young boy entered the stage with an expression that tore at Becca's heart. Three hundred silver coins. She wished she could raise the paddle, again and again, as people sold like common cows. She wanted to rescue them all. And destroy Pove in the process. But she didn't have the money or the power.

A thin pretty young woman stood on the stage. Seven hundred silver pieces. Becca ignored the tightness in her chest and focused on Caleb.

Darion leaned close. "You okay?"

"Yes. No," she whispered. "How can all these people, humans, be sold so easily? Many headed to a certain death as a Soultorn. Why do magicians need so many?"

"Do you want to know?"

"Of course."

"People have been experimenting with ways to transfer hosts. Move a demon from one person to another, in case the host is injured or not as aesthetically pleasing. The price of potential hosts has risen dramatically in the last year. Markets like these are reaping the benefits."

She noticed she was gripping her dress, above where she'd hid a knife. She placed her hand in her lap. The woman currently on the auction block was sold.

How can magicians do this? They really must think they're an entirely different species. In some ways they are.

"Not everyone agrees with Ryma's rule." Darion brushed her hand. "But enough do."

"I know."

Darion had risked everything to go against Jeremiah and help Becca. She regretted her words when they broke up, for his actions now spoke of so much more.

Caleb's number was up. He climbed the stairs, a guard at his arm. The Soultorn on stage moved toward him with a hungry look on its face.

Pove, in his smooth elegance, told of the great benefits Caleb had—muscular physic, no trace of magic, so easily controlled, strength, and not too bad to look at either. A couple buyers itched forward in their chairs. Becca straightened her back, the paddle ready.

"Let the bidding start at three hundred silvers. Who'll start at three?"

In a flash, the old magician in the front raised his paddle.

Pove didn't pause, but kept rattling off prices. "Do we have three-fifty? Three-fifty?"

And with a flick of the wrist four-fifty, five, and six hundred went in a blink. Her pulse raced as her hand tightened. The bidding finally slowed at seven hundred, and Becca joined the race. She ignored the glare from the red-haired woman to her right.

"Seven-fifty? Did I tell you what strength he had, with a defenseless mind," Pove called out.

"Eight hundred," said the old man in the front. He turned and winked at Becca.

She hesitated for a second before answering the call to eight-fifty. Darion brushed against her hand in warning. They only had a thousand dollars for this bid. No one had gone over this yet at the auction, but there were more players on the table. She focused on Pove in the front.

"Nine hundred," the woman called out.

"Nine-fifty," Becca countered. She sat at the edge of her chair, her heart thumping loudly in her chest.

The red-headed woman lowered her paddle, glaring in Becca's direction.

"Eleven hundred dollars," Abel said in the front.

A couple interested buyers lowered their paddles. Out of their price range, and out of Becca's. It didn't matter. She would give all they had and more to free Caleb. His face was stern, but those green eyes held a history she could never forget. She couldn't leave without him.

"Becca," Darion started in warning.

She raised her paddle this time, her voice loud and clear. "Twelve hundred."

People turned to stare—so much for inconspicuous. She glared at Abel in the front, daring him.

He nodded with a smile, surrendering the bid. But it wasn't until Pove uttered "Sold," with a grin that traveled ear to ear, that Becca leaned back in her chair.

Darion turned toward her, leaning in. "We don't have twelve hundred dollars."

Adrenaline from the bidding coursed through her body. She set down the paddle as Pove introduced the next person for sale. "Yeah, I know."

In the front row, Abel stood and headed to the exit, passing by Becca. He turned and leaned over the back of her chair. "Interesting to see just how much that healthy boy means to you." He patted her arm and strode out.

She grasped her purse, trying to steady her hand. If she thought the bid was hard, what about trying to collect a prize without the cash.

CHAPTER 24

Darion's tall frame kept close as they headed to collect Caleb. She could almost feel the magic from those passing by, like insects crawling over her skin. She probably was imagining it, or maybe it was her own illusion affecting her.

"Keep calm. Once they free Caleb, I'll pay them what we have, and you focus on leaving," Darion murmured as they approached the station at the side of the stage.

Becca wished she hadn't bought the amulets or the drinks. But a couple of coins wouldn't even cover a two hundred-dollar difference.

They approached the purchasing area at the side of the stage. The older woman from the auction walked out, her arms pinned behind her back. The guards brought her to the desk, where a short fat man took the payment.

Becca struggled to watch the transaction, a sick fear for the woman, and for Caleb, making it hard to swallow. Becca averted her gaze, unable to watch the new owner take her away.

"How can I help you?" a short fat man asked, sitting behind a desk.

"Number Thirteen."

The man's finger scrolled down a paper. "Yes, for twelve hundred." He paused for a moment, as if there was a problem. The attendant spoke to a nearby guard. The short man turned back to Becca. "It'll be a minute. Someone will come to escort you back."

"I can retrieve him, if security is a problem," Darion offered.

The man didn't reply, but pulled out a handkerchief and dabbed at his forehead. "It'll be a minute," he repeated then turned back to his paperwork.

Another prisoner was escorted out of the doors, a tall man, worn and beaten with age. After a few words, his new owners took him away. Becca tensed. Why weren't they bringing Caleb out like the rest of the prisoners?

Pove emerged from the closed door with his Soultorn close at hand. "Chima, wasn't it?" he said with his normal exuberance.

Becca's stomach sank at the sight of Pove. "Yes. What's the problem?"

The auction must be over. They'd been hoping to avoid Pove. His open smile and raised brow held excitement—or anticipation—while the Soultorn's black eyes had a cold steadiness to them. Darion moved closer to Becca.

"No problem. I just wanted to personally escort you to get your prize. Especially after such an exciting bid." His hands moved with a nervous energy as he spoke.

"I appreciate the concern. But I'm in a hurry." She tried to act annoyed and affronted like the witch she was supposed to be.

"I'll be as quick as possible." He clapped his hands, as if there was some sort of agreement, and headed back to the cages.

They followed Pove and his Soultorn through the row of cages. Her heart picked up speed with each step. She glanced at Darion, whose face was unreadable.

The cages were scattered with various prisoners.

Several empty. The merchandise already carried off. They approached Caleb. He stood in the middle of his cage, hands behind his back, face void of all emotion.

Her chest tightened. As good as it was to see him, she couldn't breathe easy until he was far from here.

Pove waved the guard to the side and pulled out the key. His hand stopped inches from the lock. "Where did you say you were from again?"

"Up north." Her gut twisted, knowing what he probably found with a single call. They couldn't go back. They would never get this close to Caleb again. The key held steady, mere inches from the lock.

"I recently learned that there's a bounty out on a couple of magicians," Pove continued, pulling the key back. "Said they robbed an old witch and burned the place to the ground. And I'd hate to see this fellow fall into the wrong hands."

"Are you looking for the reward?"

He beamed like a child ready to eat candy. "I figure it's only fair to get not only the bounty, but the price of the boy."

Darion shifted in front of Becca. "We don't have it."

She remained focused on the key in Pove's hand.

Darion opened his hands, a steady heat coming off of him. "No one needs to get hurt."

The Soultorn chuckled and for the first time spoke. The voice was high and smooth. "Where's the fun in that?"

The empty silence lasted only seconds but felt like minutes.

Becca discretely pulled the knife from her purse and noticed the surrounding guards. Two escorted a prisoner out a side door. Another couple of guards, both wide and tall, stood off to the side, as if awaiting Pove's command.

Not great odds with magic involved.

The Soultorn opened its mouth. In a flash of movement, Darion sent fire flying at the Soultorn, exploding in its face and spreading over Pove and the surrounding guards. The key fell out of Pove's hand as he frantically extinguished the flames.

Chaos erupted. Curses and spells shot through the air. In a fiery haze, the Soultorn launched itself onto Darion. Becca wanted to run to his aid, but the sooner they freed Caleb, the faster they could leave.

Becca darted to pick up the key and shoved it in the lock. "Caleb." His name came out in a rush.

As she turned the key in the lock, he shouted. "Behind you."

A guard grabbed her hair, pulling her to the ground. She lashed out with her knife. Blood welled up on his forearm, but he didn't relinquish his hold. Swearing loudly, he slammed her into the cage.

Pain shot through her temple. She gripped the bars to steady herself. Before she could attack again, Caleb tackled the guard to the ground.

Becca blinked several times to clear her head. Caleb pummeled the guard on the ground—punch after punch—swinging his heavy fists.

The door to his cage swung wide, the key still in the lock. She thought of the old woman from before. Was there any way to retrieve the key, and give it to the other slaves? She only made it one step, when an inhuman pain pierced the inside of her mind.

It was a sharp screeching sound, containing no words, but a throbbing so intense that it blocked out thought or reason. She staggered against the cage.

Caleb rolled off the guard, his face tight with pain. Every person except Pove and his Soultorn were huddled in pain.

The Soultorn's burnt frame was terrifying, leaving any pretense of human discarded. With hair burnt black on its skull, the once beautiful features were distorted and grotesque. What was left of the dress carried a small flame near its feet. The only feature not blackened with soot was its white teeth, its mouth open with glee.

The Soultorn stood over Darion, who lay on the ground. His chest rose and fell with shallow breaths. He lived. But with him unconscious, there was nothing left to protect them.

Becca wasn't strong enough to fight this monster. The pain from the creature reverberated off her skull, driving into the core of her being. Becca sank to her knees, watching the dark soul of the demon blaze through its human eyes.

An evil lived inside that shell, something dark and rank. Or was that the pain? She couldn't believe this was how it would end. At the hands of the one thing she detected more than anything. Demons.

Her fists, clenched in desperation, pressed against her temples. The shooting, aching pressure was unbearable.

A burning sensation slowly grew in her chest. The warm anger pushed against the pain, fighting the constant noise and stabbing agony. Her fingers began to tremble, and it traveled up her arms. Uncontrolled. Dangerous.

Becca lifted her eyes, heavy and burning, watching the Soultorn bend over Darion. Its charred hand traced his face as he arched back in pain.

Black spots filled her vision. Is this it? Her body shook. A hot sensation threatened to explode inside of her.

With her head thrown back, her body contorted in pain, she screamed without thinking. The warmth fled, exploding out of her mouth, almost tangible. A rush of adrenaline seared up her spine—and, like a fire extinguisher, muted the deadly noise.

Silence.

What the hell happened? Her breath came out in rough gasps. A slight tingling sensation coursed through her body.

The pain. The noise. Gone.

Becca slowly stood. Unsure of herself. Was it her? How? The pressure that was building inside of her was gone. It had vanished and taken the pain with it.

Scattered moans and cries of misery grew among the cells. Becca's head ached, the screeching noise echoing in her mind. She didn't have time to think about what this all meant.

The Soultorn stood in the middle of the wreckage, eyes wide and angry. Before Becca could blink, it lunged at her. It knocked the knife from her hand and lifted Becca by the neck, her feet dangling in the air.

Becca tore at the blackened hands around her throat. The Soultorn hissed in a foreign tongue. Its breath retched and foul as it began to squeeze the life out of Becca. Crushing pain pounded in her throat. Black spots clouded her vision. She flailed, kicking and struggling against the Soultorn. The monster didn't even acknowledge her protests.

A scream tore through the room. Pove.

Darion was there, behind the Soultorn. And in one quick movement, he sliced its neck. Both Becca and the Soultorn collapsed on the ground. Becca gasped, each breath laced with a throbbing ache. A dark mist rose up from the Soultorn's body, like black snow swirling in the air. It built up momentum and then exploded, the effluvia gradually dissipating before touching the ground.

Becca thought she'd seen demons killed before, but this was nothing like that. Strong arms pulled her back as the Soultorn's body lit up in flames.

"Are you okay?" Darion asked. He didn't wait for an answer, but began his next incantation.

She nodded. His arms were a warm comfort in the midst of hell. The smell of blood and burnt flesh awoke her with a renewed sense of panic.

Pove, the market manager, raced toward them, curses filling the air.

"Go," Darion shouted, his coat charred and hair matted with blood. He turned to faced Pove. Without his demon, Pove was weaker, but he had other guards rushing to his aid.

Darion didn't need her to help. They'd discussed it before. His magic was easier when he only had to focus on keeping himself free of the flames. Her stomach sank at the idea of leaving. But she must.

She found Caleb opening the other cages. "You okay?"

He continued to work on the locks. "Fine."

She reached for his arm. They had to get out of here.

Fire exploded nearby. Becca ducked down. Another explosion sounded far away.

She blocked out the cacophony of screams, shouts, and curses that filled the air and turned her attention back to Caleb. He had a cage open, pulling out a petite blonde in a short green dress. The woman's lips tightened in a fierce line as she watched chaos erupt around her.

Becca yanked on his arm. "We gotta go." Her voice was rough from when the Soultorn had almost strangled her. She grabbed her knife and purse on the floor. Darion was far from them, pushing back the guards with dancing flames. But she was never one to run from a fight.

He glanced back at her, sweat dripping down his face. He nodded, urging her to leave. She would see him again. No matter what.

"This way," she told Caleb, rushing out the door.

Once in the frantic crowd, Becca slowed her pace. She ran a hand through her hair, and attempted to blend in with the others. Shop keepers, closed up shop while wizards and witches hurried to different exits.

An explosion echoed in the back of the market. A scream escaped a woman with pink hair who knocked into Becca.

"It's okay, dear," a plump man said, patting her hand. "The coven will take care of it."

"Of course," the woman replied with a slight waver to her voice, obviously on edge. "Let's get out of here."

This upper class hasn't been shaken up for some time, Becca guessed. It might be good for them. She veered toward the main exit—more people, less chance of being singled out. The blonde from the auction trailed next to Caleb. Becca would worry about that later.

They hurried down the stone path and passed through the illusion. The smell of oil and dirt welcomed them back to reality. Becca coughed, her throat raw and pained.

They were almost there. The smoke and roar of Darion's fire was gone, replaced with cars racing out of the parking lot. Becca glanced back, the illusion gone from her eyes. She couldn't just leave Darion. He was smart and knew how to fight. He would make it out. He had to.

At the edge of the lot, Becca stopped by a large dumpster. The car was hidden a few more blocks down the street.

"Please tell me you have a getaway car," the young woman said, the strap of her dress falling over her shoulder.

Becca narrowed her eyes. She was glad the girl got out, but she didn't have time for an attitude. If Darion didn't get out, Becca wasn't leaving.

"Caleb, head south a couple more blocks. We left a car there, next to an old wash shop. Keys will be on the floor. Take…" Becca looked at the girl.

"Grace," she said.

"Take Grace and head out if there is trouble,"

He squared his shoulders, in his stubborn way. "I'm not leaving."

A few blocks off, a small store exploded, spraying debris high into the sky.

"This way." Becca's heart raced as they ran across the street. She raked her brain for a way to contact Darion.

They only made it a few feet when a blue car pulled in front of them, blocking their path. She raised her knife.

The dark window rolled down. Darion's smile rose up on one side, his illusion gone. "What? The car's not nice enough for you?"

She lowered her knife and took a deep breath. She had never been so happy to see him. Hurrying around, she opened the passenger door. "Blue was never my favorite color."

Caleb and the girl slid into the back.

The smell of smoke lingered in the car. Darion eyed her dress that was a little worse for wear. "We can't all pull off silver like you can."

CHAPTER 25

B ecca's hand tapped rapidly against her leg, while their car sped down the highway. Darion had taken off the illusion with a simple spell, evidently wanting to see the real Becca as much as she did.

Though she was grateful to return to her rugged hands and smaller frame, the unease didn't leave her stomach. She should be doing something, anything. She turned to look behind them again for signs of someone following them.

The road was empty.

"No one is following us," Darion said, keeping his eyes focused ahead.

In the back seat, Caleb looked as anxious as she did, glancing out the windows. Driving in cars was rare for both of them. A tin box out in the open left a big target.

Next to Caleb, Grace leaned back against the seat, her dress riding up her leg. She played with a strand of hair and looked bored, as if running for her life was a daily occurrence.

"We're good, Becca." Darion assured her. "We're past the city limits. They won't be able to trace us this far. I know a nearby town that we can get lost in." They needed to run. Far and fast.

"Wait," Caleb said. "Why do we have to go to a city? Can't we hide out in the country?"

Darion gave a hearty laugh. "If you haven't noticed, I'm not a country boy. I can char a good piece of meat, but that's about the extent of my talents. And isn't that where you came from?"

"I'd pick the country any day over the wizards in the city." The disgust in Caleb's voice was evident.

No one replied. Darion kept driving.

Caleb ran a hand over his face. "What about Elizabeth? What about your answers?"

Silence filled the car. Becca struggled to swallow. Her throat was tight from when the Soultorn almost choked her to death. *What I wouldn't give for ice water. Or a strong drink.* She dreaded the coming conversation, reliving it all over again, but Caleb deserved it.

She turned in her seat to face Caleb. "After Jeremiah knocked you out at Nikko's—"

"And sold me," he added with a bitter scowl.

"Yeah that too. After that, he knocked me out and I woke at his house. He said he saved Elizabeth from the fire, but she died from complications. But then, the bastard proceeded to burn off my Hand of Mary tattoo, so I'm not sure how much I trust his word."

Darion's faced tightened at the mention of what he did, even though she left him out of it. Becca didn't need a reason for Caleb to hate him.

"What?" Confusion crossed Caleb's face. "I know he always hated me, but you're family."

"Yeah, some family. Also found out my dear old uncle is a Master Magician and member of Ryma's inner circle. One hell of a family." She swallowed a lump in her throat and turned to watch the green trees pass by in a blur. "I'm not sure what happened. He must have played a role in the fires. I just can't figure out what for. Revenge from another magician on his family?"

"I haven't heard of anything," Darion said.

Caleb's face flushed with anger. "So they're just going to get away with it?"

"There's nothing we can do. We're not strong enough to take on Jeremiah." She could only wish getting to her uncle would be so easy.

Instead, Elizabeth's death felt hollow and meaningless. It festered like an open wound. Shame washed over her that she didn't save her sister. No, instead they were running from Jeremiah—the man who should pay for it.

But how could she fight her uncle? How could she fight someone who could use her, bend her will, and twist her into whatever he wanted? Becca's stomach turned at the memories from her youth and what her uncle was really capable of.

"Who's Elizabeth?" Darion asked.

"My sister, a couple years younger than me."

His eyes narrowed. "You said you didn't have a sister."

"I don't, anymore."

Darion jerked the car to the side of the road. It bounced over the uneven weeds and rocks.

"What the hell?" Grace exclaimed in the back seat.

They rattled in their seats as the car slowed to a stop by a cluster of trees.

Becca couldn't imagine this was all about omitting her family history. "What's wrong?"

Darion parked the car and turned on Becca. "You said you didn't have a sister when I asked you at Nevada's." It was more of an accusation than a statement.

"I don't. She died with the rest of my family."

She'd purposefully avoided telling Darion about her family. She didn't want to relive the past and see the pity in his eyes. It had always been that way between them. She never spoke about her past, and he didn't push her.

"What happened? Exactly."

His eyes were intent and serious. Something wasn't adding up.

"Wizards happened," Caleb answered. "They burned our homesteads to the ground. We found our parents' remains, but didn't find her sister Elizabeth. That's when we started looking for you for answers, but Jeremiah found us first."

"Your sister, does she look like you?" Darion asked.

"No," she said. A sinking sensation pulled at her.

"Blonde? Petite?"

"Yeah." Becca's breath picked up. How did he know?

"Hand of Mary tattoo, the same as yours?"

"We both got them as children." Becca could hear his words, but wasn't sure what he was saying. A sick feeling rose in her throat. "How did you know?"

Darion leaned back into the seat and let out a long breath before speaking. "Jeremiah called me up for a job. A few days before I found you. He wanted for me to remove a tattoo, just like yours, off a girl."

Her breath caught in her throat.

"I think he's building his forces," Darion continued.

"But Jeremiah said she was…"

"She was alive the day before I rescued you. No injuries from a fire that I saw. After talking to him, I think he has some big plans for her. And for his role in the coven."

She leaned forward on the dash of the car, her heart pounding. "She's alive." Her sister was alive. A rush of relief ran through her body. Silent tears fell into her lap.

"Thank God," Caleb whispered from the back row.

Darion laid a warm hand on her back. It took several minutes before her breath slowed and Becca understood everything he'd said.

"What plans?" She forced the words out as she straightened up.

"I'm not sure, exactly," Darion said softly. "He hinted at a coup or rebellion, but I have a hard time believing he'd challenge Ryma."

"Why Elizabeth?"

"He removed her tattoo for a reason. The way Jeremiah is caring for her, I'd assumed it would be to host a high-level demon."

There was a tightness crushing Becca's chest. She wanted to scream, to release the pressure building inside of her.

His eyes were sincere as he reached for her hand. "I'm sorry. I didn't know she was your sister."

She pulled back and averted his gaze. *She's a person.* It was cruel to blame him for Elizabeth's capture, but it hurt to know Elizabeth was so close. Maybe even in the same house. Darion drew back, giving her space.

"What's Jeremiah doing?" Caleb asked, anger tightening his words. "What does this have to do with my family?"

"I'm not sure how the two are connected." Darion stared straight over the steering wheel, a mask concealing all emotion. "Maybe your parents were witnesses? He's trying to gain power, make a move up in the coven. And if your families were outside city walls and stood in his way…well, Ryma won't reprimand him for it."

Becca felt as if there was more to it than that, but she could care less about politics. Her sister dying was one thing, watching her be turned into a Soultorn to be used by her uncle, that was more than she could bear.

She faced forward, biting back tears. There wasn't time for those. "We have to save her."

"We won't be able to get into Jeremiah's place, or

know for sure which one of his many holdings he's at. His wards are some of the strongest in the city."

Becca wasn't going to leave Elizabeth there. "There has to be something."

"There will be a coven meeting soon. Lots of people coming in and out. It'll be our best chance. All the thirteen leaders have to be there for upper-level magic. If he has plans for her, he'll bring her. They'll do the ceremony there." Darion stared off, a haunted look in his eyes.

Becca sat up, strengthening her reserve. She couldn't let

Jeremiah get away with this, with any of it. "Turn the car around. We're not running, we're fighting."

Caleb punched his seat. "Hell, yeah."

Grace sat up straight. "And here I thought things were going to get boring with you guys."

Becca glared at Grace. She might not deserve Becca's anger, but Becca didn't ask her to get in the car. "Who said you're coming along?"

"Rebecca." Caleb said her name as a warning. One she didn't need.

"Where I'm going next, I'm sure she doesn't want to follow. We can take her to the city." Becca glanced in Grace's direction. "Don't worry. She knows how to survive on the streets." She regretted the words once they left her mouth. It wasn't about Grace, but this little blonde was one more thing Becca didn't want to deal with.

"Rebecca," Caleb tried again.

"I gotta take a leak," Grace said casually and opened the car door. "Just so you know, I'm no whore. I was a slave."

Guilt stabbed at Becca.

"Yeah. I never chose my life. But don't worry. I don't need some wannabe magician to survive." Grace turned to

Caleb, one leg already out the door. "No hard feelings, muscles, if you're not here when I get back." She strode off into the forest without looking back.

Becca pushed her conscience away. It was only a couple miles to city limits. Grace could find work there, just like Becca had done years ago. She needed to focus on her sister.

"You kept telling me how you've changed, Rebecca. But despite your new ability with a knife, I never saw it. Until now. I'm sure you wished Darion would have helped your sister, not because he knew you, but because she needed it." Caleb slammed the car door as he left.

Becca hit the dashboard. He was right, but she wasn't ready to admit it.

"Is he always this self-righteous?" Darion said, no levity in his voice.

"He's going to get himself killed."

"Maybe. But I bet he sleeps pretty well at night."

She grabbed the door handle to go track Caleb down. She wasn't going to leave him out here and, if that included bringing Grace along, then so be it.

"Give it a bit. Cool down."

"I don't need to cool down," she huffed and wished she could have said it a little calmer. She sank into the seat, admitting defeat. "Why doesn't he understand?"

"He's a good guy. There's not much of that left out here. As infuriating as it is, he'll save every stray along the way, despite the cost. Sometimes, that goodness is worth saving."

Darion flipped his lighter again. "Damn saint."

It was true. Caleb contained something rare and pure that reminded her of home. It was that same goodness that wouldn't let him abandon a slave outside the city. Becca would always love and care for Caleb as much as family.

But was that all?

Darion studied her closely, as if trying to pick out the same thoughts she was trying to straighten.

"So back to the city?" she asked.

"I have a place we can hide out for a couple days. Up north, bordering the city limits. Who knows? By then, they might get a glimpse of what we're up against and decide to head off on their own. Run into the woods and create a little family or something."

The idea put a sour taste in her mouth. "Sure."

"You know we have to talk about what happened back there at the market."

She opened her mouth to deny it, but one glance at his face and she knew better. She had pushed away the incident, not wanting to face the truth of what she might be. "I'm not sure what happened."

"I know. But we need to figure it out before we face your dear uncle again."

She closed her eyes briefly. The idea of having this weird magic inside of her for years made her chest tighten. She didn't want to be anything like her uncle. "I'm not a magician. Wouldn't I have known it?"

"Your Hand of Mary may have suppressed it."

"But I can't be. I'm not—" Part of her knew it was a lie. Since her tattoo was removed, she had been feeling other magicians' power. At first she'd thought it was just Darion.

His magic was warm and smoothing. She'd thought he'd projected it purposely. But at the market, the prickling of magic over her skin was constant, something she'd never felt before.

His eyes narrowed. "What? You're not a lying, deranged, power-hungry wizard, constantly deceiving others?"

The words stung as much as if he slapped her. He used the same words she'd thrown at him when they'd broken up. Her face burned with regret. She hated herself, not only for possessing powers she'd always cursed in others, but for how unkind she had been to Darion. He'd done nothing to return her anger. He should have.

His lips raised in a smile. "Don't worry. We don't all turn out that bad."

⌾⌾⌾

Walking away from the car, Caleb's temper softened as he smelled the leaves underfoot and the fir trees surrounding him. A smile lit his face, and he stepped on a pine cone just to feel the crunch underfoot.

He shut out the memories of the last few days. Evil was out there. He'd been to the city before, buying supplies and bartering for his father, but being at the will of magicians—It was a whole different ordeal that he wouldn't wish upon anyone.

It was tempting to run. To flee back in the woods, live off the land like he did with his parents. But now he'd be alone. The solitude and ghosts of the past were ready to swallow him whole. The only part of his past he had left was Rebecca, and she needed him.

Even if Rebecca had changed, he felt like he owed it to the girl he used to love, the girl he used to dream of spending the rest of his life with. It might be a dream, but maybe Rebecca was still in there somewhere.

He thought back to their last day together, warm hay and her sweet kisses surrounding them. If only Jeremiah— He had to stop playing the what-if game. It would only drive him mad.

Grace startled him as she appeared besides him. "So

did you get kicked out of the car too?"

"No." He looked at her—so small, so petite but with an attitude larger than most men. "Sorry about back there."

"Don't worry. I've heard worse." She tied her hair in what looked like a knot. "I understand too. Maybe you can get your friends to drop me off closer to the city. I can manage from there."

"Doing what?"

"We don't all have the muscles to kill wild animals with our bare hands, but I've survived okay this far."

A chill ran up his back as he remembered his own confinement. "I don't call what you did surviving."

She brandished a smile that looked more sad than anything else. "It's what I do."

He wanted to help Grace. Maybe because she was the only sane person he'd had to talk to in that cage. Maybe because part of him would rather die than go back, and he couldn't resign anyone to that fate.

Whatever the reason, he cared for her, and she deserved more than being dropped off at a street corner.

"Rebecca will come around. She's not that bad. We can drop you off somewhere safe when we get a chance. I'm not sure you'll want to stay with us for long."

Grace picked up a pine cone, turning it in her hands. "So what's the deal with your girlie there?"

"I've know her since I can remember. We were pretty close for a while. I haven't seen her for years, until our parents' deaths. We're just trying to find some answers."

Grace leaned forward, too close, and gently traced a finger down his chest. "She's right, you know? You don't go picking up stray cats in the city, and most magicians don't go risking what she did, even for a nice package of muscles." Grace loved to get to him, but he wasn't going to blink first this time.

"She's not a magician."

"Your eyes must have been closed back there at the market. She's a witch. And magicians don't hang out with us normal folk. Not for free."

Caleb wasn't sure what she was talking about. He didn't know what happened at the market, or how Rebecca was tied to this magic. But it didn't matter. It didn't change how he felt about her.

Grace stared back at the car for a moment. "You might be right. It might be too dangerous for me. But don't worry, I know when to jump ship. Watch out, though, because you might want to jump too."

CHAPTER 26

B ecca leaned against the cool glass of the car window, watching the scattered stars overhead. Night draped a dark curtain over the dense trees while they drove. The serene did nothing to calm the tumultuous thoughts raging in her mind.

No one had spoken since they got gas and water at a station sixty miles back. With tempers simmering on low boil, they'd decided it would be best to stick together for a couple of days. Darion had told them about a cabin up north that should be vacant. Becca didn't like to count on "should be," but they didn't have another option.

Grace and Caleb slept in the back. Still dressed only in the pants from the market, he reclined back, Grace leaning against his arm. Becca was a bit jealous. She wished she could sleep, but her thoughts continued to twirl around her. She picked at the hem of the silver dress she still had on from Nevada.

"Do you need me to drive?" she asked Darion, wanting something to distract her.

"No. Almost there." He slowed the car and turned onto a dirt road.

A narrow path weaved through the big pines. The car traveled roughly, jerking along the path. Becca gripped the handle as the car bounced over potholes and rocks. Caleb and Grace stirred in the back seat.

"We there?" Caleb asked, rubbing his face.

"Just about," Darion answered. After a couple more miles on the washboard road, they approached a tall iron gate.

"One minute." He put the car in park and walked to the gate. He stood for a moment, hands moving, arching in the air.

"Magic can be handy," Grace said.

"I suppose," Becca replied dryly. She tried to look at magic as helpful, as something that didn't turn her stomach. She needed magic to have a chance at saving her sister. But as she remembered the demon at Nevada's house, the lines of right and wrong blurred.

Darion opened the gate and then returned to the car. "No one's home. It's all ours."

The massive home rose up two stories and was dotted with shuttered windows. A large porch framed the house and a four car garage sat to the side.

Grace let out a long whistle. "This is a bit more than a cabin."

He parked around back, and they climbed the steps to the back door. They didn't have much luggage. They'd better find supplies inside. Becca didn't want to stay in this silver dress longer than needed. Goose bumps covered her bare arm.

Darion grabbed a key under the mat to unlock the door.

"Great security," Caleb muttered.

"Any Mundane touching that gate would have been killed on the spot. And any magician who got this far could use a spell on the door." Darion opened the door and flipped on the lights. "I prefer the easy way, though."

Grace waltzed inside. "Instant death. One hell of a welcome."

Polished wood lined the floor covered by intricate rugs. Heavy leather furniture positioned throughout the great room. Off to her left, a great kitchen with shiny appliances, and large marble counters.

Definitely more than a cabin. Becca was impressed. The smell of dust and pine filled the air.

Grace brushed a leather sofa. "You have some nice friends."

"Don't we need to keep the lights off?" Becca worried about gangs or other wizards. She couldn't shake the need to keep looking over her shoulder.

Darion locked the door behind them. "No. From the gates, everything looks dark and uninhabited. There are lots of rooms upstairs. We can grab a bite to eat and get some rest."

"What about other magicians?" Becca asked. "Can't they see past the illusions?"

"They can only tell there is an illusion. If they're strong enough to break it, they will. We should be safe, no reason for anyone to look for us out here."

Pictures filled an entry table with smiling, attractive people. One showed a pretty young woman, with vibrant red hair.

Grace picked up the picture. "So, Darion, is this pretty girl yours?"

Becca looked up at him, waiting uncomfortably for the answer. She reminded herself that she'd left him. Whoever he dated was his business.

"She's a friend." He turned a corner leading deeper into the cabin.

"What a friend. Breaking in, stealing food," Caleb mumbled.

"He's doing it for us," Becca reminded him.

"You're right," Caleb agreed, though tightness

remained in his shoulders. "I'm just not sure about him yet. The way he looks at you—"

"You're starting to sound like you belong in the city already," Grace interrupted.

Tired of the conversation, Becca left to check out the kitchen. Their fridge had wood paneling on the front, but— besides condiments—was relatively empty. Becca was happy to find running water, even hot water. She searched the walk-in pantry and came back with a couple cans of peaches, tomatoes, and chili.

"Can I interest you in a culinary masterpiece?" she asked Caleb.

He grinned. "Only if it doesn't involve living insects." It stole her back to the time she'd tricked him into eating a cricket sandwich. He was so pissed, until they decided to catch some more for her sister. His smile warmed her heart, but part of her ached at everything they had lost.

"I can't promise anything," Becca told him, handing him a fork.

"I'm hungry enough to crunch through a couple legs." They sat at the bar together. He leaned back to holler in the other room, "Grace, we have some food, if you're interested."

Becca hadn't gotten use to Caleb's attachment to this ornery girl. He was more trusting that most and that worried Becca. Grace sauntered in and grabbed a glass jar of peaches.

She speared one on a fork and lifted it up. "Here's to being alive and free for the moment."

Caleb raised his jar. "Here, here."

"What are we celebrating?" Darion appeared.

"Being alive," Caleb said.

"And free," Grace added.

Becca couldn't bring herself to celebrate anything. Her

sister was still out there, and the clock was ticking. Becca looked at her cold can of peaches and couldn't find the desire to eat anymore.

"As good as anything, I suppose." Darion grabbed a can of chili and ate it cold out of the can.

"Isn't that disgusting?" Becca asked.

He shrugged his shoulders. Dark circles hung heavy under his eyes as he shoved another spoonful in his mouth.

"Rebecca, so how do you know Darion?" Grace asked as she leaned on the counter.

"It's Becca."

"Okay. Becca. How do you know Darion?"

Becca plopped a peach into her mouth, hoping to ignore the question. Everyone's gaze felt heavy, waiting for an answer. "We dated for a while."

"Really?" Grace's surprised fell false. "Didn't you date Caleb as well?"

Becca itched to slap Grace's pretty smile right off her face. "Your point?"

Grace's saucy eyebrows rose. "Nothing really. Just realizing how awkward this all must be for you." Becca smirked. She wasn't sure if this girl was trying to be funny, or what. "Thanks for bringing it up." "Anytime," Grace replied.

Caleb coughed and headed to the pantry. He returned, setting several more jars on the counter.

Grace grabbed an extra jar of peaches. "I'm going to head upstairs for a bath. Feel free to join me, if anyone wants." She winked in Becca's direction.

Becca kept her mouth shut tight. She might throw Grace into the property fence if she didn't shut up.

"She's a treat," she told Caleb.

"I'm going to warm up some chili." Caleb began

searching the cabinets, his face slightly flushed.

The clanking of pans filled the awkward silence. Becca focused on the can in front of her.

Darion filled a glass in the sink, avoiding her gaze. "I'm heading up for the night."

Caleb stood rigid. "Are you following Grace up? She's been through enough, you know?"

"Really?" Darion's jaw dropped. "After all we went through to save your sorry—"

"Just leave the girl alone, or—"

"Or what?" Darion snapped. "Go put a shirt on, buddy. I have no intention of touching that girl. Trust me. I'm not interested."

He started upstairs, stopped, and turned back to Caleb, a darkness settling onto his face. "Let's get some things straight. I'm here for Becca. And threats don't go over well with wizards." He headed up the stairs, mumbling something about ungrateful Mundanes.

Becca stood and placed a hand on Caleb's shoulder. "Let him go. He's tired."

"He's an ass."

"I couldn't have gotten you without him." She owed Darion, more than she could repay.

Caleb turned around to face her, his green eyes striking, deep, and extremely close. "He cares for you." It wasn't a question.

"As a friend," she said, not entirely believing it was purely platonic.

"Why did you break up with him?"

She froze for a moment, not expecting the question. She dropped her hand, and turned back to her seat. "He lied to me. Never told me he was a magician."

"And you trust him now?" he asked, doubt obvious on his face.

She turned back to her seat at the kitchen island. "Yes. He wouldn't hurt me." *Unless necessary.* She pushed away the memory of Darion burning off her tattoo.

"I get it, but people like him usually don't risk their lives without something in it for them."

She shrugged. Feelings aside, he'd helped save Caleb, and she needed Darion to save Elizabeth.

"Are we going to talk about what happened back at the market when you broke me out?" Caleb asked.

She picked at a tomato with her fork. She wasn't ready for this conversation, but didn't have the luxury of denial.

"Do you have magic?" His voice was soft and kind, with a slight tremble in it as if he was just as scared of the answer as she was.

"I don't know." Thoughts of that moment were clouded and confusing. "When Jeremiah burned off my tattoo, something happened. I thought he did it to control me. But the tattoo was some sort of barrier for magic."

The fork trembled in her hand, and she set it down. She remembered the sensation at the market that had coursed through her body. When she'd actually silenced the demon, she didn't realize what she had done.

The power, erupting out of her, felt strong as if maybe she was more. But what did that mean? Was she a witch? Did her parents know about it?

Her mother also had a Hand of Mary tattoo. Becca's stomach felt heavy at the idea of the possible lies that had carried her through her childhood. Remembering the paddle her mother often used on her backside, it was hard to believe all those warning and teachings were false.

Magic could be bad in the wrong hands, some types even addicting. But it could do good, even if it was born of the devil. Right?

Caleb sat down and faced her, his eyes warm and

comforting. "You're one of the strongest people I know. You can be better than the magicians in the city. Just don't let *him* convince you otherwise."

She ignored his reference to Darion. She didn't want to talk about him. The idea of becoming a witch scared her to death. Could she trust herself once magic took hold?

Leaning forward, Caleb squeezed her hand. How different would her life have been if she'd never left him? If she'd decided to settle down, make a homestead. Would she have been happy as a wife? After the last four years, she couldn't even imagine it. But here he was.

After trying to run from the life she left years ago, it had followed her all the way here. She wasn't sure who she was anymore. The farmer's daughter was so far gone, but Caleb brought back those memories, good and bad, of family and expectations. But what did he expect? What would happen when all this was over?

Inches separated them, and the air charged with an electric silence. The familiar woodsy smell clung to his large frame. She loved that smell.

Caleb finally cleared his throat then sat on the edge of his seat, his breath soft. "I never had time to thank you."

"For what?"

He tucked a stray hair behind her ear. "For coming back to get me at the market."

She itched to fall into his arms, to find comfort in being held. But as much as she wanted to, the safety was a facade. Starting anything romantic would only complicate their situation.

She stood and placed the fork and empty jars in the sink. "You would've done the same."

He cleared his food off the counter. "Yes, but I wouldn't have been able to."

She didn't want to think of that. "Go get some rest.

I'm going to take the first watch."

"I thought this place was safe?"

"Probably is. But I can't sleep, and I just want to think for a bit." She wanted to change, but didn't feel like digging through strangers' stuff. She'd find something in the morning.

"Okay." He nodded. "Wake me if you need anything."

"Will do." She didn't want to tell him of her fears: that Jeremiah was a lot stronger than a gang of Mundanes, that even though she probably had magic, she didn't trust it. She couldn't sleep, knowing what lay in wait for them and for her sister.

She grabbed a blanket from the back of the couch and sat down on the sofa, staring out the window into the dark night. How could she get to Elizabeth? And kill Jeremiah? Her thoughts continued to spin faster and faster.

The dust would settle in the coming days, but who would remain standing and alive?

❧❧❧

Becca didn't remember falling asleep. But as she stood in front of her sister, a happy weightlessness radiated all over her body. "Elizabeth."

"Becca?" Elizabeth rubbed her eyes, sitting up in bed. She was dressed in a white nightgown, several blankets gathered around her.

Becca, in her usual jeans and leather jacket, settled down on a chair across from her. "Where are we?"

The room must have been haunted by the ghost of a gardener. Dried flowers and herbs were scattered all around. Roses plastered the walls.

Confusion creased Elizabeth's brow, as if she was struggling to wake up. "My room."

"Sorry to hear that. I miss your old room." Becca brushed her hand along the desk. "I miss us."

Becca wondered if her brain was giving her what she wanted: her sister, Elizabeth, tucked away safe somewhere. The bittersweet dream had a disturbing sense of reality, though.

"You left a long time ago." Elizabeth pulled her covers up, as if cold, and pushed her hair out of her face. "It was never the same after you left."

Becca lowered her gaze, knowing what that decision had cost her. "Sorry about that."

"Why did you leave us? Leave me?" Elizabeth never beat around the bush with Becca.

Becca's stomach knotted. She tried to put her regret over leaving Elizabeth into words. She used to think it was all her fault. Part of it might have been. Either way, it was time she voiced, at least subconsciously, what really happened. "The night I left, Caleb and I were making out in the barn—"

"You were kissing?" Elizabeth interrupted. She straightened up, mouth open in shock. "I asked you about him all the time."

"I know. I lied." Becca lifted a hand to quiet Elizabeth's protests. "Sorry."

Elizabeth always got caught up in romance novels and happy ever afters. Becca hated to crush that.

"Anyways, Uncle Jeremiah caught us one night in the barn…" Becca trailed off. Flashes of memories surfaced.

Rough hands. The odd burnt smell of Jeremiah. Wordless pleadings for him to stop. Silent tears. "Let's just say, he's not the man we thought he was. He's much worse."

"Jeremiah?" Elizabeth's hands clenched her sheets. "What did he do?"

Becca's mouth opened, but the words struggled to come out. She had never told anyone. Never planned to. She couldn't face the shame and pain, even with her best of friends. But this was a dream. It shouldn't be so difficult.

"He touched me. Hurt me. I thought it was my fault for so many years."

She remembered his words, his lies. He'd told her that she was evil, that she drew out the worst in people. The lies had clouded her reason, and frozen her words. He'd convinced her she'd wanted to kiss him, to touch him. She'd believed his words, though she'd found him revolting.

Looking back on that incident, she realized for the first time what it really happened. He'd molested her, using magic. Her tattoo had protected her to some extent, but his magic had been stronger.

Tears dropped onto Becca's hands. A shudder of mixed emotions tore through her. Relief that she wasn't tainted or evil and grief for all that she lost that night. She ran because she was ashamed of her actions. Actions that she now realized were not her choice.

She'd lost not only her innocence that night, but her family too. Shame and disgust still colored the incident, but some of the heaviness of it was lifted in telling her sister and realizing Becca wasn't to blame.

Elizabeth knelt in front of Becca, holding her hands.

"Oh, Rebecca. How could he?"

Becca had to finish. She ached to protect Elizabeth and warm her of what was to come. "Jeremiah isn't the man we knew. He's a wizard, as dark and evil as they come. It's his fault our parents are dead. And now he's after you. You need to get away. Run away."

Elizabeth's nose wrinkled up, like it often did when

she was confused. She grabbed Becca's hand and turned it over, running a finger across the scar on Becca's palm. "Remember this?"

Becca nodded. When Elizabeth was seven, they were play fighting with sticks Becca had cut into swords. Elizabeth had tripped, and Becca accidentally sliced her sister's hand. Elizabeth had been hysterical. Scared she'd get in trouble from their mom, Becca cut her hand as well to appease her sister. Only a thin white scar remained.

"It was the only way to keep from getting in trouble and save my back side." Becca had gotten a few swats anyways when her mother figured out the true story, but it did get Elizabeth to stop crying.

"True. But you grabbed my hand and told me we were more than sisters." Elizabeth squeezed their hands together. "That we'll always be together, in life or death."

If only those childhood wishes were true. A sob built up in Becca's chest. She grasped Elizabeth in a hug, never wanting to let go. Both girls knelt on the floor clinging tight to one another.

"I'll save you," Becca promised.

Becca awoke back in the cabin. Silent tears streamed down her face as she stared out into the dark sky. A shiver ran down her back, though a fire now roared in the fireplace.

Was that a dream or something more? She rubbed where the scar was, barely able to feel it anymore. Was it possible that there was a connection she didn't understand? She would have to ask Darion about it in the morning.

She repeated the promise she'd made to her sister. "I'll save you."

CHAPTER 27

Elizabeth's head felt stuffed with cotton. She had spent the last two days with Paula, crammed into her bed room that grew smaller by the minute. Smoke from the herbs burning in the corner threatened to suffocate her. She hadn't seen her uncle for days.

This morning, Paula drew her a bath of rose-scented water. Elizabeth should feel spoiled, pampered, like a true bride to be. Yet in the back of her mind, the fact she had not met her fiancé kept pestering her.

She watched her reflection as Paula braided her golden hair and felt like a child. A doll to be adjusted. Lift an arm here. Pin an earring here. Rest now. Eat now.

Watching her pale reflection, an uneasy sensation washed over her. Her latest dream about Becca unsettled her. She stared at her polished hands on the table and remembered her sister's touch, and tears.

The thin scar across Elizabeth's palm was barely visible. Could those words Becca had spoken about their uncle be true? Or was it Elizabeth's own fears and insecurities?

"Can we take a break?" she asked. "Maybe open a window?"

"Tsk." Paula shoved another pin in Elizabeth's hair. "We don't want you to catch a cold. Plus, these herbs help calm nerves."

Why do I need to calm my nerves? The large garment bag on the bed may have something to do with it. However the herbs helped, they didn't ease the gnawing in her stomach.

Paula must have sensed her apprehension. "I have something you'll enjoy," she said, sticking in the last bobby pin.

She retrieved the garment bag and pulled out a red lace dress. Paula displayed the dress proudly, as if she'd made it herself. The sleeveless dress had a deep neck line, no modest woman would wear, and a tight fit, the red traveling down to the floor.

It was a beautiful dress, yet the pain in Elizabeth's stomach continued.

"You should see the back," Paula said, flipping it over. "Jeremiah had this shipped in from overseas. He spared no expense."

"Why is it red?" Elizabeth asked. "I thought it was a wedding dress?"

Paula avoided her gaze for a brief second and swallowed. "You should be grateful. Not many girls get this kind of dress," she practically spit at her.

"I'm sorry," Elizabeth replied, trying to ease the tension.

"It's exquisite."

She leaned forward to touch the gown and knocked over a cup of tea on the desk. It clattered on the carpet, splashing the tea on the dress.

Paula gasped.

Elizabeth grabbed a cloth, and attempted to clean the stain. "I'm sorry."

"Stop it, you careless girl," Paula reprimanded, stepping back. She ripped the cloth from Elizabeth and dabbed at the fabric, muttering under her breath.

The uneasy feeling grew in Elizabeth's stomach as she stared at the dress. "Paula?"

"What?" she huffed.

"When am I going to meet my fiancé?" Elizabeth needed to have something to look forward to amid the dark confusion and loneliness of the last few days.

"What?" Paula jerked back. "Really? I have enough to do without all of your questions."

The door slammed shut. The lock clicked.

Elizabeth's mind swirled in the smoky room, trying to untwist what Paula had said, or what was left unsaid. She was supposed to get married. Jeremiah had set the date only days away. But where was the groom or a white dress?

She looked up at the window. Random clouds littered the sky, unsure if they wanted to rain or let the sun come out to play. They taunted her with clean air and cool breezes.

She pulled the chair over to the window and worked on the lock, constantly listening for sounds of Paula out in the hall. After several minutes, she tugged it open. A gust of air swam into her room, carrying the smell of musty trees and fallen leaves. Memories of home tore at her heart.

As the air cleared her mind, her thoughts pieced together. Her head pounded with the events of the last couple of days. There wasn't going to be a wedding. She'd never picked a wedding cake, or chosen flowers, or even met a groom. She didn't even know her fiancé's name. Or maybe

Jeremiah told her, and she didn't remember?

Maybe her dream with Rebecca was a bigger warning than she realized. If she only had the courage her sister had. She remembered the red dress Paula showed her. It would look better on a prostitute than a bride.

Elizabeth wasn't sure of anything. She grabbed a glass of water on the desk, draining it and then setting it back down. Her thoughts jumped to Jeremiah's news of her parents' death, his promise of a kind husband to care for her, and that everything would be okay. He had a way of convincing her.

She didn't know what was real or what was part of a fabricated fairy tale. How could she get married in days to a man she had never met? She didn't want to. She could refuse, but somehow, when Jeremiah came back, he would convince her otherwise.

But where could she go? The city? With no experience and no money?

She traced the scar on her hand. Her heart raced. If she didn't go now, she wouldn't have another chance. Pearl earrings lay on the desk. She grabbed them and the matching necklace in the drawer. They were worth plenty.

She had always wanted to get married, to have the perfect family life. But not like this. Not forced into something she wasn't sure of. She looked over her room one last time— neat, well furnished, picture perfect by all means. The idea of staying to play a part she didn't choose made her ill.

She crawled out the window and didn't look back.

e/se/s

Darion stared into the fire that popped quietly in its brick resting place. With a wave of his hand, the flames danced at his command. It had been something he could do for years, and it calmed his nerves like nothing else.

Becca was the exception, except for the other half of the time she set his nerves on edge.

Fire was different. He had control of it, though

powerful and dangerous. He understood it and could control and warp it like no other he had ever met. The thrum of power was exhilarating.

For years he had flown under the radar of the coven. Now, he was getting ready to fly right at them. There would be no hiding after that. Just running.

Becca stirred on the couch across from him, and he could hear the faint murmur of the other two upstairs. They didn't understand, except maybe the slave girl. The coven was strong enough to do things to a person that would leave them begging for death for years.

Becca slowly woke, and he wished they could just run. The two of them. Give them time to discover her powers, maybe even each other again. There wasn't time for that.

And if he didn't go with her, she would be dead. She still might die, and that was another alternative he couldn't live with. How much was it going to cost to keep her alive?

"How long have I been out?" she mumbled.

He closed his hand, the flames lowered to an ordinary dance. "It's almost noon."

"Damn." She sat up quickly and grabbed the couch for support. "We need to get moving, get planning."

"We have time, and we'll need it. How about coffee first?"

Her eyes were half closed as she tried to pat down her tousled hair. "There's coffee here?"

Her vulnerable demeanor was a rare appearance that amused him. She wore the rumpled silver dress that showed one shoulder, soft and bare.

He warmed the mug by hand, before handing it to her. "Here."

"Thanks." She sipped the drink. "Hmmm. This is good." She curled her legs under the blanket and stared into the fire. "How much time do we have?"

"Three days till the full moon. We'll have to get gas but should be able to make it up to Ryma's estate in half a day."

"Why not go now?"

He scoffed. "You really think we can just stroll in there?"

"You're a magician. What do you need to break through the wards?"

He wasn't sure if he should be flattered or scared of her ignorance. "You have too much faith in my magic. Ryma's one of the Coven of Abbadon, and he rules the city coven. I couldn't step on his property without his knowledge." He ran his fingers through his hair, frustrated at the impossible task ahead of them. "Jeremiah would love to have you. And we haven't even talked about what happened at the market. Whether you want to admit it or not, you have powers. They must have been suppressed by the tattoo. Any wizard who knows you're untrained would kill to have you."

He wanted to shake her, get it into her mind what they were up against. But one look at her staring into her coffee told him she might have an idea.

Before she could answer, Grace came strolling in, clean and dressed in jeans and a dark long sleeved blouse. She plopped down near Darion. "So are you two plotting away in here without us?"

Caleb followed Grace in and sat near Becca on the couch's arm rest.

At least he finally found a shirt.

He watched Becca with a possessiveness that got under Darion's skin.

"You two both need to figure out where you want to go," Darion said. "We can stay here for a couple more days, and then I can drop you off wherever you want."

He didn't need extra Mundanes around to protect. Becca would be hard enough.

Caleb head snapped up. "I'm staying with Rebecca. I have more reason than you to find Elizabeth and to get back at these bastards."

"Possibly." Darion turned to see if Becca was going to respond, but she focused on the fire so he continued, "But only one of us knows exactly what we're up against and has the power to do something about it."

"I'm not helpless—" Caleb said.

"Why don't you tell us what we're up against?" Grace interrupted.

"There is no we." Becca finally joined the conversation.

"It's too dangerous. And I'm not sure we can trust you." Grace laughed. "The way I see it. There is us and them. Those against the market, against the magicians that rule over the city, and against them taking what they want. I know what side I'm on. Especially after being a slave to them for the last eight years. I'm just a lowly Mudane."

"I'm not a—" The words froze in Becca's throat.

With a sneer, Grace turned toward Darion. "So what's the real story?"

"We're going to Ryma's estate in the north."

"For a gathering, right?" Grace asked.

"Yes. The first moon of autumn." He had gathered the information from the market. It was surprising what security would spill with a few drinks in their belly.

"So they'll do the rising then?"

Darion cocked an eyebrow, wondering if maybe Becca was right not to trust this girl. She might have learned about coven gatherings as a slave, though.

"What?" she asked in defiance. "I already know you guys are going for her sister. But just wondering what they have in store for her. They don't go to that much trouble for just another pretty face."

He didn't have to look at Becca to feel her rage across the coffee table. He exhaled loudly. "Who were your past owners?"

"Farina's for the past couple years, and before that Zaq."

The Farina family of magicians had been in the city since the takeover, respectable with a few wayward sons. Zaq on the other hand— "Do you mean Zaqar?" he asked.

"If you mean one of Ryma's chosen thirteen, then yes. I lived with the devil himself for three years. And if it's an important gathering, he'll be there."

Darion leaned against the back of the couch. He had only met Zaqar on a few occasions. Ryma kept him outside city limits most of the time. His place was a remote land, full of gangs and savages, because his behavior could be swept under the rug. The older ruling families looked at him with a bit of disgust at the rumors of his experiments. Darion could only imagine what this girl had gone through.

"If you come, he would recognize you," Becca said. "You could ruin any chance of getting my sister."

A calmness fell over Grace as she turned to Becca. "Oh, I'm counting on him recognizing me the next time I see him. As I slowly take the last breath from his body and kill the son of a bitch, he'll know who I am." Her fists whitened by her side. "Don't worry about me, girlie. I know what I can do."

Darion stood and went by the fire. The warmth soothed the irritation growing within. "We can't even consider taking either of you, when we don't know how we'll get inside ourselves."

Flames popped, but no more ideas rushed forth. Getting inside Ryma's gathering would be almost as hard as getting out with her sister. "I'll think of something. Until then, Becca needs to start training. So we'll need some space. The sooner Becca begins, the stronger she will be at the gathering. Cramming years of training into days will be hard enough."

"Training?" Becca said, a hint of hesitation in her voice.

"Yes, training."

Grace stood, opening the door. "Well, have fun you two. Nothing like playing with demons—so I've heard."

Becca glowered in her direction. Good thing Becca wasn't a pyro, Darion thought, her temper was fiery enough. Maybe that was why he liked her.

Caleb squeezed her shoulder before leaving. "Good luck."

The fire grew slightly behind the grate. Darion calmed it down with a wave of his hand. Becca turned to face him. Her jaw tightened and her hands were clenched in front of her, as if she was readying herself for some kind of torture.

He couldn't help the smile that crept onto his face. "You ready?"

⌬⌬⌬

After a quick breakfast and change of clothes, Becca headed downstairs to meet Darion. She'd located some dark sweats and a long-sleeved shirt in a boys room, more comfortable than the dress, but a bit short on her.

She found Darion back in the front of the fire, a large book spread out on his lap.

"What is it?" she asked.

The old book had a leather cover worn with age and

lined with gold. "A grimoire. Thankfully, I found a copy in their library. Most families own one."

"A what?"

"A book of magic. A bible of sorts for black magic."

"Right, black magic. Of course."

"This explains a lot of the basics of magic. Where we get our power from, how to build basic pentagrams."

"Pentagrams—" Becca sounded idiotic, repeating everything he said. She was just struggling as magic was becoming her reality.

He set the book aside. "Do you remember at the market when you felt your magic?"

"I honestly thought I was going to die, not do magic." A cold realization poured over her. She was a magician. This monster lived inside of her, screaming to get out. Maybe it would have been better if she would have died back there. No, not with Elizabeth held by Jeremiah.

He brushed a hand through his hair. "Magic emerges gradually as a child ages. By five, most parents know if their child carries any magic. But it's uncontrollable. Wizards come into their full power by their teens. Some settle in nicely. Others lash out like you did. A power raw and uncontrolled. My coming of age was a bit of a nightmare." A briefed sadness touched his eyes.

Becca wanted to ask, but he continued on.

"There is much about magic we don't know. But most magicians focus on how to manipulate it, and how to get more.

"Figures," she mumbled.

He ignored her and added another piece of wood to the fire. He took off his long dark jacket and settled back down.

"Many magicians have an affinity for a certain type of magic. They go with the pentagram. Air, Fire, Water,

Earth, and Spirit." He flicked a hand and the fire soared, proving his point. "Not all are obvious. But my guess, after the display in the market, would be that yours is Spirit."

"Spirit?" Her jaw was slack. "What does that mean?"

"Your talents lean toward controlling the demons, Soultorns. The Soultorn in the market was extremely powerful. Only one with great power for Spirit work, could command that."

She turned her gaze to the fire. It was like being told that, not only were you inherently evil, but you have a power that called on the devils of hell themselves. It wasn't comforting.

"Demon work is extremely difficult and complex," he continued. "You have to gauge the power of the demon, the host, create the pentagram—"

"I'm not conjuring a demon." Fear coursed through her body, like ice water. The idea of calling and controlling a tool so evil was revolting.

"I'm not expecting you to conjure a greater demon. Even if you had the power, you aren't practiced enough. But if you want to stand a chance, you need—"

She stood up. "I. Am. Not. Conjuring. A. Demon."

"If you want to save your sister, you will." His brows were tight with frustration, though his words were soft.

There it was. If she wanted a chance at saving Elizabeth, she would have to dance with the devil. Despite her protests, they both knew she would do it.

He handed the book to Becca. "This is The Lesser Key of Solomon. Read it."

The book was heavy in her hand. "Solomon as in the Bible?"

"Known as one of the first magicians. He taught us much about magic, before the portal was even opened. Now that the portal's open, we have the power to fuel the magic."

"That must have been left out of my mother's Bible study." She sat down and opened the book. Diagrams and small text littered the page.

"I'm betting a lot of stuff was left out." He stood next to her. A smoky smell clung to his clothes.

"Is there anything about dreams in here?" Becca said, remembering last night's dream. It was so lifelike, it scared her.

"Some, why?"

"Lately, my dreams have been really intense. They're mostly about my sister, but they're just…different." She felt awkward talking about it. Of course she would dream of her sister. She had been on Becca's mind nonstop.

"There can be magic in dreams. Seers often use their dreams to interpret the future." He pointed to the book. "I don't know much about dreams or seers. They usually didn't train with other wizards. Check out the book and see what it says."

She nodded. Maybe it was all in her mind, reliving the nightmares in her past.

Darion didn't press her. "It'll explain a lot, and I can fill in the blanks."

She read the first line. "'The Book of Theurgia Goetia from Solomon the King. Translated into the English tongue by a dead hand.'" That's not creepy at all.

"I'm going to gather supplies and be back in a bit. Okay?"

"Yeah."

He left, the door clicking shut. The room felt unnaturally quiet, only the soft crackle of fire filled the air.

She continued on to chapter one. An index of known demons: King Bael, Duke Aguares, Prince Barbas, President Pruflas, Marquis/Count Amon…

The list went on, accompanied with pictures, descriptions, and their preferences in destruction. Reading through the names and imagining demons waiting to be called, she no longer desired a nap, or wished to close her eyes at all.

CHAPTER 28

Dry leaves crunched loudly with Elizabeth's every for step. Her heart pounded in her chest, loud enough the birds to hear. She hid behind a tree on Jeremiah's estate. Barreling through the forest like a pig wasn't going to help anyone. Blood trickled down her stockings. She must have cut her leg on the window sill. She glanced behind her, hoping there wasn't a trail.

Idiot. Might as well paint them a sign.

Sitting down, she used her long skirt to mop up the blood on her leg. She needed to calm down and think. She didn't know where she was, where she could go, or what to do. Every nerve was on end, pushing her forward, to run, to get free. But running into the wilderness, to get picked off by city urchins, wasn't going to help her.

She scanned the horizon for any sign of life. A neighbor maybe? There was nothing but hills and trees. Without food or water, she wasn't going to last long out there.

Her sister had always loved the woods, but Elizabeth hated fishing or hunting when her father took her.

There were a couple of cars in the garage. She had only driven her father's tractor twice, but she understood the concept. And while she didn't love the idea, it was the fastest way out of here.

She checked the back of the house, no sign of anyone. "You can do this," she whispered to herself. Then with a deep breath, she took off. Her hair whipped in the wind, as clouds rumbled overhead, threatening a storm.

She slipped inside the garage, panting slightly. Silence filled the dim room. It held two different vehicles: a dark sedan, and an older truck. The doors were locked.

Keys. I need keys.

She flipped on the overhead light. She was worried about it drawing attention, but she would have no chance finding the keys in the dark. She hurried to a nearby workbench and began searching. She dug through old tools. Grabbed a screwdriver thinking maybe it could break into the vehicle if needed. Her thoughts became more and more panicked.

Maybe she should have just run for the woods. It was cold, but the first freeze hadn't come yet. She could survive for some time. But not without water.

She tipped over an empty can, and nails rolled across the metal work bench. Above her head, hanging on a nail were two sets of keys. On tip toes, she grabbed the keys and rushed around the car to the driver side. The first key slid in effortlessly with a click.

"Leaving the party so soon?" It was one of the guards, the one with a tattoo on the back of his neck. He said something else, but it was too quiet for Elizabeth to hear.

The next moment her hands froze in place, along with all of her limbs. She tried to scream, but couldn't form the words.

Magic. What was her uncle doing with magical guards? Maybe that dream held more truth than she wanted to believe. Horror flooded her body as she struggled against the invisible restraints.

He strode over and plucked the keys out of her hands.

He leaned toward her, his breath hot on her throat. "You know little birds don't do well outside of their cages.

Especially one smelling so nice."

He traced a finger up the side of her throat.

She wanted to scream, to cry and rage against the invisible shackles this man had placed on her. Instead, she was silenced, a prisoner in a body that she no longer controlled.

℧℧℧

The next morning, Becca struggled to get out of bed. She'd slept fitfully with dreams of being chased. It took a couple minutes to shake off the fear, but she was determined to work.

Yesterday hadn't been much better. The day had gone by in a blur of reading about demons, spells, Greek and Latin. Demon names swirled around her head. She only remembered Solomon who was a dirt-bag with too many wives. There were ceremonies, spells, commands, seals, but she never would be able to keep them all straight. Darion had talked through her questions and issues. But they put off actually using magic, until today.

She took a long shower, trying to prolong the inevitable. She tied her wet hair up in a bun and wore a robe while scrounging through the closets for some clothes.

Grace appeared in a doorway. "I'd try the room next to the bathroom. She has a lot of clothes, but they may be a bit tight on you," she said, looking her up and down. Then with her full lips painted bright pink, she flashed a sly smile and disappeared.

"Thanks." Becca should have looked harder yesterday for the girl's room. She might have a chance of something fitting her, despite what Grace said.

In the next room, she did find a pair of jeans that sort

of fit and gray shirt. It the back of the closet was a worn jean jacket. The shoes were too big, but with a couple pairs of socks, they worked. Dressed, she headed downstairs, the smell of coffee calling out to her.

"Hey, stranger." Caleb sat at the kitchen table with a mug and tin can of peaches. He wore khaki pants and a dark blue shirt that clung to his chest. He even had hiking boots and a knife strapped to his side.

"Hey," she mumbled and reached for a mug. "Going somewhere?"

"Just heading outside for a bit of hunting."

"Going stir crazy already?" She smiled, remembering Caleb as a boy, who often fell asleep outside during the summer and would drive his parents crazy looking for him. His hair still had that same wave to it around his ears.

"A bit." He took a drink. "Just want to stretch my legs and maybe find something fresh to eat."

She stirred in some sugar. "I'm a bit jealous."

"Want to skip school for a bit and go outside?" His wide grin reminded her of when they were teens and skipping chores. He winked. "We haven't gone hunting together for a long time."

She couldn't help the smile growing on her face. Last time he tried to teach her the bow, she almost killed their family pig. She preferred a rifle. Either way she always enjoyed her time with Caleb. They could be silent for hours at a time out in the woods, a comfortable silence she'd never found with anyone else. "I miss those days, without the city or magicians."

"Maybe we can get them back one day."

"Maybe. But today I need to work inside." They only had three days left, and she had a lot to learn.

"I get it."

He put his dishes in the sink and then brushed past

her on the way out. His tender touch made her miss him already, as he headed out back without another look.

"Be safe," she said to the quiet kitchen as he headed across the backyard. How many times had she watched him walk home? Or out into the woods? She'd always taken it for granted that he would come back.

Becca swallowed some canned pears for breakfast, grabbed some coffee, and then searched for Darion.

With his hair still damp, he sat in front of the fire. He wore a tight black shirt and his same tan slacks. His back was to her as his hand reached out the fire. With a flick of his hand, the flames danced around, as if to invisible music. It was mesmerizing and artistic almost. Then in a second, they were gone.

"Ready?" he said, without turning his head.

"Can magicians see out of the back of their heads? Am I missing out on that trick?"

"No. But since you unleashed your power, you're easier to sense. Or maybe it's how you slurp your coffee."

"I don't slurp," she said indignantly.

"Whatever you say." He raised a hand in defeat. "Let's get to work."

She noticed an array of salts, potions, and small bowls that looked like something out of an alchemy shop.

He motioned for her to take a seat across from him and offered his hands, palms open. "Take my hands."

Becca perched on the edge of the seat, her pulse picking up. "What will happen?"

"Really? You don't trust me already?" He grinned. "Just take my hands. I'm going to gather my power, and if we're connected, you can feel it."

"Connected?"

"There are many ways to connect to another magician or demon. Blood, intimacy, a piece of another person."

He must have seen the disgust on Becca's face because he quickly clarified.

"A piece of hair or nail. They all form a connection if the spell is done right."

"We have touched before." They had done more than touching. The memories brought a warmth to her face.

"This will be different. Your magic is awake, and I'll use a spell to connect us as long as we are touching. There are limits and benefits to every type of combining. This will help you learn to sense magic and focus it."

She set down her coffee and leaned forward, carefully placing her hands in his. He gripped them and then said the spell. Only a few words, but the effect was immediate. A hot current pushed through her arms. Reflexively, she tried to let go.

He clasped her hands tight. "It won't hurt." He scrutinized her, as if reading something that wasn't there.

She closed her eyes and remembered to breathe. It was less intense than staring at him. Slowly, the current lessened. She didn't think it changed, but her body grew accustomed to it.

This was Darion's magic, warm and electric. Like a live wire, it trailed down her spine and to her toes, as if searching, exploring. It curled in her stomach, and she felt herself flush.

Another deep breath. A hum originated from deep within vibrating softly at first. It traveled down her fingertips then down her back, as if matching the current. Soft at first, it grew, strumming loudly.

Her eyes snapped open. It was magic. Her magic.

"You feel it?" Darion asked. His face was ablaze, full of excitement.

She nodded, unable to put into words what she felt. His magic was a part of her, consuming her. If felt intimate, more so than any of the kisses they shared before.

Her pulse pounded, matching the beating of his heart. She could feel his heart, almost picture it thumping. Her magic poured into him, flowing into to every corner and nook, relishing his warmth and power.

"Exhilarating, isn't it?" he asked.

She nodded. It was like nothing she had ever experienced, like running the fastest mile, and knowing she had the strength to do it again.

"Our power is combined. We're stronger together."

"Is it like this with every magician?"

"I'm not sure. I've only been connected to a few people. And every person is different, their magic feels different. Most protect themselves while connected, create walls and barriers. Not many magicians trust each other to share everything and be so vulnerable. "

"So, I'm doing it wrong." Panic fluttered in her chest.

"Not at all. You're just very open right now. I'm leaving myself open as well. I can feel...everything." He took a jagged breath. "I'll teach you barriers later. First, I need to teach you how to gather your magic. Pay attention."

He focused on his hands. Then his warmth, his magic, withdrew from her, stripping its heat like pulling off a warm blanket. Her body protested. She scooted closer, trying to follow it.

"Use your magic," he prompted.

She closed her eyes, trying to push herself toward him.

"Not with your body, use your magic."

She realized their knees were touching. Embarrassed she scooted back and tried again. Her fingertips sizzled, his magic nipping at them.

She focused on the sensation. Then as it traveled into

him, she followed. In the core of his being, she found his magic. Intense waves of heat and pressure, building, the power overwhelming.

"Yes," Darion murmured. "Gather your energy. Imagine winding up to throw a ball. Put all your energy toward the target."

Darion spoke in a foreign language. A rush of power and energy raced out of her. The power touched every part of her body, every nerve ending coming alive with potential. In an instance, the fire roared to life, the heat almost burning her. She turned to find a dragon shaped emerging from the flames.

Darion gripped her hands. The small dragon flew around the room, swerving between lamp posts and couches. She ducked to avoid the fiery tail. Sparks jumped off the dragon but vanished before hitting the ground. The dragon's roar echoed off the walls while fire shot from its mouth. Becca wavered between peeing her pants and amazement. The dragon dove back into the brick fireplace.

Sweat dripped down the side of Darion's face as the fire return to normal. "It's been awhile since I pulled that out of the fire."

"Can I let go?" Becca asked, her heart hammering in her chest.

"I guess." He pulled back. "Are you okay?"

"Yeah." Her hands shook as she wrapped them around herself. She struggled to find her magic. After several quiet moments, she could feel the quiet humming.

It was still there, her magic resonating deep within. She stood, avoiding his gaze. "I need a drink. It's hot in here."

"Okay. Let's take a break," he said, standing up as she hurried out the door.

The rush of power was thrilling to Becca, intoxicating

even. Her limbs tingled with each step. Fear coursed through her body—not at the show of their magic, but because she liked it.

CHAPTER 29

"You can do this," Becca told herself in the bathroom mirror. She had hidden in the bathroom for long enough. As her father had often told her, "Time to pull up the bootstraps, princess."

She pulled her hair back into a tight ponytail and headed back to practice.

Darion kept his distance and carried himself with an unfamiliar formality. They didn't physically connect magic again. Instead, they focused on elemental magic.

"There are five elements essential in completing a pentagram: Fire, Water, Earth, Wind, and Spirit," he explained as he laid out small silver bowls of water, dirt, and sticks on the coffee table. "I'm pretty sure, your affinity is to spirit, but we need to know if it entails other elements."

Becca hesitantly picked up the bowl, not sure why she was nervous.

"I want you to hold the water and repeat the word, pello," he said. "The word is Latin for to move or drive forward. But the word isn't always as important as the meaning and focus behind it. The words, often varying, help hold one's attention and focus your energy."

"So I could use any word for a spell?" *Why can't magicians simplify things?*

"In theory, yes. But common words don't hold the

emphasis for us. We need something, outside our normal vernacular to help focus the magic."

Latin it was then. Becca held the bowl, focused her power, and repeated the word. She didn't have the same rush or explosion of power as before. There was a slight ripple in the water, but it could have been her shaking hands.

"Nope." He replaced the bowl in her hands with a small one of dirt.

She tried again, repeating the same spell. Nothing. She couldn't even get the small pile of sticks to smoke. They opened a window and tried for a breeze but the air seemed to stop in its place. A small part of her was disappointed. If she was going to have magic, she would rather have something practical.

"Spirit," Darion said, scooting the bowls to the side. "I figured as much. It's just a bit more difficult to train for."

"How's that?" Becca couldn't imagine how she would train at all.

"There are several different types of magicians that specialize in spirit magic. It's more complex and difficult to determine." He shifted from foot to foot. "There are those that excel in calling the dead, in controlling demons, or control the living, an enchantress."

"Enchantress?" It sounded like some kind of prostitute.

"Yeah." He nodded. "Makes sense. It's your uncle's specialty. Granted he is gifted in several areas."

"That man is a curse, nothing more." She bit back her fury. Darion wasn't to blame for her family tree. And neither was she, she reminded herself.

"I agree." Darion's studied her closely, as if looking beyond her words. "But we need to see what you can do."

She took a deep breath. "Okay."

He closed the gap between them. "Grab my hand."

"Is this like before?" She remembered the rush of power and sizzle of magic between them.

"No. I'm won't use a spell, and my barriers are tight. I want to see if you can affect my spirit or consciousness." He held out his hand.

She grabbed it lightly. Something so simple, felt like so much more. His touch grounded her. She could feel the warmth in her face. "What's next?"

"Gather your magic, like we practiced before. Then speak the word Impero. Focus your energy on making me move or do something against my will."

"Can I do that?" As interesting the power might be, it unsettled her to control others like her uncle could. She wanted to be nothing like that man.

"I'm not sure." He stood close. His damp hair brushed back out of his face. "But we should find out."

She closed her eyes, steadied her breath, and searched for the humming deep within. She focused on the soft noise until it grew into a constant buzzing. She then opened her eyes. "Impero."

Something passed between them and Darion's eyes glossed over briefly. Confusion crossed his face as he stared at his shoe. "Why did I want my shoe?"

Becca couldn't help the smile that crept onto her face. "Because I wanted you to eat it."

He guffawed. "Eat it? Come on, Becca. I'm not going to subject myself if you're that cruel."

"I would have stopped you."

"If you could have. Changing courses can be tricky. But the fact you forced a thought into my head is impressive."

"So what does this mean?" Her smile fled. What did this make her?

His edges of his mouth turned up. "It means you won't have to ever ask twice for a date."

"Seriously."

"You have an affinity to Spirits. If developed enough, you could become an enchantress. We haven't seen your ability with the dead or a demon, but the possibilities are there."

"Possibilities…" She didn't want to control demons, but better to control than to be controlled by one. Then she thought of talking to her parents one more time. "What about the dead?"

"Calling the dead is hard, but it can be done. You need a part of the person. And the longer they're dead, the more magic is needed. You would need the strength of a demon."

She wondered about her parents. Could they tell her what happened? What she should do now? Their bodies were far away. And part of her was scared to show them who she had become.

"Raising the dead isn't a skill that will help us save your sister, so I'm not going to focus on it."

Becca nodded, pushing out the idea of her parents. Let them rest in peace. "Okay. So what's next? You eat my shoe?"

"How about some defense?"

"Sounds good."

Unfortunately, nothing was ever as it sounded.

⁂

Two hours later, Becca decided defense wasn't her forte. She couldn't gather her magic enough to block a weak spell or even freeze a fly.

It had been a long day of failures, weak attempts, and

pathetic consolation.

She leaned over panting, sweat dripping down her face, as she attempted to shield herself from Darion. "Contego," she said firmly, with a confidence she didn't possess.

Some magicians didn't need to speak the word, but that was few and far between Darion had told her. She obviously needed to scream the word for it to work.

From a few feet away, Darion threw a piece of plastic fruit at her. It hit her arm. She sank into the couch and kicked it back to him.

"I don't have anything left." She wiped sweat off her forehead. Her gray shirt was damp with sweat. "I don't feel any magic at all."

"That's when you have to push past yourself," Darion explained. "Gather the potentia around us."

"Potentia?" She was tired of this new language. "Why can't you people speak English?

"Latin for power. Imagine a fog or vapor settled all around us from the other dimension. If you can harness that power, it's yours for the taking."

"If only it was that easy."

"It's not easy. Most wizards went to school for years to master it."

"And I only have two more days."

He smirked. "You're a fast learner."

She threw a pillow. He stopped it a foot in front of his face then plucked it out of the air. "Really? You can do better than pillows."

Grace peeked her head in. "Working hard, huh?"

Becca dropped the pillow, and guilt settled in. The task ahead of her was impossible. Even if she had months to prepare, she would never be ready.

"We're trying to," Darion answered. "But Becca isn't

the easiest student." He lifted one of the pillows in jest.

"Why doesn't that surprise me?" Grace set a couple forks and jars of beets on the table. "Something to it eat?"

"Beets? Good thing my taste buds ran away years ago." Becca grabbed a fork, hoping food would ease the headache drumming in the back of her head.

"Thanks for the food," Darion replied.

Grace shrugged. "I figure it's fair for room and board."

"And all the clothes you've raided?" Darion asked, but as he dug into the food, he didn't appear bothered.

"I need them more than she does."

Becca rolled her eyes. She tried to not think the about the girl or Darion's past. This magical Darion, one with a past she'd never heard about, was like a closed box she wasn't sure she wanted to open.

Grace turned to Darion. "Caleb wanted to know if you wanted to bring the catch in before or after dinner."

"Probably after dinner," he replied.

Becca cocked an eyebrow. "Bring what in?"

His eyes drifted to the floor. "Our next lesson."

"What is it?"

He avoided Becca's eyes and turned back to Grace. "Go ahead, and tell him to bring it now."

After she left the room, Becca asked again. "What is it?"

"It's hard to explain how to contain a person or animal in a pentagram. We needed—"

"I'm not calling a demon to play with." Fear ate at her reserve. The idea of calling a demon, of pulling its power inside of her, made her insides cold.

"This isn't a game." His voice grew quiet, his eyes darkening. "I don't sit around playing with living things for the fun of it. You learn to survive."

Caleb knocked on the door and then walked in with a cage in one hand, a small red fox inside. The animal hissed at them as it was placed on the table.

She couldn't blame the fox. She couldn't count how many times she felt trapped in this crazy world, fighting to survive.

"He broke his foot on someone's trap," Caleb told her.

Becca stood up. "I'm not putting a devil in that thing." It wasn't the killing that bothered her. She'd hunted before. But how could she call on devils without some part of that darkness tainting her.

"Why not?" Darion stood, color flooding his face. "Because it's not some two-bit job Nikko is offering you? Nikko gives people drugs or supplies their dark magic."

"It's different," she said between clenched teeth. She did what she had to. She never forced anyone to take drugs. And she was pretty sure that this animal didn't want this.

Darion slammed his hand against the cage and the fox snarled. "This animal is going to die. So you can learn something that might save your sister. Or we can all die trying." He stormed out, slamming the door behind him.

"Take it out," Becca told Caleb.

"As much as it kills me to say it, he's right," he said, picking up the cage. "I was hoping to get a decent pelt off of it actually." He started out but turned at the door. "You won't become your uncle."

"I know." She touched her neck, the wound slowly healing. "But my mother gave my tattoo to me for a reason. Maybe she knew what I was going to become and wanted to save me from it, to save me from whatever twisted witch I could become."

"I don't think she wanted you to be a drug runner

either, though. And who's to say what you're going to become. Only you can decide." He paused, waiting until she looked at him. "Don't worry. I'll be around to kick your butt, if needed." He walked out the door.

They were right, both of them. But there was fear in the pit of her stomach that didn't want to do it. She remembered what Darion said back at the market about transferring a demon out of the host. Maybe she could do that and save the fox. But it wasn't the fox that scared her. It was the idea of drawing power from the depths of hell, touching it, and still remaining true to herself.

༄ঙ༄

Darion stood on the porch, watching the forest that surrounded him. Night had fallen dark and thick amongst the trees. Only a few bright stars peeked through the canopy of leaves.

He'd never felt so helpless being one of the magically strongest people in the house. And maybe that was why. He was responsible for these people, some practically strangers, and, more than likely, they would all end up dead or imprisoned by the end of the week.

And Becca!

He paced, wishing he could shake some sense into her. He would do anything for that girl, but watching her die at the hands of Jeremiah was not one of them.

Caleb came out the front door. "You want to be alone out here?"

Darion stopped pacing and held tight to the wood railing, staring out into the surrounding forest. "I'm okay."

"She really knows how to get to you, huh?"

Darion didn't answer. Becca was infuriating at every level. Her stubbornness was going to get them all killed.

How could he teach her with years of ignorance to overcome?

The heaviness of night settled around them. Darion reminded himself to breathe. Maybe this country boy had it right. Darion didn't think he'd miss the madness of the city.

Caleb relaxed on a nearby porch chair, tilting it back against the house. He was the quiet type which Darion respected, but part of him wanted to pry into Caleb's mind to see what he could find out about Becca. Maybe he didn't want to know.

"Was Becca always this infuriating?" Darion finally asked, his face turned out to the night.

"Yes, and no." Caleb chuckled. "I haven't seen her for years. When I knew her, she was impulsive and stubborn, but not so afraid or angry."

Darion would have loved to seen that Becca, but then she wouldn't be *his* Becca. The one who would infuriate him one minute then excite and challenge him the next. He admired the brave and determined Becca who would only lower her guard when they were alone. He missed his Becca, the one who trusted him without a second look. He might never get that chance back again.

He turned to face Caleb, resting on the railing. "What about her uncle? Wasn't he around?"

"No." Caleb shook his head. "He would come to visit rarely. And if so, I was always shown the door. But, man, she loved the wild. She had the sense of being a lady drilled into her along with her fear of magic. But her spirit was always free." He spoke with a longing in his voice that set

Darion's nerves on edge. "Now, she's different."

"This world has a tendency to break all of us a bit," Darion said. He couldn't ever remember a time when he thought the game of life was played by fair rules. His life was planned for him since birth, and nothing had turned out the way it should have, starting out with his parents' death. All because of their faithful service to the coven.

A dim porch light shone behind Caleb, casting shadows on his sober features. "True, but you never saw her whole."

Turning back to face the dark night, Darion struggled to find a solution that left everyone unharmed. "I can't see an answer. There's not a way inside Ryma's estate that doesn't end with us being captured." He ran a hand through his hair. "I'm going over and over the possibilities, and I don't find anything."

Caleb tipped the chair back down on all fours. A night owl sounded in the distance, accompanying the other insects' song. "I don't think any of this are under the assumption that we're getting out of this unscathed."

"You're okay with Becca getting hurt?"

Caleb flinched. "Of course not. But if you think she'll stay on the sidelines while her sister's life is at stake, you don't know her very well."

"I know her. That's the problem." Darion pulled out his lighter and flicked it on. Frustration built inside. He was ready to start this whole forest on fire. But that wouldn't help. He'd tried it before.

"We don't expect you to save us," Caleb said. "Just fight with us."

You can't fight this, Darion wanted to tell him. The coven was stronger than all of them. Thirteen of the most powerful magicians in the state compared to one pyro, one untrained enchantress, and two Mundanes. Those weren't odds, but casket options. He'd already told them several times. Maybe they didn't understand, or maybe Caleb understood and it didn't matter.

Darion closed his lighter with a click and turned to Caleb. "You know, sometimes you're hard to hate."

"I know how you feel. Then I watch you with Becca, and you make it easy."

Becca. It all came back to Becca. Darion loved her. He had to admit that to himself. Damned as he might be, he loved her. Even if he'd didn't have her.

"Caleb, if anything happens to me, you have to grab Becca and run. Okay?" He couldn't bear the idea of putting everything on the line and still losing Becca.

Caleb straightened. "What do you mean? What are you planning?"

"Nothing yet." Darion shook his head slightly. Ideas raced through his mind. He loved this stubborn girl. Admitting that to himself helped him realize how far he was willing to go for her. "Just promise me you'll get her out, with or without her sister. Even if you have to duct tape her and throw her over your shoulder."

Caleb looked him straight in the eye. "I give you my word."

CHAPTER 30

After a restless night full of dreams of being chased, Becca staggered to the bathroom. *I shouldn't be so tired when I wake up.*

The grimoire held some information on dreams. Seers had the power to see glimpses of the past and future in dreams. Also, with magic, you could share or influence the dreams of others.

Becca doubted she was a seer. She didn't understand the spells needed, either. But these dreams weren't anything she'd ever experience before.

A nagging sensation continued as she drifted toward the smell of coffee. She found the others sitting around the kitchen discussing Ryma's estate.

"It's more protected than you can imagine," Darion explained "I can't step on the property line without it killing me. Not without my magic and a demon or two."

"Is there anything I can do?" Becca asked and all three faces turned toward her. Even with her reluctance the day before, she would do anything to save her sister. "I mean…with my magic. If I learn about demons and summoning, can we get through together?"

"You could study for years, and it wouldn't matter. Ryma is the strongest wizard on the east coast." Darion's eyes were rimmed with red, as if he hadn't slept well himself. "I need to reach out to my connections. If I can get my hands on an invitation, maybe do an illusion."

"We only have two days left. We don't have the money to get illusions for everyone." Becca reminded him. "If I have to get captured to get inside, I'll do it."

Darion flinched at her words.

"It's my sister," Becca answered. He had to know she'd do anything at this point.

He stared at her, not willing to reply.

"Becca gave me an idea. Maybe the answer isn't getting in undetected," Grace proposed as she took a seat at the kitchen table.

"We can't just ring the door bell," Caleb said.

Grace flashed a smile. "Why not?"

"I'm listening," Darion added.

"I have been to Ryma's, on Zaq's arm, of course. But if they're having a gathering, and a big one at that, then they'll have extra servants on hand. And not only servants, but…" She drew out her sentence looking cautiously at Becca.

"Whores, you mean. You want me to go as a prostitute?" Becca almost dropped her cup. This girl couldn't be serious, could she?

Caleb's slammed his mug on the table. "We can't take the chance you'll be safe. It's not worth it."

"It's not like that." Grace took a drink of her coffee. "Escorts are hired for important events. Also maids, companions."

"And don't forget disposable humans," Darion said with a sardonic edge. "It'll be dangerous. Getting you hired is one thing, but escaping once you're there is another."

"You'd be surprised what servants or slaves can get away with," Grace countered. "Like little mice scurrying around. They can chew through wall sometimes."

Becca hated to agree with Grace, but it just might

work.

They had all been thinking about how they would get in, and no one had a good idea. This might be a stupid idea, but at least it was an idea.

"Why can't we be indentured to you?" Grace suggested to Darion. "You're a wizard. We can be your servants to get inside."

Darion shook his head. "I'm just as wanted as you guys are. Jeremiah and Pove will have already appealed to Ryma. You'd be taken as retribution immediately." He trailed off, a distant look on his face.

"You can't seriously be considering this?" Caleb asked Darion.

"Maybe if I can track down Nevada again," he mumbled to himself.

Caleb turned to Becca. "Killing yourself won't help Elizabeth."

She stared him straight in the eye. "I have to do something."

"How about we kill him before he gets there?" Caleb mouth was set in a grim angry line. "Get me within fifty yards of that bastard, and I can shoot him down. There can't be that many ways into the place."

"He's guarded. And it won't be a clean shot," Darion countered.

"I could draw him out. He'd stop for me." Becca turned to Caleb. "It'll get you the shot. Maybe even distract him enough for his wards to be down.

Darion was sober, but contemplative. "Maybe. Let me try to call a couple of people I trust and see what I can learn.

A fight just outside Ryma's gate is going to be dangerous."

"Every option will be," Becca reminded him.

He nodded but remained silent. Did this mean Darion thought it could work? If he thought so, this might be their chance.

"We don't have much time, if we're to get there early to intercept Jeremiah." Darion got up from the table. "In the meantime, Becca needs to train."

He was right. The more she trained, the better chance she had of surviving, of them all surviving. That meant doing things she didn't want to think about.

"Can you grab the fox, Caleb?" she asked, heading for the door. She'd seen him caring for it out back before. "We're going to need it today."

ℓ∕⊃ℓ∕⊃

The pentagram was set. Becca dusted the chalk off her hands. In each tip, the elements sat in silver bowls. For wind, the window was open, welcoming in a cool breeze. And, in the spot reserved for spirit, Becca stood.

A small fox crouched in the middle circle of the pentagram. She imprisoned the fox inside the pentagram, which came easy, a little too easy for her taste. Darion appeared encouraged by it, though. Whatever his reservation was before in the kitchen, it was gone. Only the tired eyes remained.

"Remember one of the most important parts of the evocation is choosing the right demon," Darion said, a few feet beside her. "Magicians spend years studying demons, searching for new names, torturing other wizards and demons alike to find them."

She hid her speeding heart behind a sarcastic smile. "So my two days of preparation should work wonders?"

"Precisely." He nodded, no humor on his face. "You're calling a weaker demon. One that teenagers call to

242

booby trap their bedrooms. Nothing too complex."

"So then how can I make him obey?"

"That's where magic comes in. No negotiations. Just imprison him and link him to you with the spell."

"What's the point of this?" She wiped the sweat from the back of her neck. The fire was roaring in the room, keeping it warmer than necessary and setting her on edge. "It's not like this fox can take on Jeremiah."

"You need to practice controlling a demon, drawing power from it, and protecting yourself from one. Magicians can learn to store a demon and can siphon power from it where ever they go."

"If it's that simple, why don't magicians have a ton of these things all over. I didn't see any at Jeremiah's"

"They're hard to control, and names are hard to come by. But trust me, they were there." He wiped sweat from his forehead and the fire dimmed slightly. "Names stay with families and are extremely expensive."

"How did you get this one?"

"I have several names memorized. If you dismiss a demon and don't kill it, then they can be reused. This demon I called several times through school."

"Do you have a demon hidden somewhere?"

He paused for a moment, hesitating, as if the answer would offend her. "No, but I plan on doing it. I'll need to hide a stronger demon somewhere for strength later on. If I thought you could control a level-three demon, I'd have you do the same, but you're not ready. Demons have to be strong enough for the tie between a demon and magician to carry across great distances."

"Okay." She turned back to the pentagram, not sure if she wanted to be tied to a demon. She swallowed, a slight pain in her throat, reminding her of the last run-in she had with one.

She wiped her hands on her jeans. "Let's do this." *Before I lose my nerve.*

He nodded slightly, urging her on. "You know the words."

The Latin they had rehearsed poured from her lips. Slow and steady, she made sure she enunciated each syllable correctly. The words were an evocation for the lesser demon, Talpha. When she finished the incantation, nothing happened.

Before she could step back, Darion raised a hand. "Don't move."

Pinpricks ran up and down her arms, and the fire grew ever so slightly. The demon materialized above the space where the fox huddled on the ground.

It hissed at her, speaking a language she didn't understand. Its small dog-sized body housed an elongated jaw with oversized teeth. Its eyes were dark and shadowed by a heavy brow.

Her breath caught at the sight of it. She focused on the humming power deep within. Projecting her power, she silenced the demon. Its jaw opened in a silent howl. Then it repeatedly snipped at her, the snapping of teeth filling the room.

"Good," Darion said from the sidelines. "Now, do you feel its power? Follow the lines of the pentagrams to the source."

This was nothing like Darion's magic. As she drew closer to the demon, a dark cold substance hung in the air. She worried she would get lost in that darkness, that it would swallow her whole.

"Remember to draw it out. Focus on the edge of the circle. It will be attracted to you—despite itself. Your magic is warm and bright." His voice had an edge to it. Maybe he wasn't enjoying this either.

She nodded, not trusting her voice. Staring at the chalked line, she waited. After a few minutes, its magic flowed toward her. Its bitter edge was nothing she wanted to pull to her, but it had a strength she couldn't deny.

"Do you feel the power?"

"Yes." The word came out as a whisper.

"If you gather that power and focus it, you can use it like your own. You can drain the demon dry."

A repulsion rose in her stomach. She didn't want to take the demon's power inside of her. She wanted to kill it.

"Keep a hold on the power. You'll need it to place the demon in the fox."

She gathered the power and completed the spell. A rush of exhilaration and magic flowed through her body. The fox sprang to life, eyes flashing a pitch black, and a yowl erupted out of its throat. She quickly silenced the fox.

The control, the power, felt like a whole different world coursing through her body. The fox silently screeched and threw itself against the barrier to no avail. Becca took a shaky breath. She could feel Darion's heavy gaze and struggled to remember what came next.

She recalled the words to force a demon to obey. She closed her eyes, picturing the words in her head, but as soon as she said them, she knew she'd pronounced them wrong. The fox sprang forward. She raised an arm to protect herself. But with a demon infused inside, this fox was beyond ordinary. Its jaw, stretched wide, froze inches from her face.

Darion grabbed the fox and, with a simple spell, forced it back into the pentagram. Becca tried to slow her racing heart, a bit embarrassed at her failure. After it was securely placed back inside, Becca acknowledged the burning sensation on her arm. Long deep cuts welled up with dark blood.

"You okay?" he asked, handing her a small towel.

"Yeah. It's only a scratch."

He helped her sit up, his magic radiating around her. "I'm sorry."

"For what?" The words came out harsher than she intended. "It was my mistake."

Closing her eyes momentarily, She tried to pull herself together. She had fought lesser pet demons that were found in the slums. Frustration built at how remedial she was with her powers.

"It's okay." Darion placed a hand on her shoulder. His touch brought a warmth and comfort she missed. "I shouldn't have pushed you so soon."

She opened her eyes. It was one thing to take comfort from Darion, but another to let herself be babied when things needed to be done.

"No." She stood up. "I need to do it again. I was stupid. I messed up."

"You should take a break. Get that wound cleaned."

She held his gaze, not backing down. "It can wait."

"All right," he said. "Let's work on manipulating this beast."

Her stomach twisted with uneasiness, but this would be the least of her fears in the days to come.

❧❦❧

It had been a quiet couple of days for Caleb. He'd barely seen Becca, Grace was elusive, and he could only go as far as the property line would allow him. It wasn't fair to be annoyed with Becca, though. She needed to focus on her magic.

He tried not to compare her to how she used to be, how they used to be together. It had been too many years

246

for that. But it was hard, when he continually glimpsed a bit of the girl he fell in love with years ago—that girl he would go to the moon and back for. If only they could connect, start over, then maybe they could find each other again.

He finished resetting his last snare and picked up the dead rabbit. Rabbits were abundant, but any bigger game was kept out. It wasn't much, but better than nothing. Fresh rabbit actually sounded good. He hadn't had any since before the fire, which felt like forever ago.

His eyes burned, and his chest tightened every time he remembered his parents buried in the cold earth. He closed his eyes and reminded himself how he was going to make this all right. Get revenge on those who took their life so carelessly.

"I miss you guys," he whispered to his parents.

They may no longer be living, but he liked to imagine their spirits were in the woods, free and ever watching him. Waiting for him to start his usual conversations he had whenever he went hunting.

His mother always chided him that the chipmunks heard more about his day than she did. Maybe she could hear him now too. He paused at the edge of the tree line just for a moment.

Grace sat on the back patio smoking.

"You would have liked Grace," he told his mother. "She has a spirit to her. Just like you, except for the clothes, smoking, and occupational hazards."

He said goodbye and then headed toward the house. A cold breeze bit through his jacket as he eyed the sky for a sign of what was to come. The clouds were heavy but no sign of rain yet.

"What did you catch us there, muscles?" Grace said as he approached, taking on a horrible country accent.

He lifted the rabbit high.

"Yum—mmy," she announced with an oversized grin.

He took a seat next to her on the wooden bench. "How do you keep up your spirits?"

She finished her cigarette, rubbing it out on the side of the bench. "What?"

"You know. You're always smiling, joking, and carrying on, ignoring the possibility that we'll end up dead or worse by the end of the week."

She pulled out another homemade cigarette. "I'm alive, free, and rolling old pipe tobacco. What's not to be happy about?" She lit the smoke before continuing. "And then there's the next part. I get to kill my past owner, the devil itself, Jaqar. That would make any girl happy."

He had numerous questions he wanted to ask about her past and how she was going to manage to kill Jaqar.

But she beat him to it. "How about you? How come you haven't run for the woods yet? I can tell how much you love them."

His eyes drifted to the multicolored trees, and he couldn't help the longing he felt. "I'm needed here."

"A boy with no magic powers, sneaking into Ryma's estate. How do you think you're going to help?"

He didn't have an answer. As much as he'd thought about it, he wasn't sure. But he wasn't going to stay behind and do nothing.

"Take a good long look at that rabbit," Grace said, pulling her hair back. "You might be him in a couple of days."

He leaned back in the seat, looking at the woods. His death had crossed his mind more than once. And, for some reason, he wasn't afraid. His family was already there, why not him? He felt like he cheated death at least once. "What about you? How are you going to manage to kill off Jaq?"

"I play dirty." She exhaled a large cloud of smoke. "Don't worry, muscles. I have a few tricks up my sleeves."

He raised an eyebrow in question. She winked, but didn't explain further. She had survived this long, maybe she did have a few surprises left.

"Have you thought about after all this? What you want to do?" He wanted to see past the next few days. If he didn't die, was there a chance for a life in this chaotic world?

"Nah." She stared out into the wilderness, a softness falling onto her features. "I learned long ago, not to plan too far ahead. If there's no hope in tomorrow, there's no disappointment either."

"That's a depressing way of looking at things." He couldn't help the pity that crept into his voice. He wondered who this young woman could be in a different time and place.

She shrugged, and her lips curled up into a large smile. Her confident facade snapped back into place. "That's life, muscles."

CHAPTER 31

B ecca's body protested as she headed upstairs. She desperately needed a shower. Who knew magic could make her sweat? Magic had drained her energy in a way nothing else had.

Becca rubbed out her tired muscles under the hot shower, the long shallow cuts burning from the soap. She still had to be careful with the burn on her back as well.

After working with Darion all day, she still didn't feel confident with her magic, but she'd finally controlled the demon. It was something.

They planned on getting to Ryma's early. Maybe even intercept Jeremiah before he got through the door. Would it be enough? She ignored the sinking sensation in her stomach.

The water began to cool. She reluctantly stepped out of the shower and dried off. Her arm burned as she dried it, but at least it had stopped bleeding. With a towel wrapped around her, she dug through the bathroom cabinet in search of a first aid kit.

Someone knocked on the door. "Done yet in there, princess?"

Becca rolled her eyes at Grace's mocking tone. "One sec." There it was, in the back behind a variety of fragrant lotions. Becca grabbed the kit, and opened the door. "It's all yours," she said, squeezing through the door. She headed to her bedroom, and Grace followed leaving the door open behind her.

"Muscles wanted you to know it's dinner time. Guess he likes you well fed." Grace looked her up and down as if criticizing his decision.

"I'll be down in a minute." Becca opened the first aid kit on the bed. She reached for the antiseptic for the cuts. And then realizing the injury was on her right arm, her dominant hand, she switched hands.

"Demon claws can be nasty. Let me do that for you," Grace offered, stepping closer.

"I got it." Becca's wet hair fell into her face as she struggled to keep her towel up.

Grace grabbed the tube out of her hand. "I'm not nice very often, why don't you take me up on it while the mood strikes me?"

"Uh, okay." It seemed as if Becca didn't have a say in the matter.

Grace carefully dabbed the ointment over her cuts. Her touch was gentle, unlike anything else about Grace. She reached for the bandages—it would take a few. The shallow cuts ran long down her arm.

"So why the good mood? Figure out how to break into their liquor cabinet?" Becca tried to joke.

She had steered clear of Grace as much as she could while here. Grace only appeared when she wanted to make snarky comments about her, and Becca loved to return the favor.

Grace's focused on the wound, her face soft. "Guess I figure we're on the same team, maybe it's time we started acting like it."

She pressed the wound closed as she taped it down.

Becca winced. "One hell of a truce."

"I'm sorry," Grace said as she adjusted the bandage.

Then, catching Becca's gaze, added, "Not only for the bandage. I guess growing up in a magical household has given me a few reasons not to trust others."

"Don't apologize. I get it." Becca had her share of trust issues.

Grace finished taping down a white bandage. "Don't get the wrong idea. I will criticize your poor fashion sense at every turn, and I don't do braids."

Becca let a laugh escape. "My clothes aren't that bad."

"Really? There's a whole wardrobe in there and you pick the colors of a drab sky." Grace motioned to her dirty shirt on the floor. "I don't understand what these guys see in you."

Becca ignored last sarcastic comment. Grace loved to make her squirm for fun. What did the woman think? It was time for a fashion show?

Caleb's heavy steps sounded on the wood staircase. "Hey, ladies, this rabbit isn't going to eat itself."

"Just because you're all domestic, doesn't mean you can order us around," Grace hollered back.

He peeked into the bedroom. "What's going on?"

"Just finishing up." Becca tightened her towel. "Rabbit sounds great."

Caleb reached for her. "What happened to your arm?"

"Nothing really," Becca said.

She couldn't help but notice Grace, stepping back.

"It's just a scratch. Grace was helping me bandage it."

Caleb turned, not hiding the surprise on his face. "Really? Thanks."

"No problem. I'll go stir the soup." Grace headed out of the room.

Becca wondered, not for the first time, what Grace's relationship with Caleb was.

"It was the fox, wasn't it? I shouldn't have let you do

it." Caleb kept his hand on Becca's arm, focusing on the wound and ignoring the fact she wasn't dressed.

She didn't forget and used her other hand to make sure the towel stayed up. "It's just a scratch. I had more control by the end."

Becca was grateful for Darion's support. Caleb couldn't back down now because of a few scratches.

Without warning, Caleb pulled her into a warm embrace. "I don't know if I can lose you again. But I know I can't convince you to stay behind." He knew her better than that. Emotion tightened his voice, something she hadn't seen from him since they were rescued.

She relaxed into his arms and let herself feel the worry and grief that had been plaguing her for days. His shirt smelled of the forest, crisp wintergreen trees, fallen leaves, and that special something that reminded her of home, of the countless days running free with Caleb at her side. Everything she would never have again.

He kissed the top of her head as he held her close.

"Promise me you'll be safe. You have to survive this."

She rested her cheek against his chest, wishing she could promise that. What hurt her was asking her friends to come along. Was she willing to sacrifice her friends in order to save her sister? No. But she wouldn't leave her sister there, either. Words failed her as she couldn't think of anything reassuring to say.

He stepped back, but kept her in his arms and forced her gaze up, brushing back her wet hair. "I won't lose you Becca. Not again."

Such a simple action, that took this embrace to a different level. One she wasn't sure she was ready for. It was wonderful to have Caleb back. He was her best friend first.

Anything more, she wasn't sure about.

Pulling her close, he closed the gap between them. He leaned forward as if he was going to kiss her. Turning her head, she laid it on his chest—not ready to hurt Caleb or commit to something between them.

There, in the mirror, was Darion's reflection watching from out in the hall. His face held a pain that crushed Becca. She broke the embrace.

"What's wrong?" Caleb asked, his face fallen a bit.

By the time she turned again, Darion was gone. Dammit.

"Nothing. Just seeing things," Becca lied and continued, trying to be truthful. "Caleb, I'm not ready for this, for a relationship. Things have changed."

A cold bucket of ice water would not have been as effective. He dropped his arms and stepped back. "I understand. We better not keep that rabbit waiting." He quickly turned down the hall, but not before Becca glimpsed the pain of rejection on his face.

Guilt sank deep into her bones. How could she manage to not only put Caleb's life in danger, but make him feel like crap too? Lately, she felt like a disaster, hurting everyone nearby.

She headed down stairs. How could she explain to Darion what was between Caleb and her when she didn't know herself? They had grown up together for years. He was the closest thing she had to family right now. She couldn't push him away.

And why was she so worried about Darion? The obvious truth slapped her in the face. She cared for Darion. If she really wanted to be honest, she'd never stopped. She left because she didn't trust him. Two completely different things. And now she trusted him with the life of Caleb and her sister. Where did that leave her?

Forget it. She needed to focus on her magic, and

saving her sister. She'd worry about the rest in a couple days—*that is, if I'm still alive.*

She wore black jeans and a red shirt as she headed downstairs, just to show Grace she could. The smell of onions and cooked rabbit welcomed Becca to the kitchen. Her stomach growled with approval. "That smells amazing."

Caleb stood in front of the large gas stove, a tall pot in front of him, while Grace rolled a cigarette at the table. He grabbed a nearby bowl to fill, avoiding Becca's gaze. "Can't beat fresh."

"You're right." Awkwardness settled among them. She needed to clear the air between them tonight, before they left. Even if she wasn't sure how to do that.

Grace lifted her head, watching them back and forth as if deciphering what she missed. "What happened?" she asked. She was never one to beat around the bush.

"Nothing," Becca snapped. She headed over to grab spoons and bowls.

"How boring," Grace said, the unlit cigarette resting in her lips.

Becca glowered at Grace and wished she could use her magic to shut Grace up. Instead, she set out dishes for dinner.

"Hey, guys." Darion stood at the doorway to the kitchen, no trace of what he saw upstairs bothering him. "I just got off the phone. We'll need to head out of here by noon tomorrow. I talked to some people. I'll be allowed at the gathering and can bring you three as my indentured servants."

Grace slapped the table. "That's great. I knew you could maneuver something."

"Sounds better than offering up Becca on the side of the road to Jeremiah," Caleb said.

Darion forced a smile, but his eyes hid an uneasiness only Becca would recognize. The other two didn't know him. This wasn't as good of a thing as he was trying to sell.

"How?" she asked.

"What does it matter?" Grace asked. "He figured it out. Be thankful."

"I just wanted to give you a heads up. I'm going to grab a shower before dinner." He hurried upstairs.

Becca started after him. The uneasiness in her stomach would not settle down.

"Becca, what is it?" Caleb stopped her.

She paused at the door. "Something isn't right. There's something he isn't telling us."

"He'd tell us if we needed to know," Grace said.

"Maybe..."

Caleb grabbed a nearby bowl. "Grab a bite first. He'll be back down soon."

She was too restless for dinner. "Save me some. I'll be back."

Heading upstairs, she wondered how and why Ryma would now let Darion into the meeting. She knocked on his door. There wasn't an answer. It turned with a click, and she barged in.

"Hey," Darion shouted his shirt in his hands. "I didn't say you could come in."

She closed the door behind her. His room was spotless, even his bed was made. She'd forgotten how meticulous he always was. She sat on the bed. "We need to talk."

He put his shirt back on and leaned on the desk across the room. "Come on in. Make yourself comfortable, why don't you? I shouldn't have to remind you what a double standard this is."

She knew Darion well enough to know something

didn't add up. "What's going on?"

"Ha. What isn't going on? Jeremiah is after us, you're a magician, barely trained, and we're going to visit Ryma and Jeremiah tomorrow." He ran a hand through his hair, pulling on it. "Is that not enough for you? Want more drama? Maybe you could be carrying Caleb's child too."

"What are you talking about?" His dark humor had a biting edge that Becca had rarely seen. "I haven't even kissed Caleb."

Relief briefly crossed his face and then he resumed pacing. She'd never seen him like this, except for when he first found her at Jeremiah's.

She approached him and grabbed his hand, forcing him to look her in the eyes. "How did you get us into the coven meeting?"

"I pulled in some favors, and got an invite." He raised a cocky brow. "I know some people who know some people."

She searched that false bravado for something more. "You told us you're just as wanted as we are. That there's no way you could get in."

He pulled back, shaking off her hold, and went to the window, staring out into the graying night.

"Just tell me." Her voice rose, tearing a bit. Silence filled the room. Why wouldn't he just say it? Was it that bad? "Do you want to know why we really broke up? It's because you wouldn't talk to me."

A warm wave of magic rippled through the room. He turned, all pretense gone. His eyes held an angry spark to them. "We broke up because you couldn't stand to date a magician." A sarcastic smile lit his face.

"Maybe. Or maybe you could have trusted me enough, to tell me the truth."

"Yeah. You can barely trust your own magic. You're

going to trust mine?"

He might have a point. She thought back to the training, when she felt his magic. It was warm and strong. Nothing like the demons. "I'm sorry about how I acted. I trust you, magic or not. How did you get us in?"

He closed the gap between them. Inches from each other, he stared fixedly at her. The electricity, which Becca knew was magic, grew heavy between them.

"I gave them what they wanted," he said.

It took a moment to catch up, and she prayed she was wrong. Her words crawled out as whisper. "You gave them you?"

"Bingo." He turned away, grabbing a nearby towel, and attempted to walk around her to the door. "Now if you'll excuse me."

She grasped his hand, not ready to let this go. "You're not leaving until you tell me what that means."

His mouth drew down in a scowl. "I don't have time for—"

"Please," she pleaded. She wasn't great at begging, but she'd do it if she had to.

He threw his towel on the floor. "I'll pledge my loyalty to Ryma. That way we'll have his protection against Jeremiah."

"Okay. So we'll pretend to be on his side, then grab Elizabeth and take off. What's the problem?" She didn't understand.

"There is no leaving for me, Becca. Ryma has wanted a willing blood pledge from me for years. I'm the best pyro this side of the country. My parents' allies are the only reason it hasn't happened sooner. Why do you think I met you at a Mundane bar?"

When they had broken up, she'd figured he was some sick magician who preyed on weaker Mundanes. But now, holding onto his hand, she knew that wasn't true.

"I'd been hiding out as much as I could, avoiding the coven's attention for the past few years."

What did she do? In an effort to save her sister, she'd just put Darion up on a platter for Ryma. She squeezed his hand. "Don't do it. You don't have to go. I don't want—"

A warm current of electricity passed through their hands. "It would have happened eventually. Don't worry about it. We'll get your sister and get you a car out of the city. I'll feel better knowing you're out of their grasp."

A hallow coldness settled in her stomach. He couldn't. Her mouth opened but the words didn't come. What could she say? Not goodbye. She wasn't ready for that. And thank you was far from adequate. She couldn't let him do this.

Before he could say anything else, she pulled him close and kissed him. It wasn't because he was sacrificing himself, because he had helped her save Caleb, or because he saved her from Jeremiah. She hadn't stopped thinking about those lips since she'd kissed them last. And she would hate herself if she didn't.

His body froze at first, his mouth non-responsive. She leaned in closer, a pleasant warmth coursing through her body. Then in a rush of hot magic, he wrapped an arm around her waist and kissed her back with an impatient hunger.

She wasn't ready to let him go. Ever. As if sensing her thoughts, he pulled her tight against him. His body was so close that it set her skin ablaze with insatiable hunger. He traced her body, down her back, then grasped her waist, leaving a trail of heat.

She had missed Darion, longer than she'd admitted. Every touch, every kiss, made her realize how she couldn't live without him. He began kissing down her neck, and all conscious thought fled for a moment. She held him tighter, knowing it would never be tight enough.

"Don't go," she begged. "We'll figure something out." She couldn't leave him with Ryma. She couldn't imagine leaving him period.

He paused and leaned back slightly, the familiar distance seeping into their embrace. "How come I feel you want me the most when you can't have me?"

"That's not it," she protested. It had taken her time to trust him again, to realize why he lied in the first place. But she wanted him, today and forever. "Can't you see how I feel?"

He silenced her word with a gentle kiss. It held a distant goodbye that broke her heart. She'd had a glimpse of being back with him, only to have it ripped away.

"Don't worry, Becca, I don't take it personally." He picked up his towel and left the bedroom.

She sank onto the bed, a cold loneliness enveloping her. Her heart shattered into a million pieces. When she first left Darion, she promised herself she'd never get back together with him. Leaving him hurt too much. So much for empty promises.

She struggled to imagine leaving the city, moving on without him. She had taken it for granted that he'd always be there. His warm strength had carried her more than she realized.

He might think he was going to be this sacrificing hero, but she wouldn't let that happen. She couldn't. Ryma couldn't have him without a fight. Too bad she didn't have an idea of how to stop him.

౿ఎ౿ఎ

After a quiet meal, Becca headed to bed early. She was

asleep as soon as her head hit the pillow, too exhausted to process all that had happened throughout the day. Unfortunately, her dreams provided her no respite either.

She wandered around, lost and confused, in a dense fog. Cries for help pierced the air. Elizabeth's voice. Becca searched and searched, panic overcoming her senses, but her sister was nowhere to be found.

"Elizabeth!" she screamed until her voice went hoarse.

The cries grew to shrieks of pain. Becca ran until her legs collapsed, and she sank on the misty floor, crying and screaming for it to stop. Where was her sister?

Becca bolted up in bed. Sweat plastered her shirt to her skin, and a scream stuck in her throat. "Just a dream," she told herself.

She needed to talk to Darion. Despite the lack of magic, what if somehow she was connected to Elizabeth? She needed to make sure. Or she would be leaving to find Elizabeth tonight.

When she closed her eyes again, the cries echoed in her mind. She jumped out of bed and went to Darion's room. She stopped, hand poised to knock.

How could she bother him again? There last conversation flooded her thoughts. He was giving everything as it is.

She'd read the book. There was no way the dreams could be connected. Becca didn't even have magic until recently. She dropped her hand. She had more to worry about than some bad dreams.

Since she wasn't going back to sleep soon, she figured she'd grab a bite to eat and work over the plan for tomorrow. Maybe there were some leftovers in the fridge.

Dim lights led the way down the staircase. Her bare feet slapped the frigid wood floor. The first floor was completely dark. Becca felt along the walls for a light.

"Where are those damn lights?" she muttered, following the wall around to the kitchen. Finally, she found the switch and flipped it on. She blinked several times, adjusting to the light.

A man with long hair sat at the island. He held a type of thick gun in his hand. A short dark man, actually a Soultorn, stood behind him.

She blinked again, wondering if this was still a dream.

The guy took a swig from his flask. "So glad you could make it down on your own. It saves me the trouble."

Her heart raced with panic. Everyone else was asleep. How did they find them?

The Soultorn winked. This wasn't a social call.

She turned to run, her mouth open to scream, but nothing came out.

CHAPTER 32

D arion's head pounded as he struggled to wake up. He briefly opened his eyes then snapped them shut. Panic struck him to the bone. He wasn't at the cabin.

That meant someone with enough strength broke into the cabin and grabbed him without even waking him. Darion couldn't believe he could be so stupid. The call with Ryma and fight with Becca threw him for a loop. After not sleeping for several nights, he passed out last night without setting sufficient wards. He didn't think he needed them.

Before he opened his eyes, he pushed out with his magic. There was one other magician in the room. The wards were some of the strongest he'd ever encountered. He knew where he was. Darion wasn't leaving soon.

"Are you finally awake?" a deep voice spoke from across the room.

No point in feigning sleep anymore. Darion sat up on a couch. A tall wizard Darion didn't recognize stood on the other side of the room.

"I'll let Ryma know you're awake," the wizard said before leaving.

A small ripple of magic flowed from the door, after he shut it. There was no getting out, especially if he was already at Ryma's estate.

Becca. The idea of her in the hands of other magicians

sent his pulse racing. He had to find a way out. Darion rose on wobbly legs. He needed to get his blood moving.

The room was a den of sorts, or small library. Books lined one wall, while large maps hung on the other. Pins marked the locations of major covens. And it looked like the Western War still raged on across the ocean.

A massive desk filled up one corner. But it was sealed tight, containing its secrets inside. How did he get to Ryma's? And why? Darion was planning on coming willingly tomorrow.

There was no time to find out. He had to get the others. If Ryma broke the truce they agreed on, all bets could be off.

Darion attempted to gather his magic, to push out at the wards around him, but his power was as slow to wake as the rest of his body. Closing his eyes, he searched for any other weakened exit in the room. He felt several exits, complicated with layers of magic. Not easily downed without help.

Forget undoing wards, he'd burn down the door. He always had enough magic for a spark or two.

He reached out around him, pulling in whatever potentia he could find. The door began to warm, and a wisp of smoke escaped. This was harder than it should be. He was only creating a sauna to roast himself in.

The door opened without warning.

Ryma looked the same as Darion remembered from the last time he saw him, at his parent's funeral. He wasn't tall, but the power that leaked from him gave off the feel of a giant. He had a heavy brow and protruding jaw but his shaved head, with a thick scar traveling down the side of it, stole most of the attention from his face.

Darion heard he displayed it as a reminder he was not easily killed. Supposedly his brother, who was now dead, gave it to him.

"Didn't your parents teach you it was rude to burn down doors?" Ryma closed the door behind him and, surprisingly, didn't look upset. Why should he?

"Not as rude as kidnapping," Darion countered.

"You're probably right." Ryma went to the small stand with drinks. "The Stevenson's weren't happy that you decided to borrow their cabin without asking."

"They'll get over it." Darion didn't care about the Stevensons. "I was going to come in willingly tomorrow. What was the hurry?"

Ryma poured a couple of drinks, motioning Darion to a nearby chair. "You have to understand. You called me, thinking you had the upper hand, bargaining from a position of power." After handing Darion a drink, Ryma took a seat, crossing his legs. "You're young, so I'll forgive you. But you need to know who has the power in this city. We'll negotiate, but on my terms."

Ryma grinned, his face remaining pleasant. Even Darion, who was not gifted in reading people's magic, could feel the power Ryma contained. He had probably a dozen or so demons in this house loyal to his command, nevertheless wizards and their demons that were loyal to him. This man had the fate of Becca resting in his hands. Darion best remember his manners. So he remained silent, waiting to hear exactly what Ryma wanted.

"I heard you haven't been playing nice lately," Ryma continued.

"When has being nice mattered?" Darion replied.

"True, but we should always act civilized with our fellow coven members. From what I hear, you've been stealing from other magicians and burned down the market." Ryma took a drink. "We have rules in this city to keep things running smoothly. We cannot let chaos take over. Hence I have to enforce the rules."

"I understand." Darion had witnessed Ryma's hand of justice since he was a child. Magicians wanted to claim that their justice and prosperity surpassed that of the age of the Mundane. That opinion varied on who you were. "I stole from Jeremiah, what he had stolen himself."

"As I understand, the girl is his niece," he said. "Family overrides any claim you may place on her."

"But he killed her family. His own sister and brother-in-law. A family member like Jeremiah shouldn't have a right to anything."

"They were living outside the coven's protection. But they weren't the only ones." Ryma smiled, as if recalling a happy memory. "You should have seen him when I first discovered Jeremiah, stuck in a ragged home run by religious zealots that tried to beat the magic out of him. He was all too happy to kill his own parents to prove his faithfulness to me. Just be grateful, you're not related to him."

He killed his own parents? Darion was disgusted, but not completely surprised. Becca didn't belong to this man, her uncle.

Ryma didn't see it that way, though. And his was the only opinion that mattered here.

"What of our deal? I was to join you willingly in exchange for my claim on the other three." Darion had thought Ryma's offer was sincere at the time. How stupid could he have been, to think Ryma would play fair? He didn't count on Ryma locating him so easily. Now, he was bargaining for more than his life.

"The two Mundanes are yours after the ceremony tonight. But you can't claim Jeremiah's niece." Ryma looked down his thick nose at Darion, lecturing him on well-known rules.

Darion sat up straight on the end of his chair, almost jumping up. "But he plans to kill her!"

With a wave of Ryma's hand, Darion was pushed back into the chair, his drink spilling slightly. "It's best if we stay calm about these things." Ryma reminded him. His eyes darkened in warning. "The girl is his niece, and, with no other family, he has the claim on her."

Darion wished he would have thought of marrying Becca earlier, anything to keep her safe and out of Jeremiah's hands. They would have had to been married by Ryma, though. And she might prefer death than to be married to the coven. There had to be some way to convince Ryma.

Darion took a sip of the expensive liquor. It warmed his throat and steadied his nerves. "I fear Jeremiah is planning a coup against you." Jeremiah had almost told Darion exactly that when he worked on Elizabeth.

Ryma's brows raised in mock surprise. "Oh, so all of this is for my protection?"

"No. But I found out that he has been grooming these two girls for years, binding their magic. He has his sights on a level-six demon." That had to concern Ryma. He was the only other magician in the city with the power to summon a level six.

"I know about Jeremiah's ambition. You're a bit late for concern," Ryma said. "We have reached our own agreement, part of which is he gets custody of his nieces. And I'll help him raise his own level six demon."

Darion's almost dropped his glass.

Ryma leaned forward, an earnestness filling his face. "Don't doubt my abilities. I'm not threatened by Jeremiah. I'm going to give him his own city to run. There is enough for all. Don't you understand?"

Darion nodded. Jeremiah didn't want to replace the

coven leader, but become his own. And Ryma was dumb enough to let him.

"In a few hours, you will be joining the order," he reminded him. "You'll feel the power we wield. We're stronger together. Stronger than you know."

You mean you're stronger. Darion couldn't imagine being tied to this group for the rest of his life. "And what if I don't?" he had to ask.

"I've been patient with you for years because of your parents. Their power and loyalty was without question." Ryma glared at him, though a smile remained on his lips. "If you join without persuasion, you'll keep the two Mundanes and your freedom in the city. If you don't, then get comfy, because this will be your home for a while."

"Quite the choices you've laid out."

"I am truly sorry for your parents' deaths. They were powerful allies." The iced clinked in is glass as he finished his drink.

Darion put his drink down on the table, unable to control the tremble in his hand. *Allies. That's all they were to him.* They died on coven business, fighting demons on Ryma's behalf.

The ache of their deaths was ever present and always would be. And now, he was forced to join their murderer. There was no other answer he could give but yes.

"I'll pledge tonight." He was going to be forced to join. At least this way he would have a better chance in protecting Becca.

"Glad to hear it. I'll have someone escort you to your rooms." He stood, smoothing out his suit, and headed for the door. "You'll come to find the coven is a brotherhood like no other."

∽◈∼

Becca's head pounded as if she was hung over. She rolled over and remembered the last few moments of conscious thought. Adrenaline shot through her body, and she struggled to keep her breath quiet. Where the hell was she?

This is why magicians get a bad name. They never fight fair.

Instead, she searched her surroundings. She lay on a mat in the corner of a large bedroom of sorts. Furniture was scattered around the room.

A woman stood over a large table working on something. A heavy looking vase held a large bouquet of flowers nearby, perfect for smashing someone's head in.

"Don't get up too fast or you'll be sick. And I'm not cleaning up after you," said the stocky lady with curly brown hair.

Becca almost wanted to puke, just to piss the old broad off. Becca stood quietly and inched toward the vase. After two steps, she hit an invisible barrier and was thrown back. She shouted in pain and rubbed her head. "Thanks for the warning."

The woman looked over her shoulder. "Please. That's the least of your concerns."

"Then what should I be concerned about after being kidnapped and trapped in an invisible cage?"

The woman, whose eyes creased with age, glimmered with an evil light. "Tonight, dearie. Tonight." She turned back to her work, ignoring any more of Becca's questions and protests.

Where were the others? How did anyone find them? Was this part of Darion's deal? She stopped focusing on what she didn't know and what she could do.

Magic, idiot. Becca focused inward, searching for that strumming magic inside of her. For some reason, she struggled to gather the magic. It was slow, unresponsive.

"What a surprise." Jeremiah appeared by the door. "You've taken a magic lesson. You were always a resourceful girl."

Becca ignored her vile uncle. Her gaze was locked on her sister who hung calmly on his arm.

CHAPTER 33

Caleb paced the confines of the magical cage while Grace sat on the concrete floor, picking at her nails. He could feel the electricity and heat coming off the shield when he got too close. Four steps, then turn. Four steps, then turn. One zap was enough for him to know he didn't want to do it again.

There were trapped in an invisible barrier inside of an old bedroom that was small and simple, stripped of decorations. A single bed covered only in plastic lay centered against the wall. There were two doors, one that opened to a bathroom, the other shut tight, and a drain in the center of the floor.

The drain disturbed him the most. "Stop wearing yourself out." Grace looked up at him. "They'll unlock us at some point. They better before my bladder explodes."

Maybe that's what the drain is for? "How can you be sure we're at Ryma's?"

"Trust me on this one. I've been here before. He has a knack for decorating."

"And you're okay with this?"

An iciness spread over her features, smoothing out her skin and pulling her lips into a wicked grin. "I'm one step closer to killing Jaq. So, yes. Wasn't this the plan? To make it to Ryma's?"

"Not exactly." He pulled at his hair in frustration. He

itched to have a weapon, a bow or rifle was his preference but he'd take a steak knife right now. "Where's Rebecca, do you think?"

"You forget Becca's in a different class than us. As a witch, she gets the five-star treatment."

He couldn't help the guttural sound that came out of him.

Muffled voices traveled through the door. He couldn't wait to tear into whoever was out there.

"Play dead," Grace ordered as she rose to her feet and undid the top couple of buttons on her blouse.

"What? No." He wasn't going to let Grace fight this alone.

"Cut the chivalry. I'll get the guard to drop the shield, and you kill him. Got it?"

"That I can do." He dropped to the floor, relaxing his body and slowing his breath. It was harder to do than he thought when he wanted to fight someone.

"About time you came in. I'm bored as hell." Her voice had a light air to it. He remembered it from when he first met her at the market.

"Not my problem." The gruff voice didn't sound terribly interested.

"No. But maybe you could help me think of a solution."

Silence. Caleb kept his breaths shallow and slow.

"What's that guy's deal?" the man asked.

"Dunno. He's been out since I woke up. But I'd appreciate a different cell. I think he's pissed himself."

"If I open your cell, you may not like what'll happen." The man's voice was husky now.

"It has to be better than this." Grace's playful tone bristled against Caleb. He knew it was an act, but she was good at it.

It took another minute until Caleb felt the electricity near his legs vanish. The shields were down. He knew better than to move right away. Caleb had hunted enough to learn not to scare away the prey.

"You're all man, aren't you?" Grace said. Her light laughter sickened Caleb.

It took all he had to remain still. The flirting soon died, and he dared to crack his eyes. He heard the plastic on the bed and took it as his cue.

He silently stood, moving to the bed. The meaty man with short dark hair pinned Grace down. He forced his mouth on hers while his meaty hand ran up her thigh.

Red flashed before Caleb's eyes, and, without a second thought, he attacked. With an unknown fury, he grabbed the man's head and yanked it at an unnatural angle.

There was a sickening crack, and it was over.

The man slumped down, and Grace pushed him off the bed. Caleb stumbled back against the wall, his heart pounding in his ears. He'd killed a man with his bare hands.

He shook uncontrollably. He thought he should feel something, remorse, guilt maybe. But he didn't. Granted he had killed before with his bow and had snapped the neck of an injured doe once. But this was a human.

Grace straightened her clothes and smoothed out her hair. "You okay there, muscles?"

He nodded, unable to put into words what he was feeling. He rubbed his hands. A numbness traveled through them.

She went to the bathroom for a moment. It gave him a chance to shake off what just happened. Returning fresh faced, she had an enthusiasm that unnerved him. "I'm going to head out for a while. I'll head to the garage if I make it out."

"You know you don't have to go through with it."

She flashed him an empty smile, but he could see her thoughts racing behind her pretty eyes.

Caleb met her at the door and grabbed her hand. "Please stay. Why can't we go together? I can help you, just like now." Even though this last encounter felt like luck more than anything else, he couldn't imagine her facing a wizard and walking away.

"I have to do this alone."

"Why?"

She stepped into him, looking even smaller than before. So easily over powered. He didn't want to let her leave, but he knew he wouldn't force her to do anything. She had lived with enough of that in her life.

She placed a soft hand on his cheek. "I don't think you're strong enough for this kind of work. Thanks for everything, muscles. It's been one hell of a ride." Then pulling him down, she kissed him.

Short, but intense—just like Grace.

She was out the door before he could say another word. His lips tingled where she pressed against him. Her lavender perfume carried in the air. He had known her for such a short time, but had grown to care for her more than he realized.

He punched the door and welcomed the pain. He hated feeling helpless while those he cared about faced death.

℘℘℘

Grace walked through the estate undisturbed. Funny how even the most dedicated service man let her pass. Some recognized her and must have assumed she was working again for a new owner. With the men, a slight touch of her hand or an innocent catch of breath worked wonders. That was what parents should really teach their daughters.

Granted, she had been here before and recognized many of the servants and guards. She headed down the stairs to the basement, to the complex system of servants washing, cooking, and mending—whatever was required of them. It took an army to run an estate this size. That was what this was, an army of ants, buzzing around, and unseen, for the most part.

She arrived at the kitchen that was teaming with servants and hot dishes. Cooked tomatoes and garlic filled the air. She hadn't eaten all day, but that didn't matter. She couldn't lose this opportunity.

She caught the eye of a sandy-haired man. "Hey, is there any way I could get some drinks and snacks for Jaqar."

The man's eyes widened slightly at the name.

"He works up quite the appetite, you know?" Grace twirled a piece of hair, acting bored, while the man looked her up and down. *Yeah, buddy, soak it in, 'cause it's the last you'll see of me.*

She couldn't blame him too much. The green blouse she slept in clung to her chest, and the black soft pants fit like a second skin.

The man looked over at an older woman, with silver hair wrapped in a bun.

She nodded. "I'll get you a plate of muffins and coffee."

"Fruit too," Grace added. "Jaq loves his fruit."

The man chuckled and ordered a young homely girl to put together the plate. Grace leaned against the wall, waiting. She almost envied these workers hidden below. Most were too plain, or marred, to be presented in the estate. Down here, people lived a simple life with a decent wage. Grace always imagined her mother working at a place like this.

Never meeting her mother, Grace's imagination was all she had.

Instead, she found herself barely nineteen and plotting her first murder. Actually, she'd been planning it since she lived at Jaq's. But this is the closest she had ever come after years of dreaming about it.

"Got a smoke?" she asked a bus boy as he went by, but he shook his head. She continued to twirl her hair, forcing herself to stay calm. No use in tripping before the finish line.

They finally handed her a tray, and she carried it back upstairs. She passed a guard who told her Jaq's room number. It was the farthest from the dining area. The same room he stayed in before.

Being he was the black sheep of the coven, Ryma often hid him away. Ryma ignored the girls Jaq tortured and people he hurt. This time, the isolation would make things easier.

Before she got too close, Grace set the tray on an entry table. She pulled a tiny vial from her bra. It contained three small white balls that she'd procured earlier from the cabin. She'd found them when digging around in the master bathroom.

It was a sign, a gift that she had been waiting for since she first met Jaq. She crushed one bead in the bottom of each mug and poured the steaming hot coffee on top, dissolving the last trace of poison. The last bead rolled around in the vial.

Before she could think too much, she popped the bead into her mouth, carefully tucking it under her tongue. She didn't want to think what would happen if she was caught. A murderous servant received a grisly reward.

She wiped her damp palms on her skirt. She couldn't tell if it was excitement or nerves. Picking up the tray, she continued forward.

A tall security guard stood in front of the door. He was a lithe man, with wide shoulders. Jaq usually had a guard outside his room. Not for magical protection—he was strong enough on his own—but to help cover his extracurricular activities from the more prominent straight-laced members of the coven.

Grace flashed the guard a sexy smile. "Room service."

"We didn't order anything."

"I'm an old friend, hoping to reconnect," she tried again. "Thought he'd like his usual coffee and Vodka. I know it's his favorite."

The man stared intently at her, as if trying to decipher her true intentions. He looked over the tray and popped a blueberry in his mouth.

"So, you just show up and think you can get an audience with Jaqar. You may want to try another door, or maybe wait till I'm off work." He smirked, picked up a spoon from the tray, and stirred in a bit of sugar.

Her heart picked up its pace. "This isn't for you," she told him, stepping backward. "I came for Jaq."

It wasn't quick enough. The man picked up the mug, with a cocky eagerness.

"Stop—"she said. She couldn't let this man ruin her plan.

He ignored the warning and took a drink. "You think a two-bit girl like you isn't worth my time or money. Always wanting the big fish, but I'll tell you—"

The man slumped to the ground, the coffee spilling. He twitched for several moments then stilled. The first man she had ever killed lay at her feet, and all she could think was that it was the wrong one.

CHAPTER 34

"Elizabeth," Becca cried out.

But Elizabeth didn't move. She was focused on some spot in the distance, but thankfully her eyes were still clear blue. She wore a red lace dress that clung tight.

"Elizabeth," Becca screamed louder, hoping to jar her sister out of whatever trance he'd put her in.

"Please. She's not going to respond to you," Jeremiah said.

"What did you do to her?"

He rubbed her sister's arm. "Just calmed her down a bit."

Becca banged on the invisible barrier, ignoring the pain shooting up her arms. "Why her?"

"Because it couldn't be you. The day I found you in the barn with that boy, I knew I had to find someone else."

She froze, the truth of those words stabbing at her. She had been trying to find Elizabeth, save her, and now, she realized she gave her sister up to this monster years ago. Guilt stabbed at her.

He dismissed the older woman in the room and then proceeded to sit Elizabeth down in a chair. Becca's rage flared. How dare he touch her, and treat her like something he owned. He sat himself down in the chair across from Elizabeth. He had no right to be near her sister.

"Why don't you use me instead? Let her go." Anger laced every word. "A willing volunteer has to be worth something."

He scoffed at the idea. "Rebecca, that ship sailed long ago. You tarnished yourself with that farm boy. A demon of Bael's power demands a clean, pure sacrifice. And that was no longer you."

He smiled, and Becca wanted to claw the image of his face. Was that why he abused Becca years ago, because she no longer matched his definition of pure? He made sure of that.

The upside, though, was that maybe Jeremiah hadn't touched Elizabeth. He better not have.

She pushed back those memories. She had given them too much power over her life. Pounding on the cage walls, she poured her magic into her fists, She couldn't sit here watching her uncle. He needed to die.

In a flash, she flew to the back of the cage. It felt like a hundred ropes pulled her back, her body struggling to move.

"Let's not hurt yourself. You still have some worth. You're a present really, to help secure my place." He poured himself a drink, while Elizabeth sat in a frozen stupor.

"You're sick." Becca panted, struggling against the magic that bound her. "You're my uncle."

"I'm strengthening our family name. Our magic has been repressed for too many decades by religious bigots. But don't worry. We'll be known again. And your sacrifice will be considered noble by my descendants."

"My mother trusted you. And you killed her, and my father. I'll spit on your dead body as you rot in hell." She would use her last breath to kill him, if that was what it took.

"If I do, I'll be welcomed there like the royalty I am." He raised his glass in the air as if toasting his own grandeur—or psychopathic greatness as Becca thought of it.

She struggled to keep her face empty of her emotions, fear eating away at her from the inside. Darion and Caleb were gone, probably murdered by the monster in front of her.

Even Grace deserved more than ending back up for sale. And all three of them, even Elizabeth, would have been better off without her. The ache in her chest made each breath difficult.

Her dark fears surrounded her, closing in. As much as she loathed to admit it, she was powerless against this monster. Though she'd sacrifice it all for her sister, her all wasn't enough.

∞∞∞

Grace froze. She had seen dead people before. After all, she had lived in Jaq's house. But she'd never killed someone. Did he have a family? Loved ones?

He worked for Jaq, she reminded herself. Grace had been handed off to several of Jaq's men to be raped more than once. Jaq would say it was her job. But no more. This man sold his soul to the devil already. She just moved up the appointment.

A muffled noise came from down the hall.

Crap! A dead man in the hall was going to create a problem. She set the tray down, hooked her hands under his arms, and pulled. Damn, this man was heavy. She remembered a sitting room off the hall and dragged the body down there. Her arms strained as she hurried into the room.

It held a coffee table and a couple of chairs. She rolled him under the table, shoving his legs in tight. The pearl shaped poison slid from under her tongue.

She froze, a hand covering her mouth. She had to be more careful. One small bite and she would be lying next to this man. She tucked the pill carefully back under her tongue.

She grabbed a nearby duvet, spread it on the coffee table, and placed the centerpiece back on top. *I'd hate to be the cleaning person to find that mess.*

It was getting late. The darkness of night shadowed the room. If she didn't hurry, she might miss Jaq. She took a deep breath to slow her shaking hands.

Hurrying back to Jaq's room at the end of the hall, she steeled her courage. She picked up the empty mug off the floor, and hid it in a nearby flower arrangement.

She closed her eyes and swallowed carefully. *I can do this.* She had to do this. Or she would never forgive herself. Before she could bend down to pick up her tray, the door opened.

It was him, Jaqar—the monster who had haunted her sleep for years.

"You're not Eddie." His brows raised in question.

Looking Grace up and down, he straightened slightly, adjusting his clothes. His long blond hair and muscular body were set off by a dark suit. Licking his lips, he acted as if she was his next meal. His ego demanded a whole separate room.

Grace consciously slid her mask in place. She lifted her chin and bit on her lower lip slightly. "Remember me?" Her insides churned at her velvet voice.

His eyes flashed in excitement. "Barbie, was it? Or

Candy?"

"Candy," she agreed. She easily donned a different name, she actually preferred it. Then they never touched her, the real Grace. Just the name she pretended to be.

He reached for her arm. "Good to see you again."

Her blood boiled, but she kept that tapped down. She had years of perfecting that ability. "Wish I could say the same," she said with a smile.

"I always liked that attitude of yours." He pulled her in close as her heels dragged on the heavy rug.

"I am someone else's property now, Jaq." She held back the revulsion. He was sweaty with a slightly floral smell, sickening sweet. "I am not yours anymore."

He laughed loudly, getting more excited by her refusal. She'd watched him play this game more than once. Like a child, Jaq always wanted what wasn't his. She tugged against his grasp, but he just tightened it, pulling her close, his vile breath hot on her neck.

She closed her eyes briefly for what was about to happen. She was ready, she told herself. It was worth the price to see him dead. Worth the countless hours of torture, rape, and murder she had witnessed and endured at his hand. This was a cost she was more than willing to bear.

He forced his mouth hard and heavy on hers. And before doubt entered her mind, she bit down on the capsule, a tasteless fluid flooding her mouth. Without swallowing, she pushed the poison into his mouth.

He was briefly excited, thinking somehow she was participating in this sick game. He paused for a moment, and fear coursed through her body. Could he taste it? Could he stop it in time?

He began kissing her harder, his hands digging into her arms. She struggled under his grasp, not needing to pretend anymore. She wanted away from this man, and the poison in his mouth.

It had to work. She'd been planning for years. Once learning of the poison, she'd thought about taking it herself. That was before she met Caleb. Pure, innocent Caleb that saw her as more than she ever was.

By the time Grace had counted to six, his body tightened around hers. His eyes, pale and wide, showed the surprise the rest of his paralyzed body could not. Grace untangled herself from him and began spitting out the poison from her mouth until there was nothing left.

Jaq's body trembled on the floor, face down. He deserved to die that way. After several long seconds, his body stopped moving. She'd done it. He was dead.

"My name's Grace, you bastard," she spit.

A slight tingling began in her fingers. Nerves, she told herself. Raising her hand, she noticed it shaking uncontrollably. She grabbed the wall to steady herself. Her legs were no longer under her control.

She must have swallowed some of the poison. The small amount of poison she might have absorbed couldn't kill her. Right?

Watching Jaq's dead body, she couldn't muster any regret.

CHAPTER 35

I ndecision racked Caleb. He wasn't sure where to go next to find Becca. He'd be best to follow Grace's lead and poise as a servant, but he didn't know exactly how to do that. Hiding out in this bedroom with the man he just killed wasn't a good option.

He would borrow his clothes, though. The man's dark buttoned shirt looked like some type of uniform, with a crisp collar. Caleb cringed at the smoky smell of the man, as he undressed him. The sleeve fell above his wrists and the material stretched tight across his shoulder. It would have to do. He pushed through his uncertainty and left the room, locking the door behind him.

It was a hallway with plush carpet and scones lining the beige walls. To his left the hallway dead ended, so right it was. He meandered through the halls for time, trying to get a feel for where he was at. He passed a couple ladies that had a similar dark uniform. They watched him, but didn't say a word.

At a window, he peered through the heavy curtains. This was more than a home, they were at an estate, a mansion.

Grace had to be right. There were at Ryma's. He'd better move fast.

After talking to a young servant, he realized he needed to go upstairs for Jeremiah's private rooms. He slowly made his way up and began searching that floor. Unfortunately, it was a little more crowded. Anxiety bubbled up in his stomach, as he approached a couple, obviously dressed for the party. They passed by without a second glance.

The man behind them though had a similar black shirt and clipboard in hand. Giving Caleb a double take, he stopped him in the hall.

"What are you doing way up here?" The man was shorter than Caleb but somehow managed to still look down his nose at him.

"I was told to come up." It was the simplest lie he could think of.

"By who?"

"Jaqar." It was the only name he could use besides Ryma or Jeremiah. And maybe he could help out Grace.

"Maybe…" The man wasn't buying it. He flipped through papers on his clipboard. "What's your name?"

With a hand clenched into a fist, Caleb prepared to answer the man the hard way.

"Caleb, my man" Darion called out to him from down the hall. "I've been looking everywhere for you. Did you get lost again? I swear you're as dumb as a minor demon."

The small man gave Caleb a dirty look. "Get your act together or I'll feed you to a minor demon." He stormed off before Caleb could reply.

"Have you seen Becca?" Darion asked, beating Caleb only by a second.

"No. I was searching for her now." Caleb wondered how Darion made it out.

He appeared to be in okay shape.

Caleb grabbed his arm, pulling him in close. "Did you do this?"

"Yes and no." Darion didn't flinch. "I didn't want for

us to come this way, but we can fight about it later. We need to find Becca. I have a sinking feeling she's part of the festivities that are due to start soon."

As much as Caleb wanted to hate him, Darion was their only way out. Releasing his arm, Caleb stepped back. Darion wasn't the enemy, not now. "Lead the way."

"This is the back way to the ceremonial rooms," Darion explained as he maneuvered the hallways. "Less people this way. If we see Jeremiah before the ceremony, I'll distract him with magic, and you grab Becca. Then don't stop running, got it?"

"Yeah, I got it." Caleb flexed his hands by his sides. "What if we don't?" Things hadn't been working out as planned lately.

"Then we improvise—" Darion stopped short.

Caleb put a hand out to stop from running into to him. "What?"

It was Grace. She lay motionless in a pile on the floor. Next to her was a man, unconscious or dead.

Cold dread spread over Caleb's body, as he rushed to her side. This couldn't be happening. Not so soon. He'd just spoken to her less than an hour ago. She'd just kissed him.

The reality of what they were doing hit him. As Mundanes, maybe this was all a suicide mission.

"She's not dead, yet," Darion murmured as he looked over her body. He opened her mouth then checked her pulse.

"Come on, Grace, wake up." Caleb brushed the hair off her face. "Can't you give her something…a remedy, a spell? Dammit, you're a magician."

There was a slight pulse, weak but there. Her breath was slow.

Darion's blank face was void of any response. Caleb

wanted to shake him, wanted to make him feel for this girl next to him dying.

"I'm not that kind of magician. And I'm not sure there is one who can help. But she wouldn't want her body here, dead or alive."

Caleb's fist tightened. How dare Darion write her off so easily? Just another dead Mundane to him.

Darion checked the man behind him. "He's gone."

"Is that him?" Caleb asked. If he was Jaqar, the man who did this to Grace, he wanted to revive him just to kill him again. If only Grace would have let him help in the first place.

"Yes. I need to get rid of his body." Darion stood and put a hand on the door next to him. After a moment, he opened the door and pulled the man into the room.

"We need to get her out of here," Caleb said, pulling Grace up in his arms.

Her eyes fluttered open. "Hey, muscles."

His heart raced with joy. "Hey."

Her skin paled against her lips that were tinged blue. "Did I get him?"

"Yeah. He's dead." Caleb forced a smile on his face to hide what was really happening. "Why didn't you let me help?"

She closed her eyes for a moment and swallowed. "My demon to kill. No one else could have."

"You brave, stupid, wonderful Grace." He pulled her into his chest, kissing the top of her head. This small girl who could barely weigh a hundred pounds just took out one of the deadliest magicians in the city.

She closed her eyes. Her breath came out in short gasps.

"No, Grace. Stay awake. Stay with me." He rubbed her bare arm, trying to give her warmth and life. "We need to get her out of here. Now," he hollered to Darion inside the room.

Darion returned, a couple girls at his side.

"Here," Darion put some money into their hands. "Take the service stairs straight down. Good Luck"

"Who are they?"

"What Grace used to be? Servants of Jaq. I figured Grace would have wanted them saved as well."

The girls quickly left down the hall. This is what Grace did. Saved these girls. He wished she could have seen it. "How's she doing?" Darion asked kneeling next to them.

"Not good. She needs help."

Darion put his hand on her chest. "I can't do anything. I'm not a healer. But it shouldn't be long."

"Long?" The realization of her death slowly sank in. He prayed to whatever or whoever was listening. But it went unanswered. Grace's labored breathing eventually stopped.

"I'm sorry, Caleb," Darion said.

Caleb placed her on the floor and prepared to give her CPR, anything to keep her here. He didn't want sorry, he wanted her alive and well.

Darion stopped his hand. "Anything you do will just prolong the pain. There is no antidote. She knew that."

"How can you be so casual?" Caleb wanted to throttle him. Make him feel something for this girl that had been through so much.

"This isn't the first casualty and probably won't be the last." Darion's face hardened. "If there's any way of saving Becca or her sister, we have to move. And Grace wouldn't want her body used after death."

Caleb wiped away the tears on his cheeks. Not because he was embarrassed. Grace was beautiful inside and out. He would mourn her death. But this wasn't over. He needed to focus on the task at hand. He would make these magicians pay.

Darion handed him a couple of knives. "I found them in the room."

They were light, for throwing. Caleb sheathed the knives and then picked Grace up in his arms.

"You'll need to take the servant's back entrance. If they ask, tell them you're taking the body out to the cooler for Jaqar. Then go to the garage and secure a vehicle."

"What about Becca? The meeting is starting soon. She'll be there. I'll come back up. You'll need my help." Caleb wasn't about to leave knowing Rebecca and her sister were still here.

"You're a Mundane. You won't be allowed in the room, unless you're a sacrifice."

"And Rebecca's there." He felt almost hallow, as if death was mocking him, taking away everyone he cared for.

He couldn't sit in a car, waiting for Rebecca to be killed. Darion didn't know him very well if he thought he'd agree to that.

"Just find us a way to get us out of here, okay?" Darion asked. "Trust me. I won't be leaving this place without her."

CHAPTER 36

Becca's mind pounded with magic. A fog of confusion layered her reality. A loud door shut somewhere in the distance. She was sitting in a cold dark room. The daze slowly lifted as Becca took in her new surroundings.

The night sky darkened the long windows while several candles littered the floor and walls. It was a large room, mostly empty. The bare brick walls and concrete floors seemed to echo a past filled with hellish ceremonies Becca didn't want to imagine. She was in the center of a deathly assembly hall.

On the floor, she found herself trapped in the very circle she just learned how to create, a demon's pentagon. Too bad her lessons with Darion never covered how to escape one. As she reached out, magic sizzled against her skin like an electric brick wall, lighting her nerves on fire.

She slowly stood and turned around. She wasn't alone. A gangling teenage boy sat in another pentagram and, in a third one, Elizabeth still wore the red dress.

Becca screamed for her sister and reached out. She ignored the pain burning up her arms. Elizabeth was slow to respond, looking around, confused, as if she couldn't figure out who was speaking.

"Cut it out," a guard said. "No one can hear you. And we'll have to sedate you, before you can hurt yourself." Two of them stood by large wood doors.

The pentagram surrounding her was a complex barrier. She could hear them, but they couldn't hear her, convenient when trapping people against their will. On second look, the taller one had the pitch black eyes of a Soultorn.

Becca pressed the tight spot between her brows to relieve the tension. She needed to think, to figure a way out of this.

She couldn't help but test the circle again, this time, though, with one of the protective spells Darion had taught her. She inched her foot forward only to jerk it back at the pain that traveled up her leg. She stifled a cry.

The human guard laughed at her attempt. She swore at the guards, before remembering they couldn't hear her. She noticed Elizabeth staring at her.

"Elizabeth," Becca said, facing her sister. Would she even recognize Becca now? "Elizabeth, please."

Becca sat down in the circle, reviewing every spell, even throwing some toward the guards. But they didn't flinch. Nothing could leave the pentagram. It was how magicians were protected from the demons they summoned.

'Rebecca?' The word rang out in her mind, as clear as if Elizabeth has said it aloud.

"Elizabeth." Becca spoke the word aloud, but her sister didn't respond. She tried only thinking the word instead. *'Elizabeth.'*

Her sister's eyes lit up in recognition.

How was this possible? How could they talk, not only through the pentagram but in each other's mind? Was it one of the spells Darion taught Becca? Or maybe a sister thing?

She didn't know or care how, she was just grateful that she could.

'*Is this a dream?*' Elizabeth's voice sounded again inside Becca's mind.

'*Sorry, but no.*' Becca shook her head. '*Do you have the dreams, too?*' Maybe this connection between them was stronger than she knew. It was bitter sweet, finally talking to her sister, before they were both put up to slaughter.

'*What's happening?*' Elizabeth rubbed her hands together, folding and refolding them in her lap. '*I thought you were dead.*'

'*I thought you were dead, too, for a bit.*' Becca didn't know how to warn or prepare her sister for what was to come next. '*But the night's not over.*'

'*The fact we're both sitting inside pentagrams doesn't look too good,*' Elizabeth said in earnest.

Becca chuckled slightly. She could only laugh or cry at this point.

Without notice, the large doors slowly opened, creaking against the hinges. Magicians filed into the room, each one with a grace and reverence that unnerved her. Several had Soultorns trailing behind them, their dark eyes a portal to hell.

'*We'll figure something out,*' Becca told her sister, wishing she believed it.

Jeremiah entered with an entourage of two younger magicians and a Soultorn trailing behind. With his head high and chest puffed out, he looked like a buffoon as he took a place close to Elizabeth's pentagram. Becca couldn't stand to watch him.

Scanning the room, her breath caught as she found Darion. There were a million questions she needed to ask him since their kidnapping. She tried speaking to him, in the off chance, this new mental telepathy worked on him. It didn't.

He avoided her gaze and spoke quietly to a beautiful

redheaded young woman at his side.

A trickle of fear stabbed at Becca. When Darion talked of his plan, he said he was going to turn himself in. He never mentioned being attacked at the cabin or turning Becca over to Jeremiah.

Darion stood relatively free now, and she couldn't help but wonder if this was part of the plan? She glared at him. Why wouldn't he even look at her? Maybe he realized what side he needed to be on to stay alive.

Calm down. She ignored the pain in her chest, and focused on getting Elizabeth out alive. She needed to think.

Silenced filled the room and every head turned as a black robed figure emerged. Though never having seen his face, Becca knew it had to be Ryma—the coven leader. His scarred head and grisly face looked as if he earned his position the hard way.

He projected some kind of energy. She could almost feel his magic like an electrical current. He reached the front of the room, and his two Soultorns stood behind him, reverently.

She stepped back, instinctively, her body telling her to run.

'This is bad.' Elizabeth's voice echoed in Becca's mind. Elizabeth was on her feet and, like Becca, as far as she could get from Ryma.

'We're not gone yet,' Becca reminded her. *'We fight to the end, okay?'*

The sisters shared a quick glance. Tears swam in Elizabeth's eyes, but she straightened her back. *'Okay.'*

Becca wasn't sure if it was the candles or maybe incense, but the strong warm smell reminded her of death, of rotting flesh, of the hell from which they called these demons.

Ryma bent his head and so did the rest of the room, respectfully. Then he began chanting in another language which sounded like a prayer or some kind of rite. Yet it didn't have the feel of the religion her mother taught her. It was cold and vile, but taken as serious in every other respect.

Ryma lifted a hand to silence the crowd. "We will have the pleasure of creating three Soultorns tonight, calling on the demons of the highest levels. Then following, Darion will be giving his blood pledge tonight."

Several heads turned to Darion in surprise.

Ryma raised a wide goblet high in the air. "He will be bound to me and to the coven."

"To the Coven," the magicians replied in unison.

This has to be a joke. A fake. Darion can't pledge to this man.

She knew he planned on it, but he couldn't follow through. At Ryma's command, Darion moved to stand behind Ryma just like another puppet. Another magician at Ryma's beckoning call. Rage seeped into her body, taunt and ready to strike.

"Farina." Ryma called a beautiful witch with porcelain skin and thick red lips forward. Hand in hand the two magicians moved toward the pentagram that held the young man.

They had to be combining magic, like Darion and Becca had done. But not quite the same. Darion said magicians put up guards, protected themselves so the other magician couldn't take them over. Only a child would ever trust someone like that and not guard themselves.

And me.

Her blind trust in Darion tore at her. How could she have let him hurt her again?

Ryma spoke a few words, and the young man stuck his

hand through the pentagram. The rest of his body remained stiff like a soldier at attention. Ryma sliced effortlessly across the boy's palm and dark blood dripped into the glass goblet.

The witch cut herself next. Her crimson blood dripped into the glass. Ryma gently twirled the liquid like a fine wine. The witch quickly dealt with her wound. The stunned boy dropped his hand to his side where it continued to drip blood onto the cement floor.

Ryma spoke over the cup then handed each of them a turn to drink from the goblet. He continued the summons, calling a demon that hovered in the air.

Becca couldn't watch. She focused on the silent drops of blood that slid down the boy's fingers and fell to the floor.

Drop by drop, the crimson beads pooled on the floor.

It was the blood that tied them together, Becca remembered. That was why her connection with the fox was so weak. She had not shared blood with the animal, since Darion had worried the animal may not be clean.

Blood. The one thing I share with Elizabeth. Becca rubbed the scar on her hand from that summer day they became blood sisters. That was how she was communicating with her sister. It had to be. Could they do more?

Elizabeth's blood ran inside her veins. That had to be something.

'Elizabeth,' Becca called to her sister.

'Am I next?' Elizabeth's voice trembled with fear.

'Elizabeth. We need to focus. We have to get out of this.' Becca wondered if Elizabeth had magic like she did. There had to be a reason Elizabeth had a tattoo. If only they could combine their magic like Becca did with Darion? Becca didn't know the spell, but she had to try something.

'What are we going to do?' her sister asked.

'I'm not sure yet. But we have a bond and combined strength. We'll figure out something.' Becca forced her voice to have more confidence than she felt.

Ryma finished the ritual, and the small boy now stood with pitch black eyes. A faithful servant. Becca tried to ignore the sickness creeping up her throat as the boy took his place with the other Soultorn.

A smug satisfaction crept into Jeremiah's face as he relished her dismay. Darion stayed neutral, not even an ounce of disgust. How could he stand it? How would he look as they turned Becca into a Soultorn?

"Jeremiah." Ryma called him forward. A servant handed Ryma a new glass goblet and together they started toward Elizabeth.

No! Not Elizabeth first.

Becca had counted on being first, on utilizing their combined power to attack. She couldn't do anything if they opened Elizabeth's pentagram first.

Becca began shouting spells to her sister, over and over. *Just say it. Project. Use my power'* The same cues that Darion had taught her days ago.

Frantic, Elizabeth tried to repeat the words. But Becca couldn't feel any power leaving. It wasn't working.

When Jeremiah opened the pentagram, Elizabeth froze, her body stiff and eyes glazed over as before. Ryma took her arm.

Becca continued talking to her sister. *'Listen. Try to gather that humming power inside of you. Try it. Please.'* Becca pleaded, but there was no response. Not anymore. Becca spoke the words over and over, in vain.

Jeremiah cut Elizabeth's hand then proceeded with his, collecting the blood in a goblet. Ryma began the incantation.

Becca screamed. It bounced inside her pentagram, no

one else hearing the pain and heartache.

Without warning, something exploded outside the room. The candles flickered briefly. Murmurs broke out among the wizards—possible spells of protection.

Ryma paused the incantation and, with a flick of his hand, Darion rose off the ground. He writhed in pain, but he didn't make a sound. The other magicians backed away from him.

"You really think you had a chance against me. You're a child," Ryma said, almost amused. He threw Darion against the wall, where he stayed, held a foot off the ground. "I will deal with you after I'm finished here."

He'd tried. Darion tried to save her sister, but it wasn't enough. Becca's heart sank. Smoke lingered in the air, but Darion didn't move, his muscles straining.

She never should have doubted him. He had always been at her side. She was grateful for his sacrifice, but wasn't sure it was worth it. Now his neck was on the chopping block too. She pounded against the portal, using every curse she could think of.

Jeremiah continued the ceremony. Becca ignored his words and kept repeating the basic spell. It couldn't end like this.

In a blink, a demon larger than life filled the room. It had numerous heads. One, almost human like, held a crown.

Its legs or arms—she couldn't make out the difference— were huge pincers. The demon roared. The voice pierced her to the depths of her soul. A few other wizards winced in pain.

Jeremiah stood proud, a touch of blood in the corner of his mouth. "Bael, by the power of the coven, I command you to enter the vessel I place before you."

Ryma placed a hand on Jeremiah's shoulder, she

assumed, to combine their magic. He finished the spell in another language.

In a mere blink, the demon was gone.

Becca's scream raked her body, a pain she couldn't describe. Her sister, beautiful Elizabeth, had lost those innocent sky blue eyes. In their place, a monster stared out, showing the depth of hell itself.

Becca felt as if her whole body was going to tear in two as Elizabeth or the demon Bael stepped outside the pentagram. A voice cut through her cries, strong and deep.

A deep chuckled sounded in her mind. Becca spun around, wondering where it was coming from. No one else seemed to hear. *'What do we have here? Ties to multiple magicians?'*

Jeremiah and Ryma faced the group of magicians and spoke of strengthening old alliances. It sounded like Ryma was even giving Jeremiah his own city. The surprised crowd focused on the pair, ignoring Becca completely, which was for the best

'Who is this?' Becca asked as she turned around in the pentagram. A sinking feeling in her gut told her she had a clue.

'The great Bael, prince of hell himself.' The voice boomed inside her mind. *'And how is such a weak magician tied to me?'*

Blood. It had to be the blood. But what did this mean?

'Elizabeth?' She had to try. Maybe somewhere in that body she could find her sister.

The demon laughed, loud and deep. A darkness and power crept into Becca's mind. It tingled all the way down to her fingers. Her breath picked up. It was a power she had never experienced—the power of Bael.

Then, in the next second, she dropped to her knees, her mind traveling into a black hole. Coldness invaded every sense. If this demon was tied to her, then it could destroy her. She could barely control a level-one demon.

The demon spoke to her. It's strong voice booming in her mind. *'So open. So impressionable for a witch. And I'm in this body, so pure and strong. Time to play with these so called wizards. They think I, the great Bael, can be their servant?'* Then it was gone. She stood slowly, her legs unsteady.

What the hell was that thing? Something more monstrous than she could have imagined, and it inhabited her sister's body.

The demon didn't hesitate. Bael, in her sister's body, struck Ryma in the back with such a strong force that it had to be magical. Ryma flew across the floor, as if dragged by an invisible rope. His body smeared the pentagram.

The power surrounding Becca fled. Screams erupted. It looked as if Jeremiah's supposed Soultorn just attacked the coven leader. Gratefully, no one noticed Becca leave the circle.

Adrenaline pumped through Becca from her connection to Bael. Her fingers tingled with the magic coursing through her body.

"I'm not weak," she whispered.

CHAPTER 37

D arion collapsed to the floor as Ryma's curse finally lifted. Blood raced through his veins, his hands hot and ready to fight. His defenses were up, but where to begin?

What was happening? Magicians turned on one another without a second thought as cries and curses filled the air. Jeremiah and Ryma had just stood before the whole coven proclaiming unity. Ryma just awarded Jeremiah his own coven. Was it all a pretense for Jeremiah to usurp authority?

There was no time to think. Magicians quickly chose sides, fighting against one another. Jeremiah had more allies than Darion imagined. It was going to be a bloody fight, and Becca was in the middle of it.

Darion raced toward Becca, who was focused on her sister. Elizabeth's body took on an inhuman strength as it tore apart a young magician.

"Becca." Darion grabbed her wrist and pulled her to the side of the room, placing a protective spell around both of them. A power stronger than he imagined, emanated from Becca's skin and jolted him back.

"How?" His mind shuffled through possibilities. She now held more power in her touch then she previously had in her whole body. The only way that could be possible would be—a demon.

Bael fought with an inhuman strength, tearing into the men closest to Jeremiah. Bael, now inside Elizabeth, wanted to kill Jeremiah to be free. The Soultorn snapped a magician's neck quickly, and an intense look of gratification crossed its face. Then Elizabeth's pristine features turned ghastly as those black eyes turned on the next victim.

Becca drew his attention back. "Don't know how. I'm connected to Bael, but not in control."

Jeremiah hollered orders over the crowd and charged at the group of men surrounding Ryma.

"We have to go." Darion grabbed her hand again, but now absorbed the current off her skin. The magic was somehow consuming her. She didn't know how to control the power. If he didn't stop this soon, she would die.

He focused his energy on combining their power. Her magic contained a different, deep flavor—overwhelming almost. This wasn't just Becca anymore. He pulled on her arm, about to pick her up and drag her out of here.

In a flash, the Soultorn Bael was in front of Darion. "No hurting this one. She's mine."

This demon needed to protect Becca for the moment. If she died first, then it would be bound only to Jeremiah, who had the power to control it. And with an inexperienced master, the demon could kill everyone in the room, then save Becca for dessert.

Becca tried to step in front of Darion. "No, no." She gave the command for the demon to halt, but she was too slow.

The Soultorn punched Darion in the stomach. Darion's breath rushed out of him and pain spotted his vision. He stumbled back against a wall. Thankfully, he kept a tight hold on Becca, and pulled her into him.

He concentrated his power on controlling the demon.

Hopefully, his magic combined with Becca's would be enough. The Soultorn stopped in front of them, anger creasing Elizabeth's face. Bael paused for a moment, halted by Darion's spell.

"Are you okay?" Becca asked Darion.

Even though they were surrounded by flying spells, warring wizards, and Soultorns, now that Becca was truly by his side, he was okay. He nodded, not trusting his control over this demon.

Before they moved, a blast of magic came their way, hitting Becca's sister in the back. The Soultorn fell into them. Darion strained against the demon's power. He had to control it before it took over Becca. The demon stilled. Elizabeth's features were angry and strained, but Bael was no longer in control.

Jeremiah approached them, striking out at their shield over and over. He wasn't going to let them go.

Darion held onto her arm. "We have to keep this bond between us. All right?"

Becca nodded and briefly closed her eyes. He could feel her pushing her power into him. It was something magicians never did in a battle. Love and trust had little place in politics.

Becca and Darion carried Elizabeth's body between them and hurried for the door. They ducked behind other dueling magicians, hoping to block Jeremiah's path.

Jeremiah hit them again. But this time it barely rocked their shield. The battle with Ryma must have cost him. Jeremiah was only feet away and probably had yet to figure out what really happened to the Soultorn during the ceremony.

It was an advantage, Darion couldn't let pass.

Jeremiah's forces were scattered around the room, fighting off Ryma's men. Screams and curses echoed off the walls. And though Darion was nervous about using Bael and Elizabeth, through Becca he could siphon all the power of a prince of hell. He turned around to face Jeremiah and attacked.

Jeremiah flew back several feet. Darion hit him again, before he could retaliate. He took pleasure in attacking the man who had hurt Becca in so many different ways. Jeremiah's body crashed into the concrete. There were no longwinded speeches or goodbyes. This dirt bag didn't deserve any of it.

Becca put a hand on Darion. "Let me." She gathered her magic toward her uncle and spoke the words to compel him to do her will. She held a dark hatred in her eyes Darion had never seen before. Power coursed through her body as the spell took its course.

Jeremiah slowly stood, uneasy on his legs, his eyes wide with fear as he tried to cry out, but his body didn't listen. His armed raised and Darion noticed a small dagger in his hand. A small weapon usually carried on wizards for magic.

"Don't do this," Jeremiah mouthed, but the pleas fell on deaf ears. The battle raged on as he raised the knife and, in one swift motion, cut his own throat. Becca's chest heaved as the magic poured out of her. For such a spell came at a cost.

"You did it. He's gone." Darion focused on controlling Bael and maintaining a protective shield.

"Yes, he is." Her words held empty resignation in them.

Others pressed toward them, testing their shields. Darion pushed them back with what he did best, fire. Shouts filled the room as the smoke spread. With Jeremiah dead, his other Soultorn was set free. The large blond Soultorn began attacking everyone in its path. A guttural roar bounced off concrete walls.

Ryma was surrounded by Jeremiah's allies who realized their leader had fallen. They were no longer fighting for power, but for their lives.

"Let's go." Darion started for the door, hoping to sneak out amid the chaos, because once Ryma had squashed his opponents, Darion and Becca were dead. Even with additional magic they wouldn't survive the fight.

"We have to run. Don't break contact with me." He hoisted Elizabeth's body over his shoulder, and Becca grabbed onto his arm.

Darion set a nearby guard on fire as they raced out of the room. Spells shot through the air, threatening to trip up Darion, but none of them broke through his shields.

Once out of the room, they didn't stop. They avoided servants and ignored their questions. The Soultorn in his arms began to stir, but Darion forced the body back to sleep, trapping the demon inside the unconscious body. He didn't want to attempt to control a level-five demon right now.

They turned down another corridor. Two witches. He torched the curtains to their right and turned back. They fought the flames and didn't seem to care enough to pursue.

Finally on the main floor, they headed to the servants' exit and found Caleb. He leaned against the wall panting. A guard lay bloody at his feet.

"You okay?" Becca asked him.

"Will be. Ready to go?" Caleb took Elizabeth from Darion and glanced at Becca's grip on his arm. "Is Elizabeth all right?"

Caleb couldn't see or feel the demon inside yet. "She's—" Becca's voice caught.

"Long story and Ryma won't be far behind." Darion

pushed the two forward through the kitchen and servants' exit then stopped at the back door. He'd thought about this for a while. The best way he could protect Becca would be to stay behind. Ryma didn't know of her power and would have no reason to follow.

He avoided Becca's gaze and spoke to Caleb. "Keep going. I'll clear the way for you."

Caleb nodded and started off toward the garage. Darion couldn't help himself. He stole one more glance at Becca.

e/ɔc/ɔ

After a couple steps, Becca realized Darion wasn't following. She paused and the deeper meaning of his words sank in. He said he'd clear a path for them to escape, he never said he'd be joining them. She turned back and caught his gentle gaze—a caress almost—which looked too much like a goodbye.

The pain in her chest wasn't sadness, it was anger. "I'm not leaving you."

"I'll catch up."

"You promised to never lie to me again."

The cold night they broke up was fresh in her mind. He promised to never lie again, but she couldn't forgive his lies at the time. Now she understood. He lied to protect her from this world, and he was trying to do it again.

But she still remembered the pain of that night. It took days, weeks, no longer—she never got over that hurt of losing him. She couldn't let that happen again.

He opened his mouth then shut it.

Caleb sifted restlessly behind them. "Becca, we need to go."

"Go ahead. I'm not leaving without Darion," she told Caleb, though she never took her eyes off Darion.

"It may be everyone's only chance out," Darion said. "I've lost too many people in my past, including you," she said. He tried to interrupt, but she continued talking over him. "I can't handle the emptiness, the longing when you're not there. So it doesn't matter if I'm walking to my grave. We do it together, or not at all."

Remembering Caleb, she turned to him. "You can go ahead." Her sister was lost at this point, but maybe he'd still take her with him.

Caleb shook his head and looked at the both of them. "We're in this together."

Turning back to Darion, she tightened her jaw. He'd called her stubborn before. Well, she'd show him stubborn.

Shaking his head he stepped toward her. "Okay. Let's hurry."

She grasped his hand, the familiar twinge of magic sparking between their palms. "Glad we can agree on something."

This was her family now, and she'd fight to the death for all of them.

❧❦❧

Caleb hurried down the path, his arms burning from holding Elizabeth, Rebecca and Darion right behind him. He tried to push out the pain from the scene he'd just seen between Becca and Darion. He'd think about it later when they were safe.

The cool night provided them some coverage, but not enough. A guard appeared ahead. Caleb grabbed at the last knife. But the guard collapsed on the ground, before he got within range.

"Just keep going," Darion huffed behind him.

They made it to the garage. The two guards lay bound unconscious on the ground. Darion had been right. The guards were little more than chauffeurs and had been easy enough for Caleb to take out. Unfortunately, that probably meant driving out of here wouldn't be as easy as it sounded. Glad they were still passed out, Caleb stepped over them.

"The big black one there." He pointed to an old Humvee. It'd likely have the guts to get them out of here.

He placed Elizabeth in the back seat, noticing blood on her arm also, but no other visible injuries. Sometimes the worse kinds of wounds were those not seen. He had already tucked Grace's body gently into the back of the large vehicle. He couldn't think of that now. He had to get them all out of here.

He threw open the garage doors. Guards exited the mansion, heading their way.

"Move it," Darion said as he slid in the front beside Becca.

Starting the car, Caleb noticed the glazed over look on Rebecca's face. Shock maybe? He put the vehicle in gear, peeling out of the garage.

Darion pointed. "This way."

Caleb sped around fruit trees, wheels skidding across the loose gravel and over the paved path. Straightening out, he picked up speed.

"Ummm, Darion, do you see those massive iron gates ahead?" he asked, not seeing another road to take. "And the two guards standing in front of them with large guns?"

"I feel them." Darion focused ahead, one hand reaching forward.

Before Caleb could understand what he meant, the

small office near the gates exploded. Flames raged on the road. The two men, unloaded on the Humvee, rapid shots filling the air.

Caleb ducked down as the windshield splintered in front of them.

Darion stayed upright and spoke in a foreign language, concentrating on the road ahead. Did that mean they were bulletproof now?

Caleb let his foot up on the gas only to have Darion slam his knee back down.

"Don't stop."

"But the flames—" Caleb didn't know everything about magic, but that fire raged with an unnatural hunger. And however expensive this car was, he doubted it was fireproof.

Something hit them from behind, the wheels lifting up in the air. It fell down hard. The back of the Humvee swerved a couple times before finding traction. Caleb tightened his grip on the wheel. There was no going back.

"Don't stop or we're dead," Darion shouted.

"If we don't make it, don't let them get us." The chill in Becca's voice told of horrors unspoken.

It took a minute before Darion replied. "I understand."

Caleb pushed the pedal all the way to the floor, knowing any hesitation might kill them, if the fire didn't. As they approached the flames, he struggled to keep his eyes open against the scorching light.

Then he took a deep breath and drove straight through.

CHAPTER 38

Becca stood at the cliff's edge, the salty air pulling her hair. Morning light rose slowly over the horizon as the waves crashed against the shore with a fierceness she'd never imagined. They pounded the rocky mountain face over and over, slowly pulling at it grain by grain.

She'd never seen the ocean before. She always assumed it was peaceful and calming. This water had a powerful spirit no one could contain. She imagined jumping in, salt water tearing at her clothes. She might find peace in that destruction, for there was no peace to find here on land.

Darion grabbed her hand, pulling her back from the edge. "Ready?"

She didn't answer. She never would be ready to bury someone. They both turned to where Caleb stood by Grace's grave. Darion had already burned a molten layer out of rocks on top of the grave to keep out grave robbers or animals. Caleb planted a wildflower on top.

Did he love this girl? Becca didn't have the heart to be jealous. It hurt her to see him lose another person he cared for. There had been too much loss.

"I've never been to an official funeral." Caleb dusted his hands on his pants. "Not sure what to say."

"Whatever you want," Darion offered. "I hated all the funerals I've been too. And Grace wouldn't have liked them either."

Caleb cleared his voice. Red rimmed his eyes, his face tired and sad. "Grace was an actress. She performed a role she was forced into for years. But getting to know the real her, she had a beautiful spirit, strong enough to save many. I'll miss her."

"Amen," Darion said.

Becca bit her lip, not trusting her emotions. Grace didn't deserve to be dead. Becca couldn't avoid the guilt of her role in Grace's death. If she didn't steal this girl from the market, would she be safe? Maybe a maid for a rich lady? Becca would never know.

How many deaths was Becca responsible for? She felt a buzzing in the back her mind. It was Bael. Probably enjoying her sorrow. But it wasn't all Bael. Somehow, she still felt connected to her sister. It was the same feeling Becca would get when she dreamed of Elizabeth.

"Is it still there?" Darion asked. He must have seen her confusion on her face.

"Yeah. I feel them both. I know you told me, we can't get her back, that she won't be the same." Becca's voice broke slightly. "But I can't help but still feel like she's there, part of her, somewhere."

"People don't always want to accept it when they lose someone." The resignation in his voice crushed her hope.

"What if she's right?" Caleb asked. "You say she can't save Elizabeth, but from what you told me about what happened in that room, with Becca taking over Bael, that couldn't have happened either."

Becca looked at Darion, searched his face for any sign that these words might be true. Caleb was right. No one expected what happened at Ryma's to happen. Darion called it old magic. The grimoire didn't mention removing a demon, but magicians were trying and maybe they'd succeeded.

Darion's wind-blown hair stood on end, his face hesitant. "I don't know, Becca. Caleb's right. I've never seen or would have expected what happened in there. I'm not sure why or how you're connected to Bael. So, I don't know what the future holds."

"Maybe it means, we don't have to say goodbye to Elizabeth just yet?" Caleb proposed.

"Or maybe we're just prolonging the inevitable." She loathed the idea of keeping Bael trapped in Elizabeth longer than necessary. And what if they chanced removing the demon and found her sister dead. Becca could feel vague impressions from her sister, but not enough to know if Elizabeth was in pain. This wasn't a decision she was ready to make.

"We can search for an answer," Darion said. "Maybe ask around down south, out of Ryma's way. It will take a while."

"Nothing else to do right now." Caleb stood next to Becca, a familiar comfort helping to hoist her up.

"True." Darion reached for her hand. His warm magic soothed her ragged heart.

The wind picked up, covering the silence as the sun rose on the horizon. Its beauty mocked Becca. She had never imagined this kind of ache. Yet at the same time, there was hope. All because of the two men standing next to her. They had all lost a lot, but not everything. And that was something worth fighting for.

ALSO BY
DEANNA BROWNE

An Unholy Sundering
Dark Rising Trilogy Book2
(Out Summer 2018)

Thirty years ago, dark magicians opened a dimension to another world and unleashed a new power on the earth fueled by demons. Governments toppled, millions died and magicians became earth's most feared predator.

Twenty-four-year-old Becca spent years on the streets earning every scar, but she can't outrun her past forever. After rescuing her younger sister, Elizabeth, from the clutches of a power-hungry coven, Becca discovers her enemies have left an unholy gift behind—a demon bound to her sister's soul. On the run and determined to save the last of her family, Becca works with her best friend, Caleb, and the pyromancer who tempts her untrusting heart, Darion. When caught by an unknown faction, they're thrown in an underground community where Becca learns the price she must pay to save her sister is dear.

As they work to rid Elizabeth of the demon, the unlikely trio realizes they haven't run far enough to escape Ryma and his twisted coven. Unsure of who to trust, Becca searches desperately for answers, even as someone leaks information leaving their new found haven vulnerable. War looms on the horizon, and despite her instinct to run. Becca is forced to pick sides in a game where their survival isn't guaranteed.

A New Science Fiction
Romantic Adventure from Browne

HOOKED

When virtual reality surpasses people's wildest
dreams, many struggle to remain in the real
world. Sixteen-year-old Ari has watched the
financial and emotional cost of virtual reality
addiction for years as her father continues
barely existing in a VR coma. Unfortunately,
her only option to help her family escape
poverty is if she studies the one subject she
hates and fears: virtual reality programming.

Despite her misgivings, Ari soon develops a
rare talent that makes her question everything.
Now she must hide her ability or risk
becoming a priceless commodity that
governments and corporations will fight, steal
or even kill to possess. As officials tighten the
shackles surrounding Ari, she rebels against
her imposed future and searches for a way to
save those she loves. Yet, running proves
impossible, when the government is always
one click away.

ACKNOWLEDGMENTS

This being my debut novel, my gratitude runs deep for everyone who has helped and encouraged me with my writing. To my parents, who instilled in me a love of learning and always are willing to help me manage the chaos. To my first critique group, the Seven Evil Dwarves, who told me to keep on writing. To Jami Gray, who told me to not give up on this novel. A big thanks to everyone at Black Opal Books, for believing in my novel and working hard to see it in print. To my sister, who was my first reader, and Marci, who was my first cheerleader. And lastly, to my husband Spencer, who never doubted my dream.

ABOUT THE AUTHOR

DeAnna Browne graduated from Arizona State University with her BS in Psychology. She finds it helps to corral those voices in her mind and put them to paper. An avid reader and writer, she has a soft spot for fantasy with a touch of romance. Despite her love for food and traveling, she always finds her way back to Phoenix, Arizona with her husband, children, and pet dog.

You can find DeAnna at www.deannabrowne.com for upcoming projects, free short stories and up to date releases.